WILLIAM SHAKESPEARE'S

HAMLET

CAMPFIRE®

KALYANI NAVYUG MEDIA PVT LTD

WILLIAM SHAKESPEARE'S
HAMLET

Adapted by
Malini Roy
Illustrated by
Naresh Kumar
Colored by
Ashwani Kashyap & Vijay Sharma
Cover Art & Design
Naresh Kumar & Vijay Sharma

CAMPFIRE®

www.campfire.co.in

Mission Statement

To entertain and educate young minds by creating unique illustrated books
that recount stories of human values, arouse curiosity in the world around us,
and inspire with tales of great deeds of unforgettable people.

Published by Kalyani Navyug Media Pvt Ltd
101 C, Shiv House, Hari Nagar Ashram, New Delhi 110014, India

ISBN: 978-93-81182-51-2

Printed in India

SEPTEMBER 2019

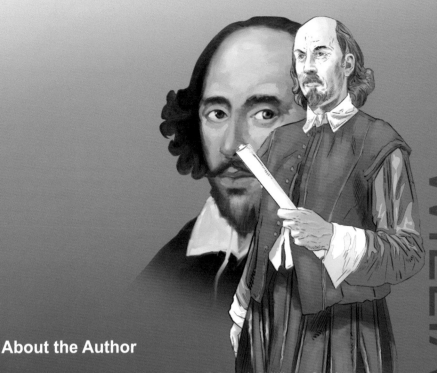

About the Author

Famously known as 'The Bard of Avon', William Shakespeare was born in Stratford-upon-Avon, most probably on April 23, 1564. We say probably because till date, nobody has conclusive evidence for Shakespeare's birthday.

His father, John Shakespeare, was a successful local businessman and his mother, Mary Arden, was the daughter of a wealthy landowner. In 1582, an eighteen-year-old William married an older woman named Anne Hathaway. Soon, they had their first daughter, Susanna and later, another two children. William's only son, Hamnet, died at the tender age of eleven.

Translated into innumerable languages across the globe, Shakespeare's plays and sonnets are undoubtedly the most studied writings in the English language. A rare playwright, he excelled in tragedies, comedies, and histories. Skillfully combining entertainment with unmatched poetry, some of his most famous plays are Othello, Macbeth, A Midsummer Night's Dream, Romeo and Juliet, and The Merchant of Venice, among many others.

Shakespeare was also an actor. In 1599, he became one of the partners in the new Globe Theatre in London and a part owner of his own theater company called 'The Chamberlain's Men'—a group of remarkable actors who were also business partners and close friends of Shakespeare. When Queen Elizabeth died in 1603 and was succeeded by her cousin King James of Scotland, 'The Chamberlain's Men' was renamed 'The King's Men'.

Shakespeare died in 1616. It is not clear how he died although his vicar suggested it was from heavy drinking.

The characters he created and the stories he told have held the interest of people for the past 400 years! Till date, his plays are performed all over the world and have been turned into movies, comics, cartoons,

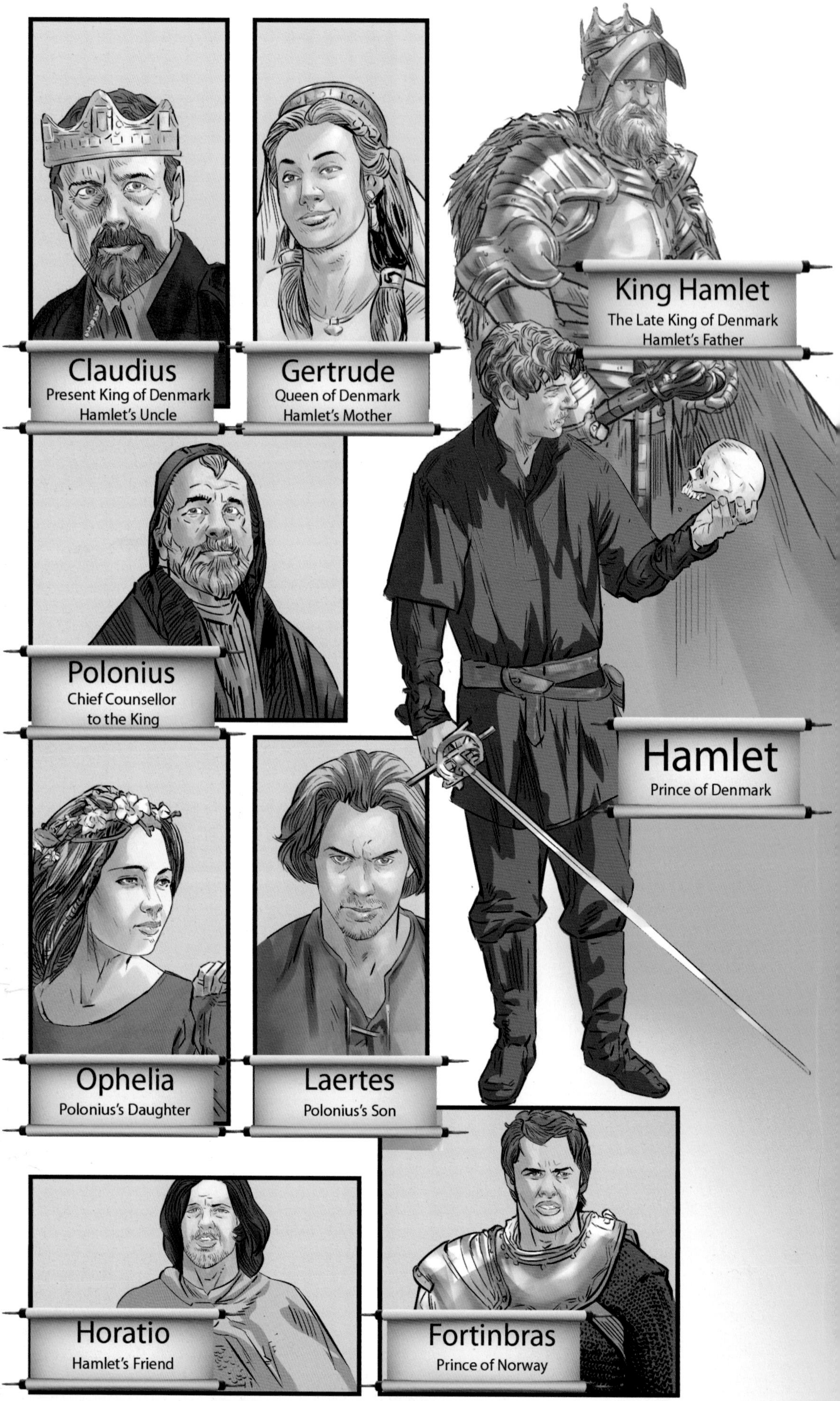

Claudius
Present King of Denmark
Hamlet's Uncle
Gertrude
Queen of Denmark
Hamlet's Mother
King Hamlet
The Late King of Denmark
Hamlet's Father
Polonius
Chief Counsellor
to the King
Hamlet
Prince of Denmark
Ophelia
Polonius's Daughter
Laertes
Polonius's Son
Horatio
Hamlet's Friend
Fortinbras
Prince of Norway

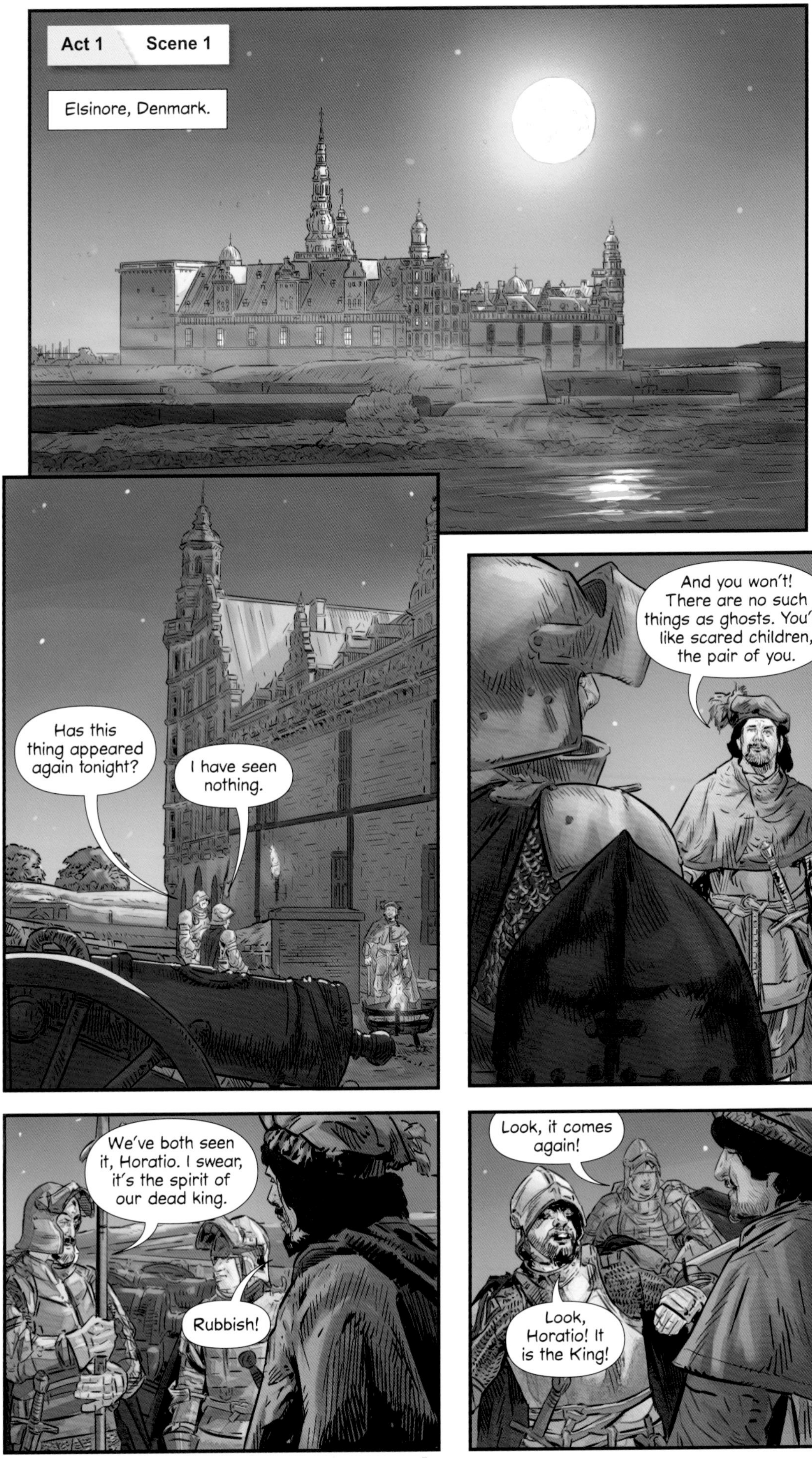

Act 1 Scene 1
Elsinore, Denmark.
Has this thing appeared again tonight?
I have seen nothing.
And you won't! There are no such things as ghosts. You're like scared children, the pair of you.
We've both seen it, Horatio. I swear, it's the spirit of our dead king.
Rubbish!
Look, it comes again!
Look, Horatio! It is the King!

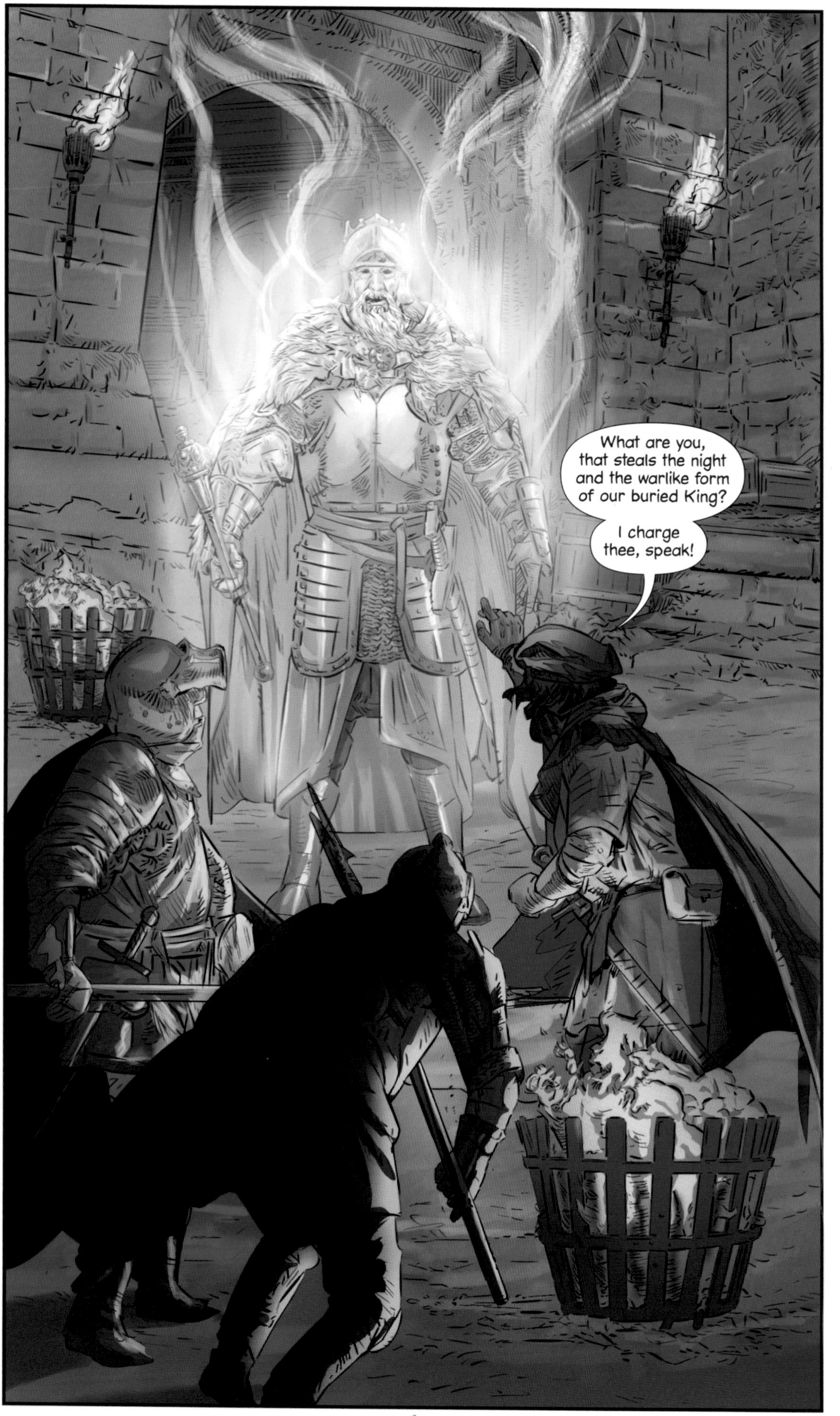
What are you, that steals the night and the warlike form of our buried King?
I charge thee, speak!

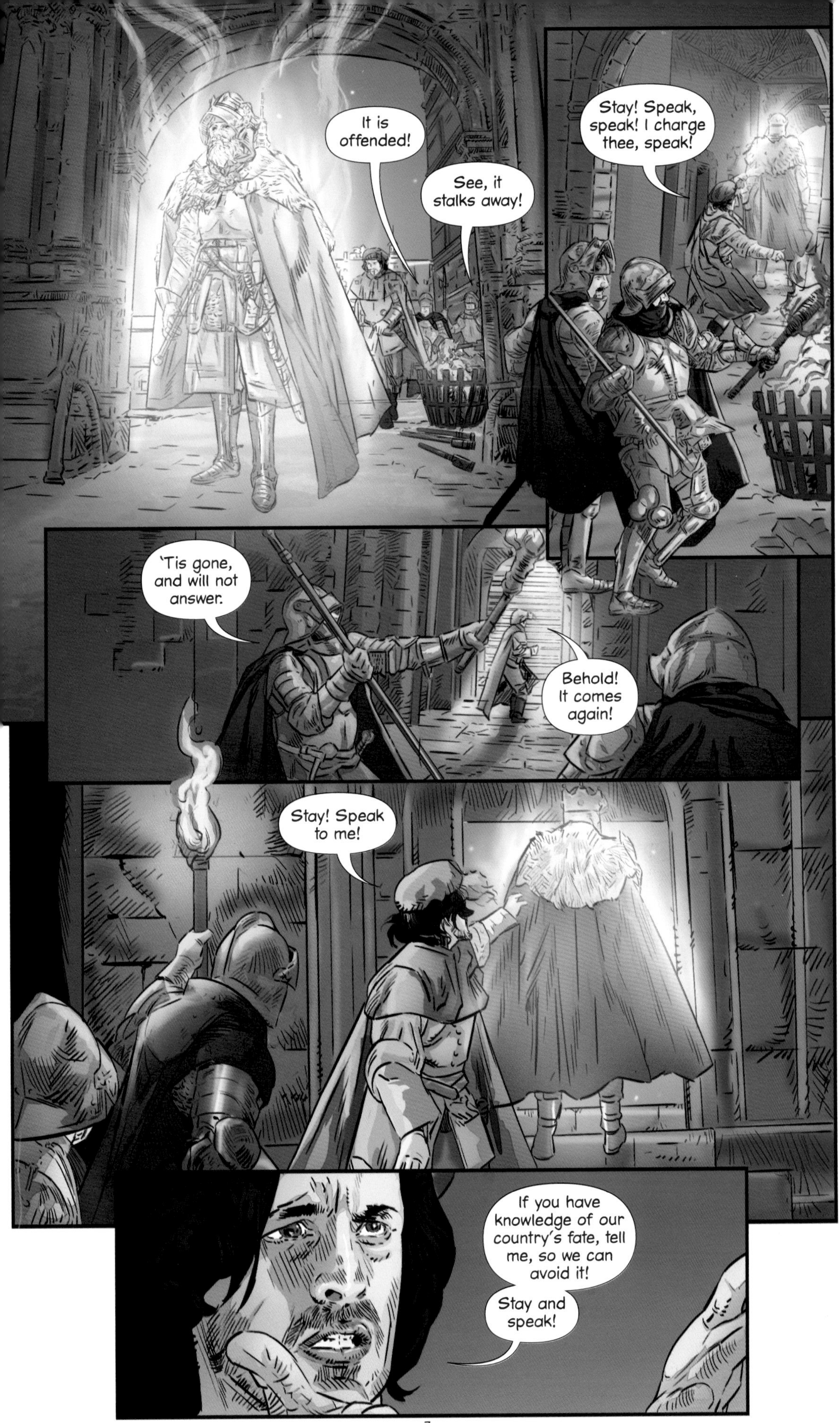
It is offended!
See, it stalks away!
Stay! Speak, speak! I charge thee, speak!
'Tis gone, and will not answer.
Behold! It comes again!
Stay! Speak to me!
If you have knowledge of our country's fate, tell me, so we can avoid it!
Stay and speak!

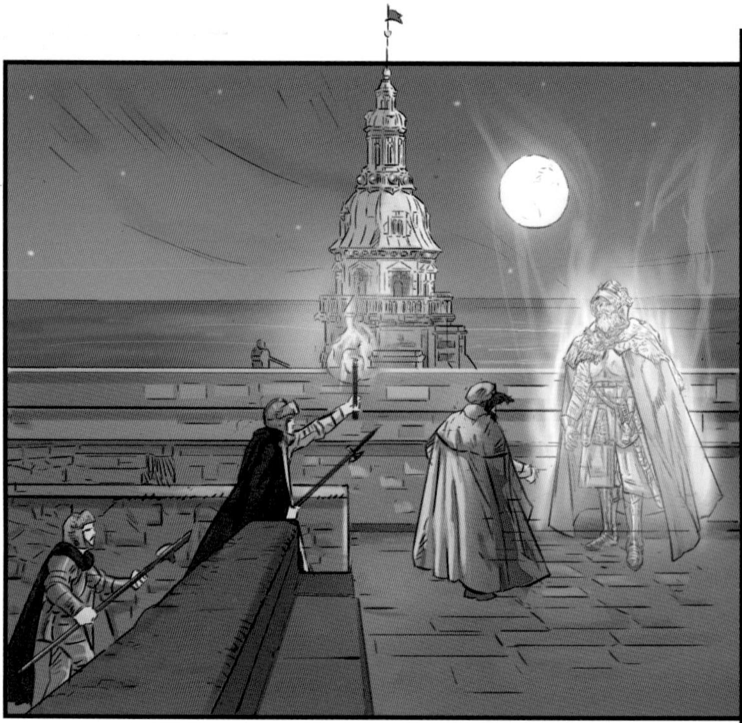

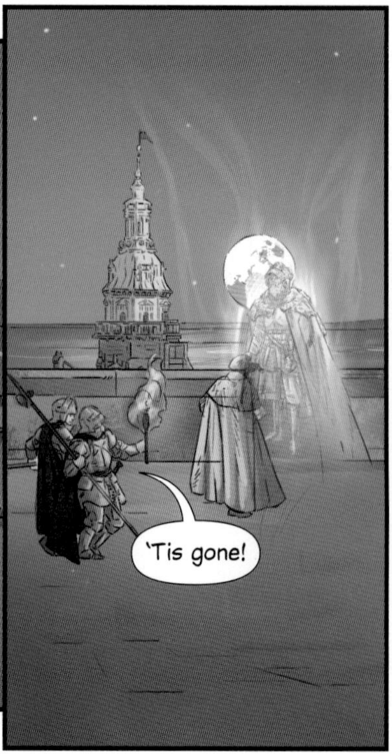
'Tis gone!

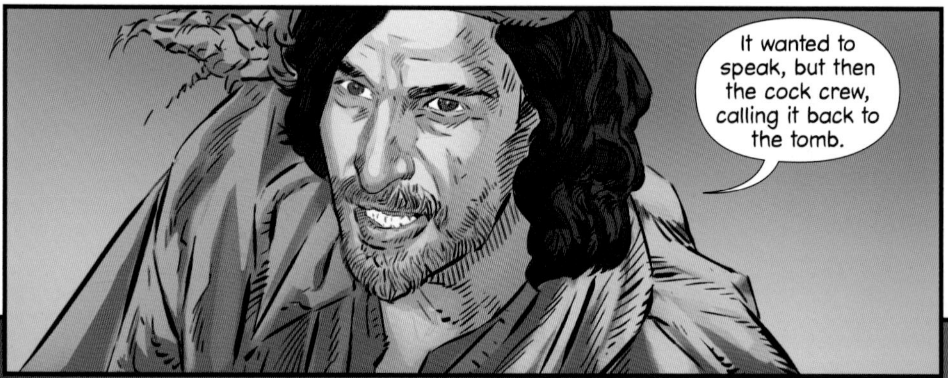
It wanted to speak, but then the cock crew, calling it back to the tomb.

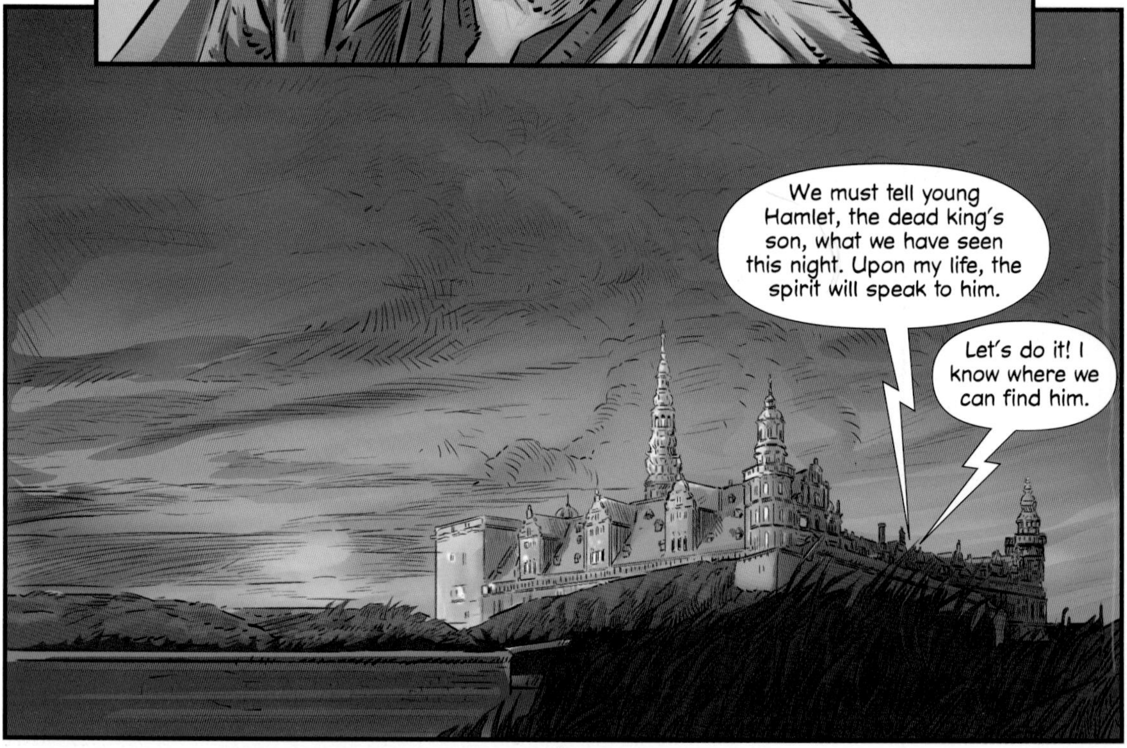
We must tell young Hamlet, the dead king's son, what we have seen this night. Upon my life, the spirit will speak to him.
Let's do it! I know where we can find him.

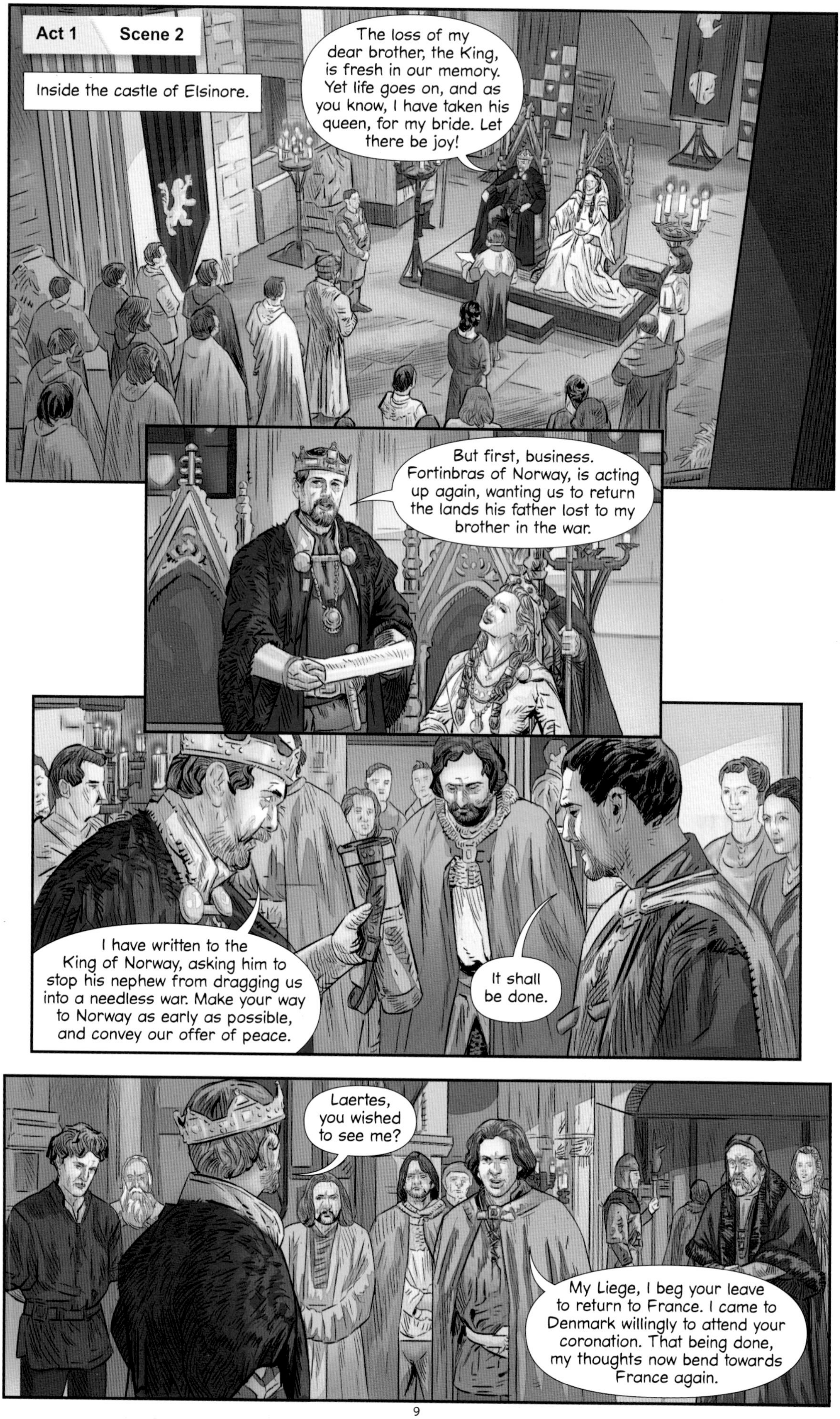
Act 1 Scene 2
Inside the castle of Elsinore.
The loss of my dear brother, the King, is fresh in our memory. Yet life goes on, and as you know, I have taken his queen, for my bride. Let there be joy!
But first, business. Fortinbras of Norway, is acting up again, wanting us to return the lands his father lost to my brother in the war.
I have written to the King of Norway, asking him to stop his nephew from dragging us into a needless war. Make your way to Norway as early as possible, and convey our offer of peace.
It shall be done.
Laertes, you wished to see me?
My Liege, I beg your leave to return to France. I came to Denmark willingly to attend your coronation. That being done, my thoughts now bend towards France again.

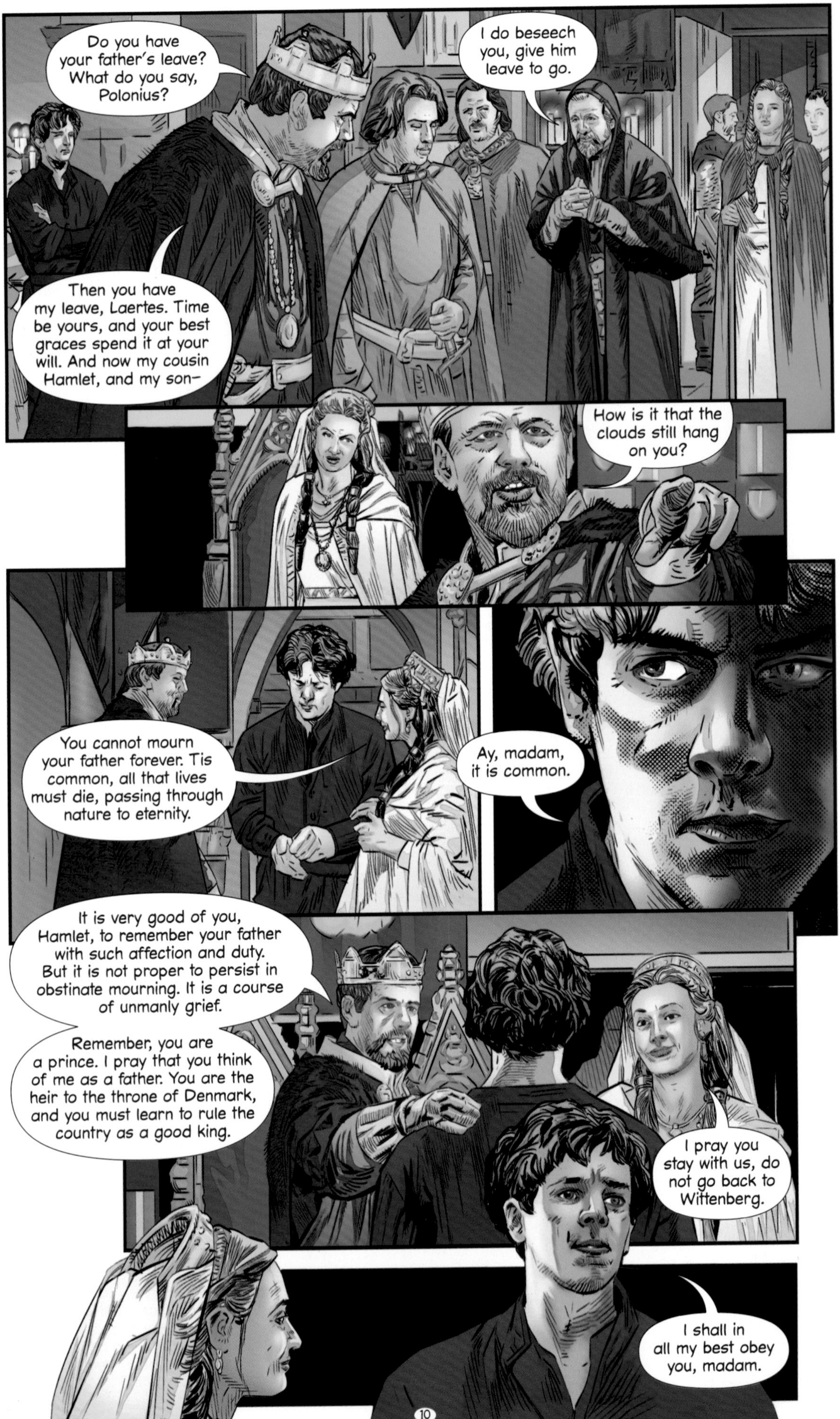
Do you have your father's leave? What do you say, Polonius?
I do beseech you, give him leave to go.
Then you have my leave, Laertes. Time be yours, and your best graces spend it at your will. And now my cousin Hamlet, and my son–
How is it that the clouds still hang on you?
You cannot mourn your father forever. Tis common, all that lives must die, passing through nature to eternity.
Ay, madam, it is common.
It is very good of you, Hamlet, to remember your father with such affection and duty. But it is not proper to persist in obstinate mourning. It is a course of unmanly grief.
Remember, you are a prince. I pray that you think of me as a father. You are the heir to the throne of Denmark, and you must learn to rule the country as a good king.
I pray you stay with us, do not go back to Wittenberg.
I shall in all my best obey you, madam.

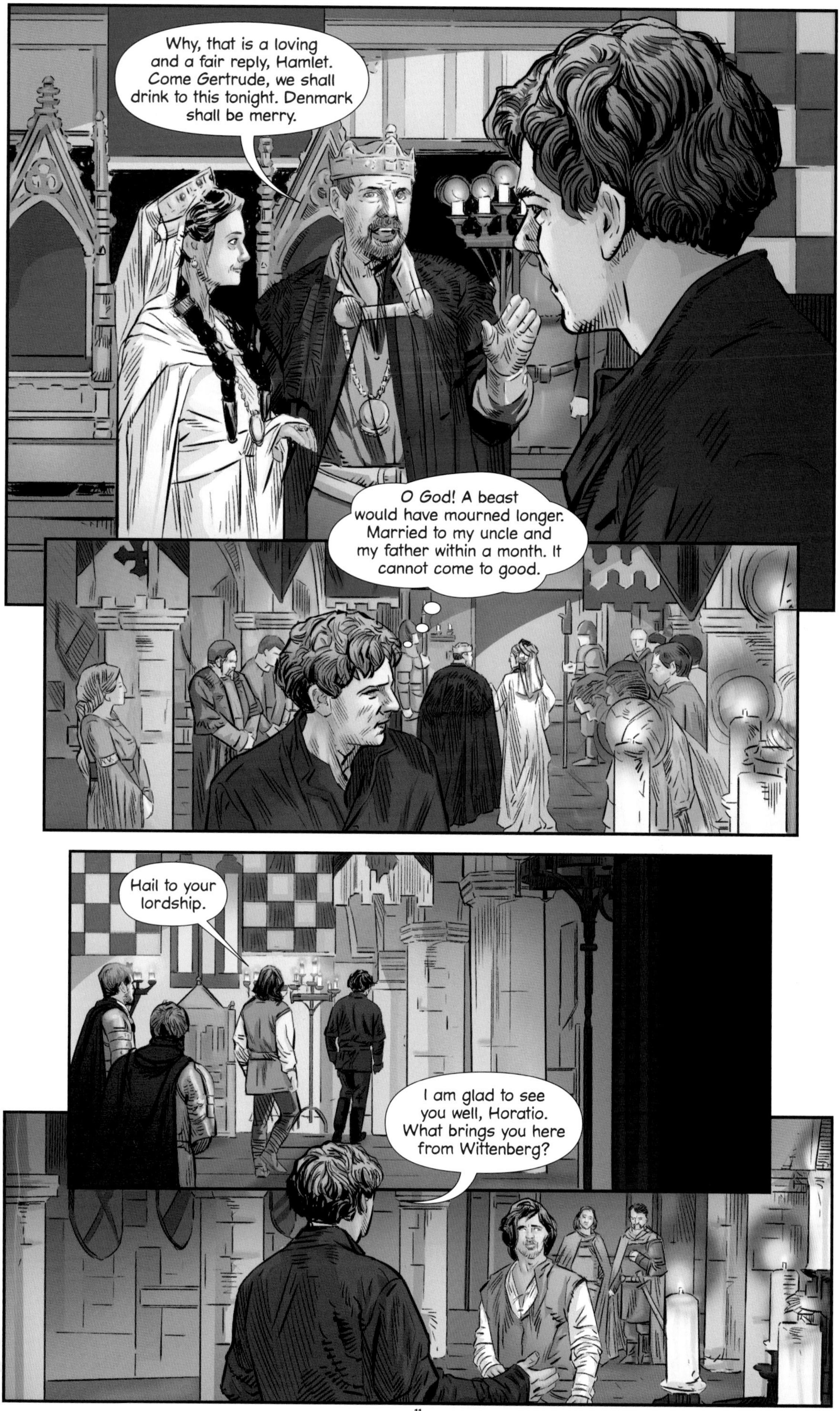
Why, that is a loving and a fair reply, Hamlet. Come Gertrude, we shall drink to this tonight. Denmark shall be merry.
O God! A beast would have mourned longer. Married to my uncle and my father within a month. It cannot come to good.
Hail to your lordship.
I am glad to see you well, Horatio. What brings you here from Wittenberg?

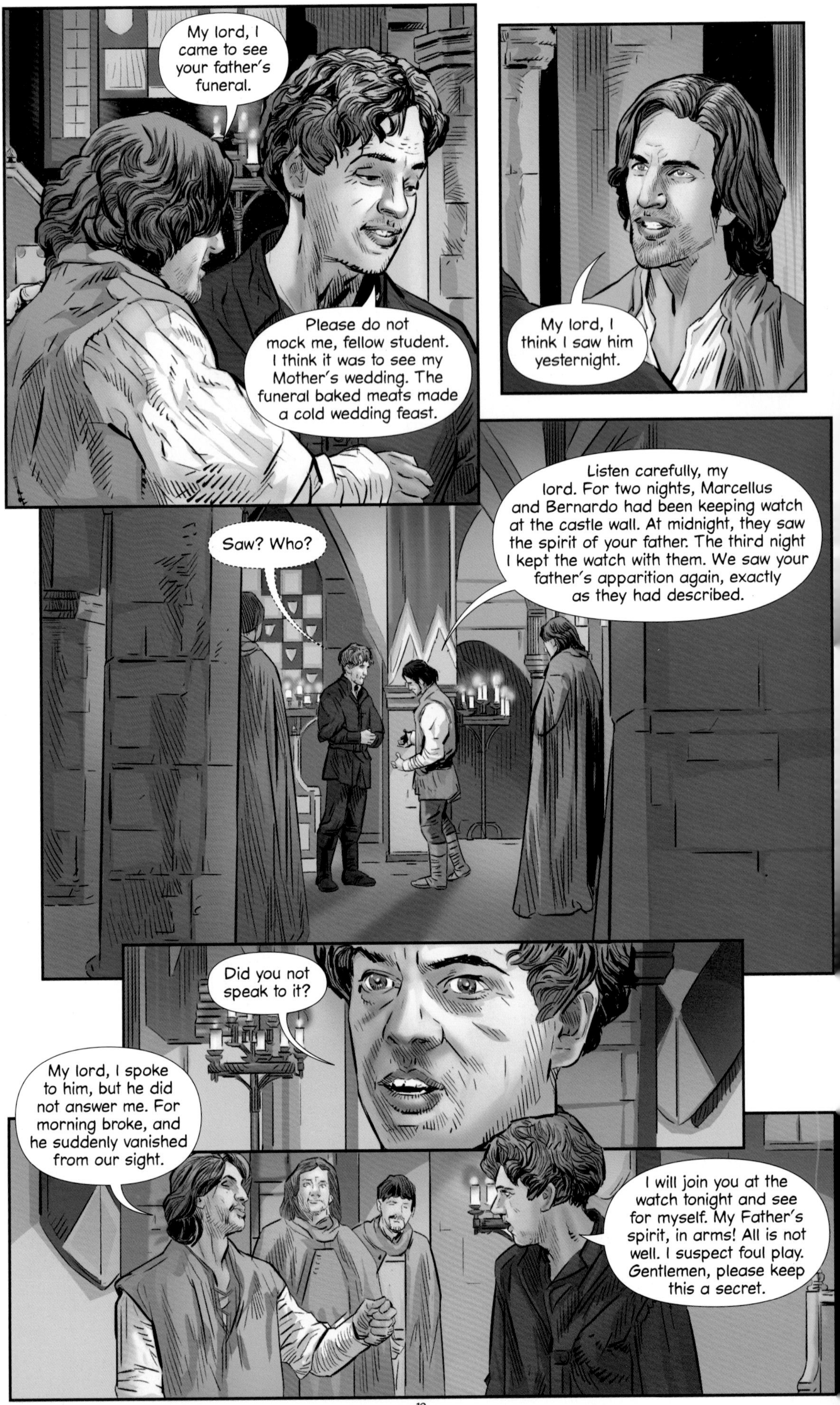
My lord, I came to see your father's funeral.
Please do not mock me, fellow student. I think it was to see my Mother's wedding. The funeral baked meats made a cold wedding feast.
My lord, I think I saw him yesternight.
Saw? Who?
Listen carefully, my lord. For two nights, Marcellus and Bernardo had been keeping watch at the castle wall. At midnight, they saw the spirit of your father. The third night I kept the watch with them. We saw your father's apparition again, exactly as they had described.
Did you not speak to it?
My lord, I spoke to him, but he did not answer me. For morning broke, and he suddenly vanished from our sight.
I will join you at the watch tonight and see for myself. My Father's spirit, in arms! All is not well. I suspect foul play. Gentlemen, please keep this a secret.

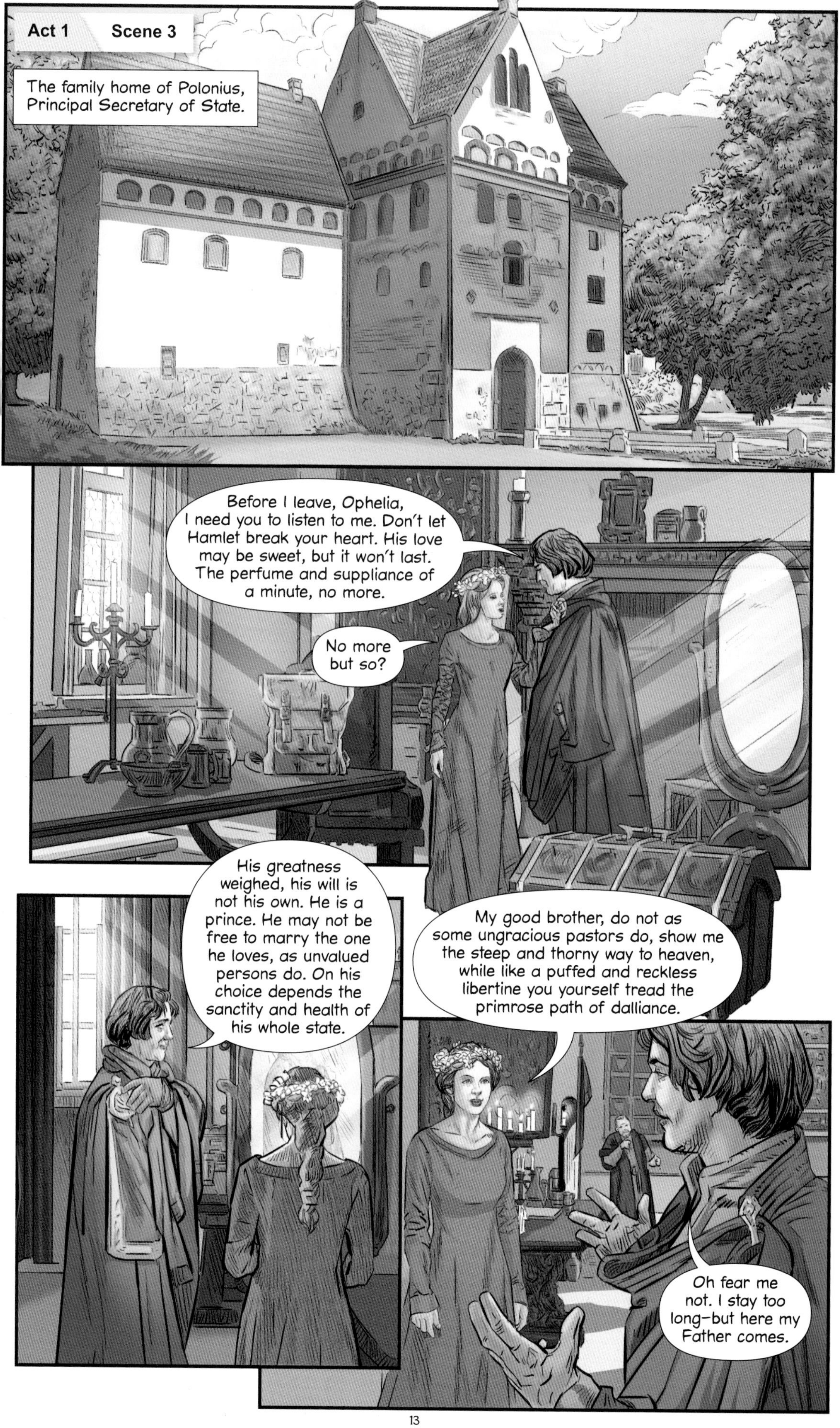
Act 1 Scene 3
The family home of Polonius, Principal Secretary of State.
Before I leave, Ophelia, I need you to listen to me. Don't let Hamlet break your heart. His love may be sweet, but it won't last. The perfume and suppliance of a minute, no more.
No more but so?
His greatness weighed, his will is not his own. He is a prince. He may not be free to marry the one he loves, as unvalued persons do. On his choice depends the sanctity and health of his whole state.
My good brother, do not as some ungracious pastors do, show me the steep and thorny way to heaven, while like a puffed and reckless libertine you yourself tread the primrose path of dalliance.
Oh fear me not. I stay too long—but here my Father comes.

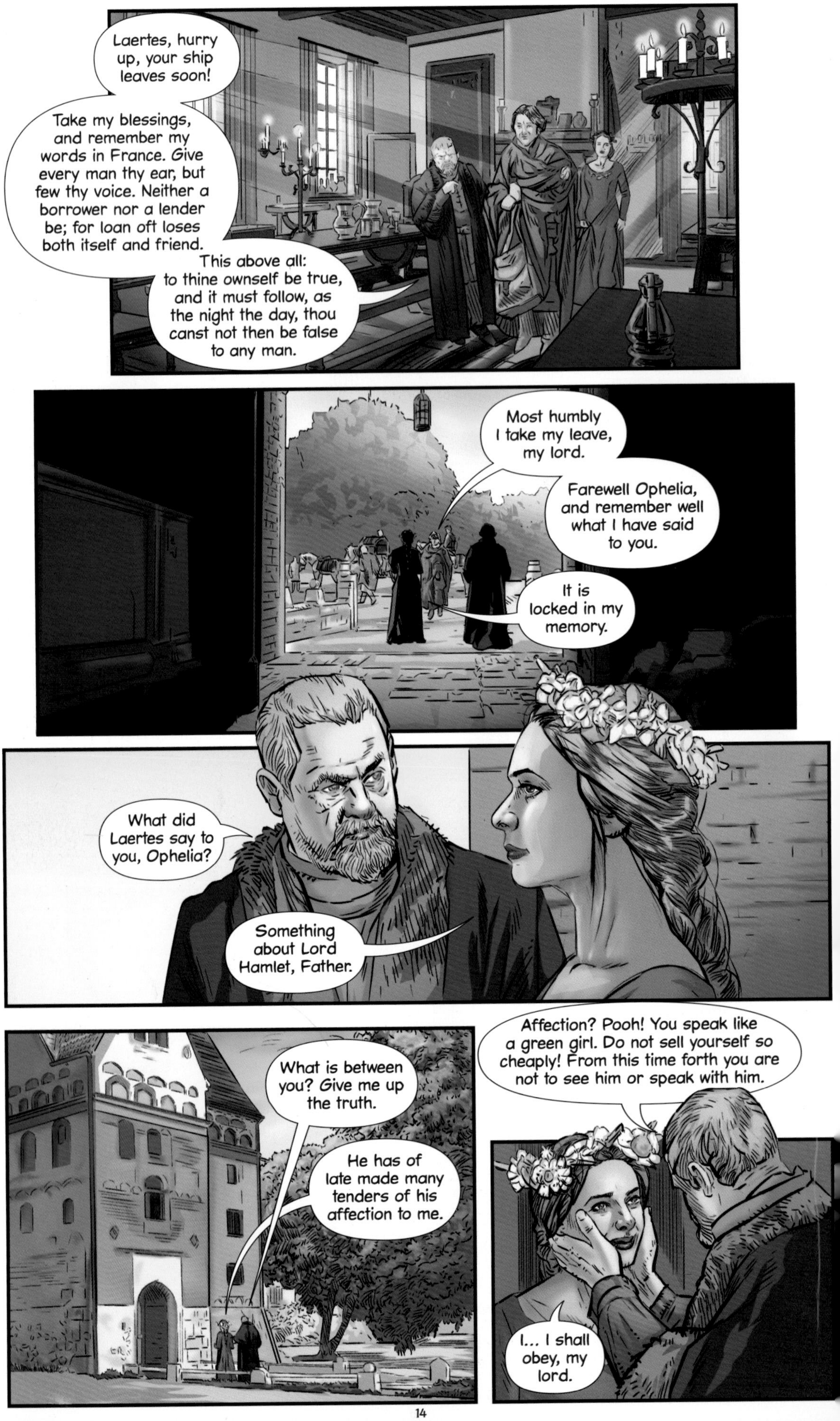
Laertes, hurry up, your ship leaves soon!
Take my blessings, and remember my words in France. Give every man thy ear, but few thy voice. Neither a borrower nor a lender be; for loan oft loses both itself and friend.
This above all: to thine ownself be true, and it must follow, as the night the day, thou canst not then be false to any man.
Most humbly I take my leave, my lord.
Farewell Ophelia, and remember well what I have said to you.
It is locked in my memory.
What did Laertes say to you, Ophelia?
Something about Lord Hamlet, Father.
What is between you? Give me up the truth.
He has of late made many tenders of his affection to me.
Affection? Pooh! You speak like a green girl. Do not sell yourself so cheaply! From this time forth you are not to see him or speak with him.
I... I shall obey, my lord.

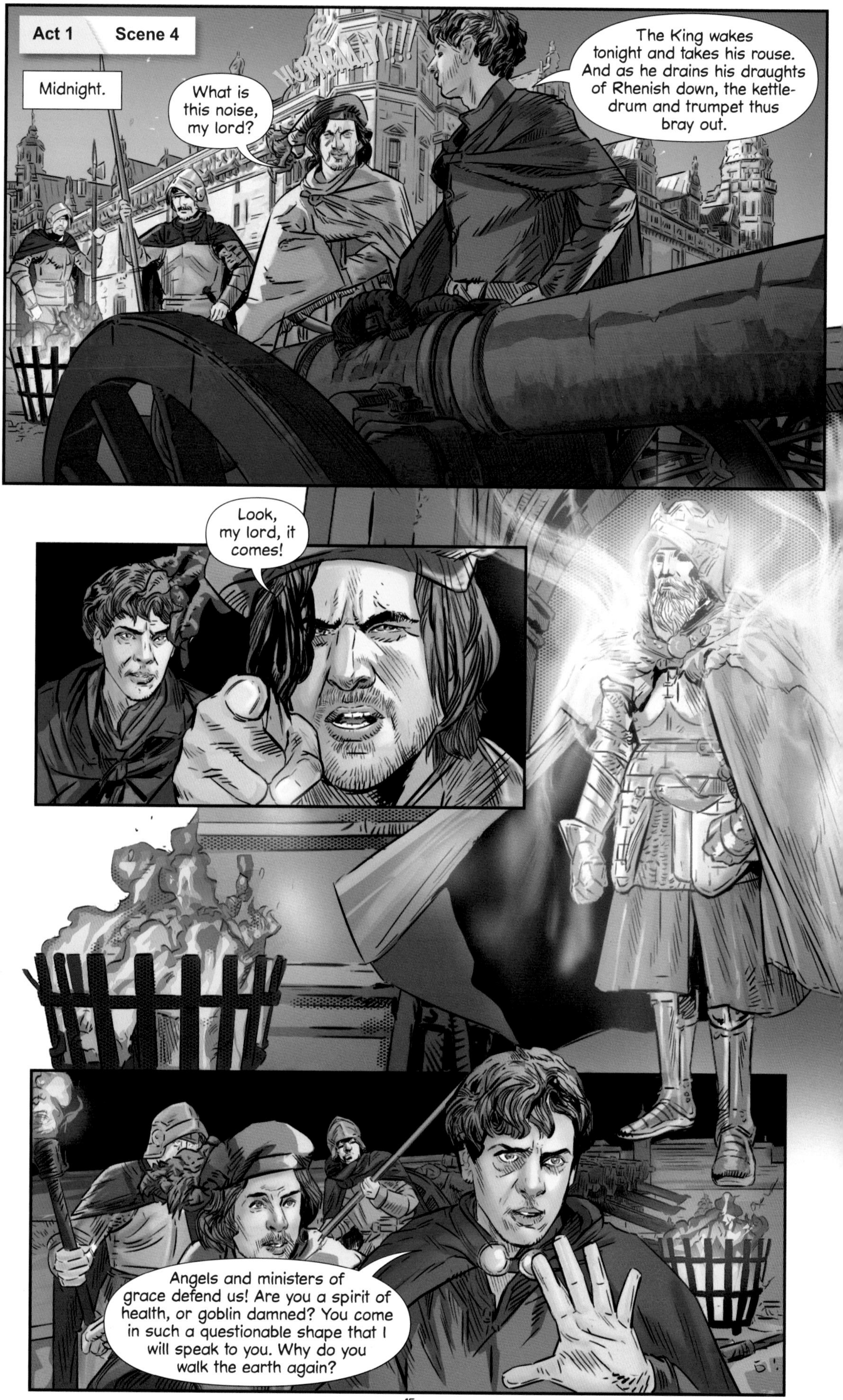
Act 1 Scene 4
Midnight.
What is this noise, my lord?
The King wakes tonight and takes his rouse. And as he drains his draughts of Rhenish down, the kettle-drum and trumpet thus bray out.
Look, my lord, it comes!
Angels and ministers of grace defend us! Are you a spirit of health, or goblin damned? You come in such a questionable shape that I will speak to you. Why do you walk the earth again?

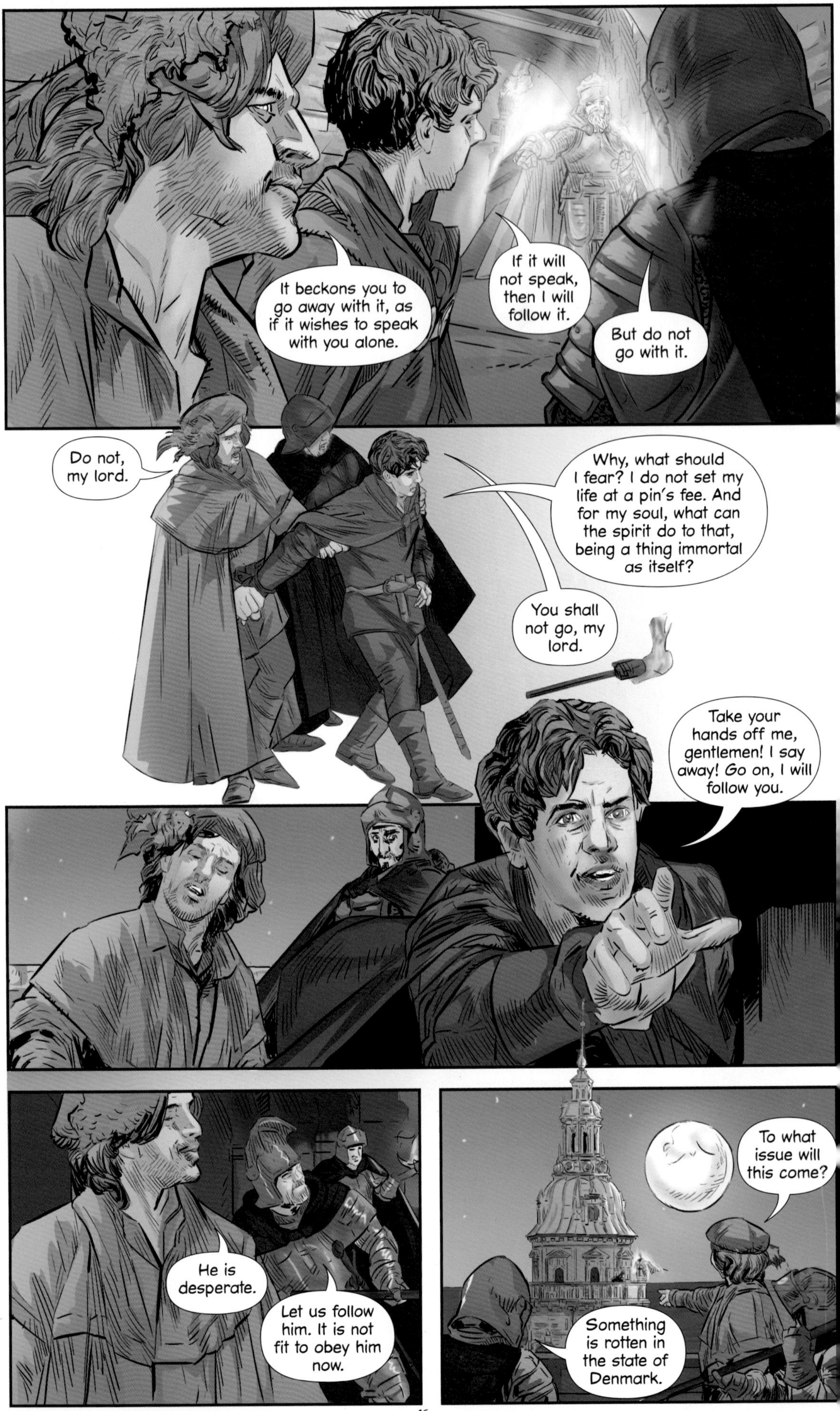
It beckons you to go away with it, as if it wishes to speak with you alone.
If it will not speak, then I will follow it.
But do not go with it.
Do not, my lord.
Why, what should I fear? I do not set my life at a pin's fee. And for my soul, what can the spirit do to that, being a thing immortal as itself?
You shall not go, my lord.
Take your hands off me, gentlemen! I say away! Go on, I will follow you.
He is desperate.
Let us follow him. It is not fit to obey him now.
To what issue will this come?
Something is rotten in the state of Denmark.

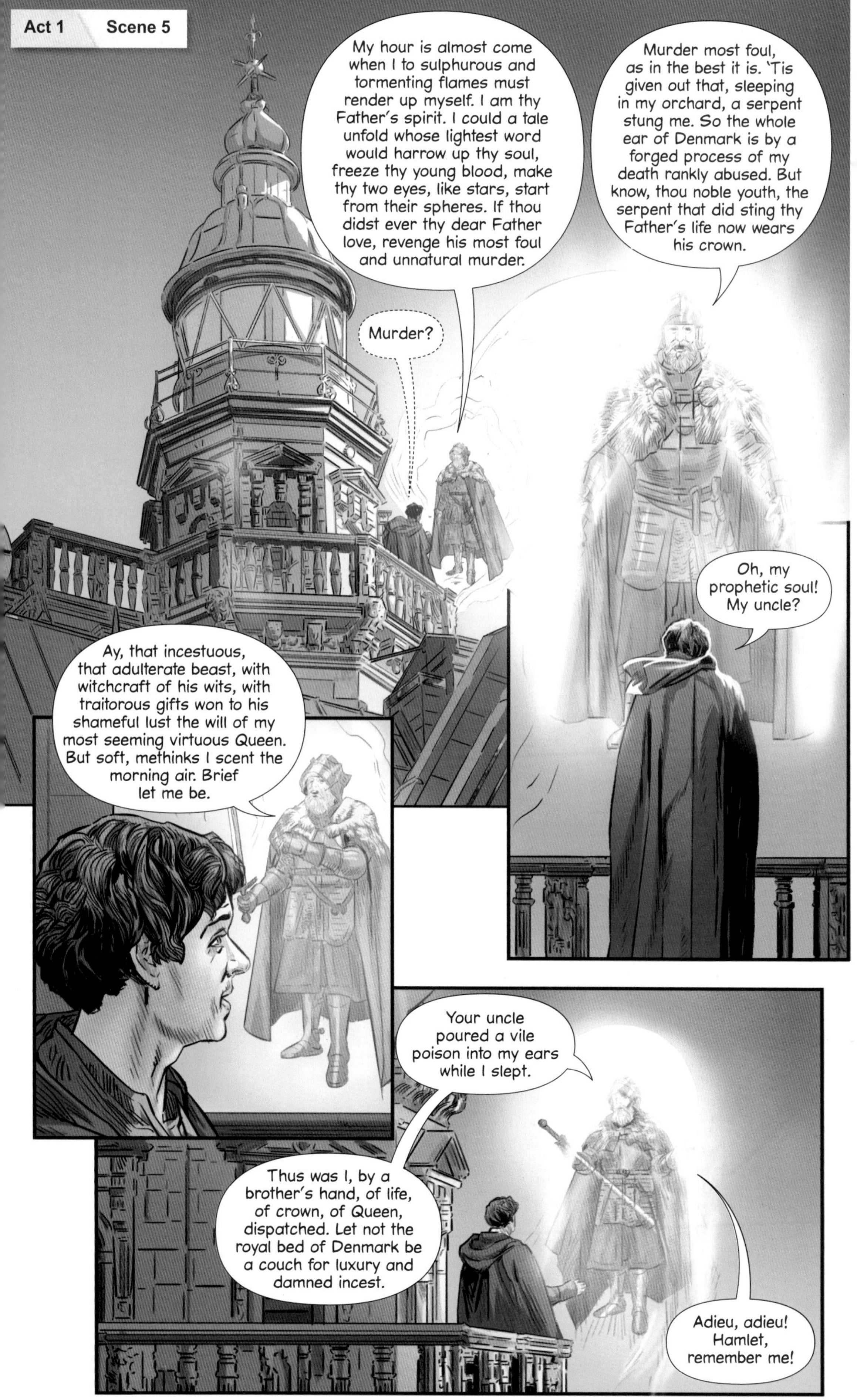
My hour is almost come when I to sulphurous and tormenting flames must render up myself. I am thy Father's spirit. I could a tale unfold whose lightest word would harrow up thy soul, freeze thy young blood, make thy two eyes, like stars, start from their spheres. If thou didst ever thy dear Father love, revenge his most foul and unnatural murder.
Murder?
Murder most foul, as in the best it is. 'Tis given out that, sleeping in my orchard, a serpent stung me. So the whole ear of Denmark is by a forged process of my death rankly abused. But know, thou noble youth, the serpent that did sting thy Father's life now wears his crown.
Oh, my prophetic soul! My uncle?
Ay, that incestuous, that adulterate beast, with witchcraft of his wits, with traitorous gifts won to his shameful lust the will of my most seeming virtuous Queen. But soft, methinks I scent the morning air. Brief let me be.
Your uncle poured a vile poison into my ears while I slept.
Thus was I, by a brother's hand, of life, of crown, of Queen, dispatched. Let not the royal bed of Denmark be a couch for luxury and damned incest.
Adieu, adieu! Hamlet, remember me!

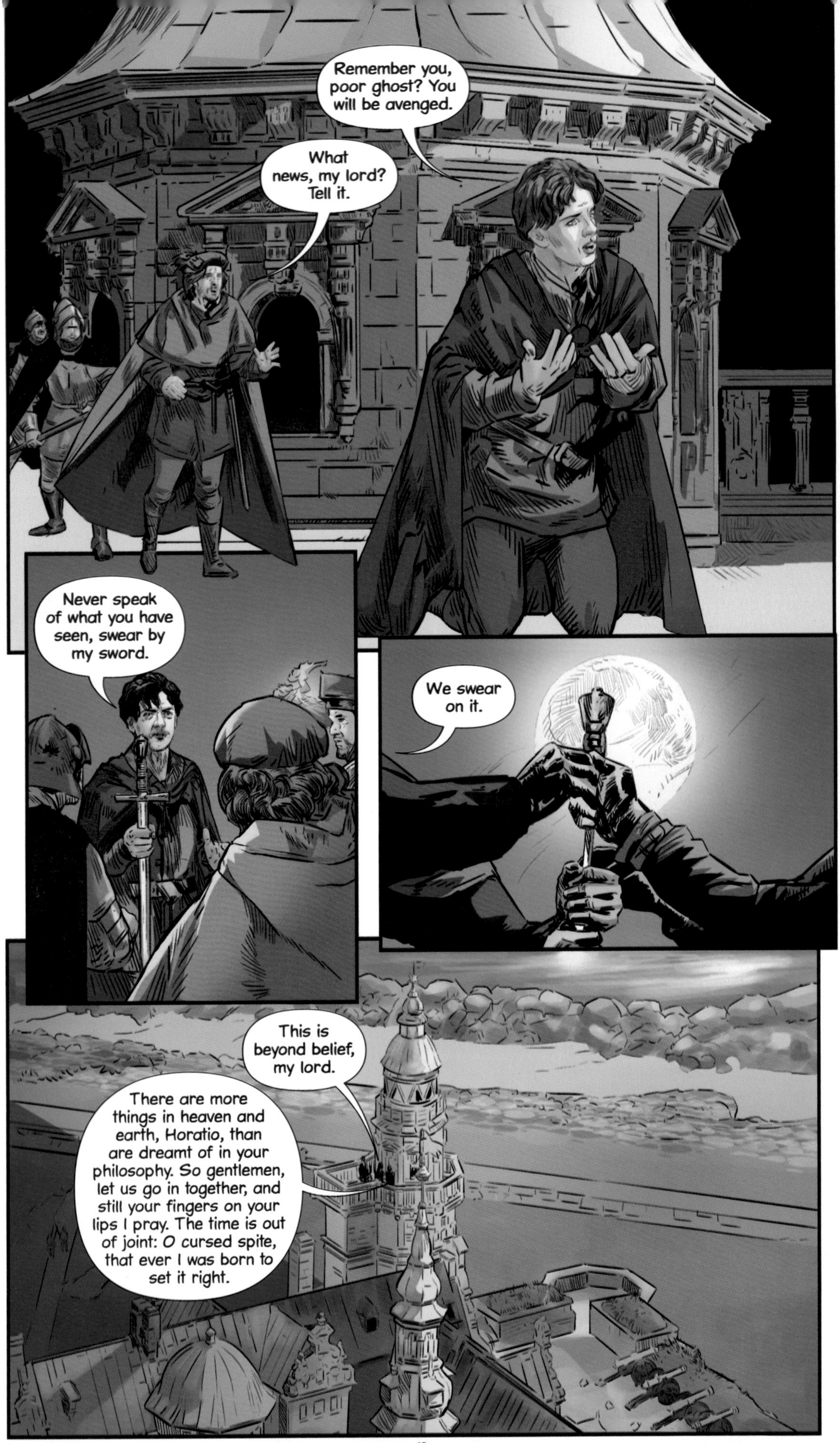
Remember you, poor ghost? You will be avenged.
What news, my lord? Tell it.
Never speak of what you have seen, swear by my sword.
We swear on it.
This is beyond belief, my lord.
There are more things in heaven and earth, Horatio, than are dreamt of in your philosophy. So gentlemen, let us go in together, and still your fingers on your lips I pray. The time is out of joint: O cursed spite, that ever I was born to set it right.

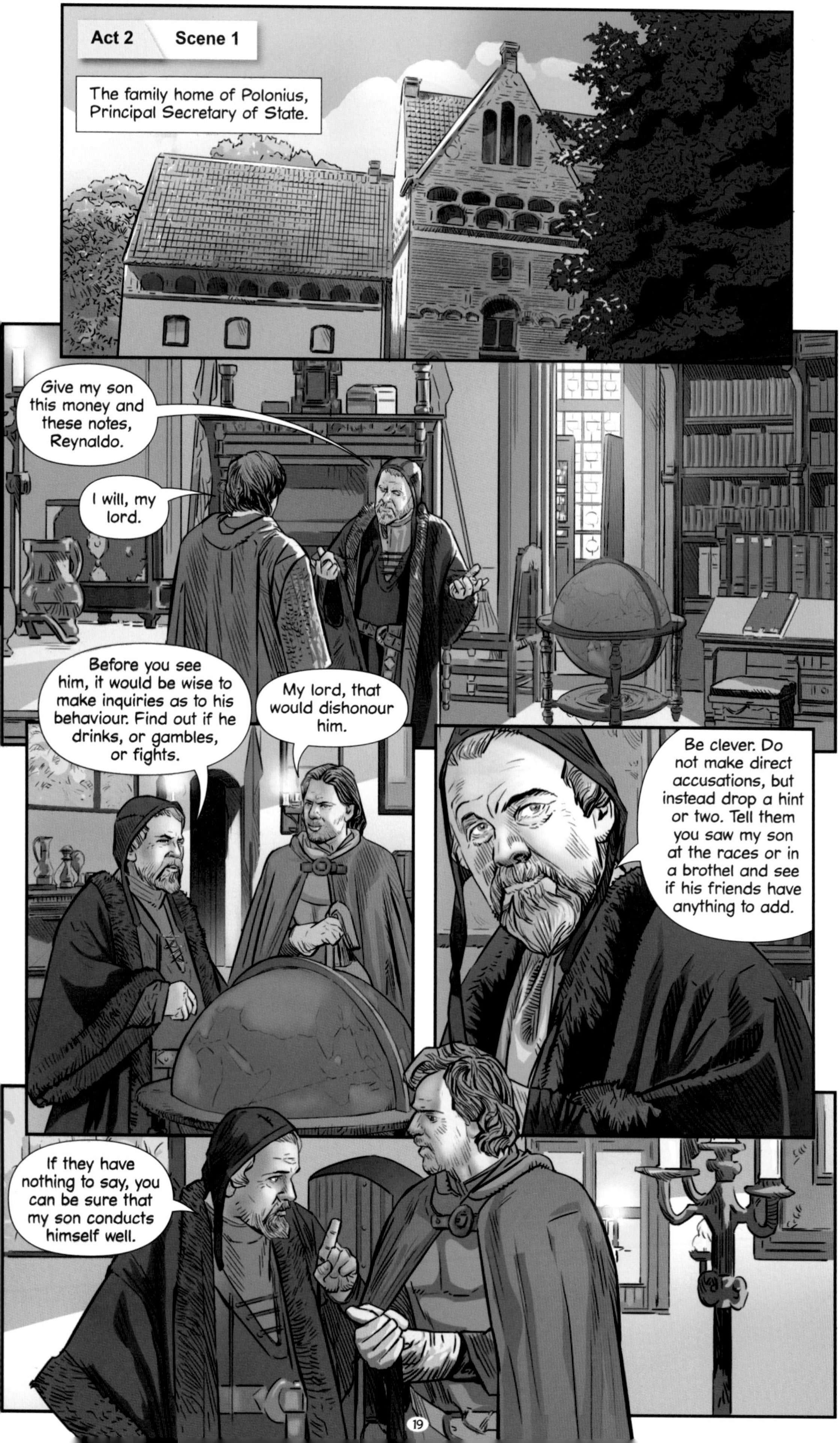
Act 2 Scene 1
The family home of Polonius, Principal Secretary of State.
Give my son this money and these notes, Reynaldo.
I will, my lord.
Before you see him, it would be wise to make inquiries as to his behaviour. Find out if he drinks, or gambles, or fights.
My lord, that would dishonour him.
Be clever. Do not make direct accusations, but instead drop a hint or two. Tell them you saw my son at the races or in a brothel and see if his friends have anything to add.
If they have nothing to say, you can be sure that my son conducts himself well.

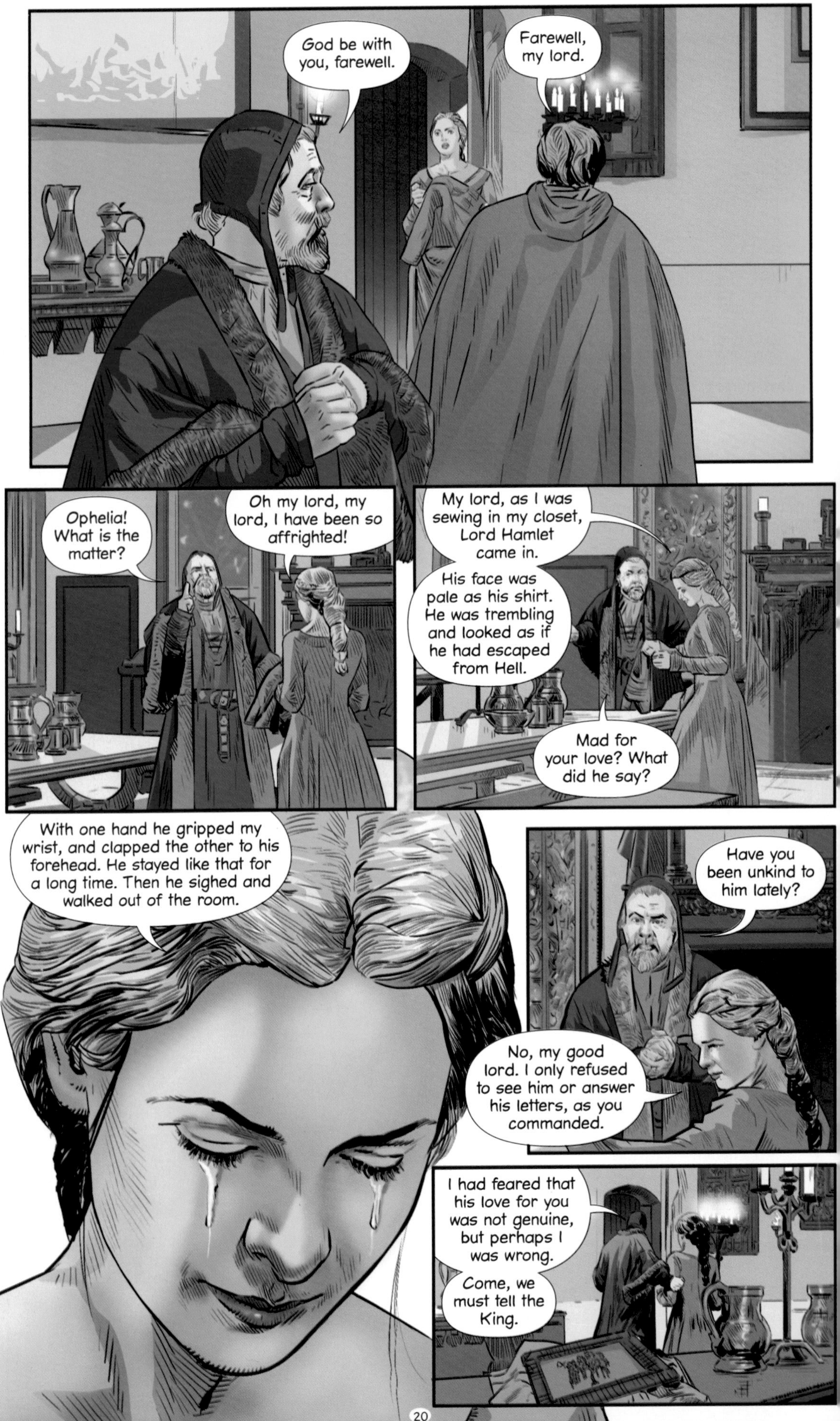
God be with you, farewell.
Farewell, my lord.
Ophelia! What is the matter?
Oh my lord, my lord, I have been so affrighted!
My lord, as I was sewing in my closet, Lord Hamlet came in.
His face was pale as his shirt. He was trembling and looked as if he had escaped from Hell.
Mad for your love? What did he say?
With one hand he gripped my wrist, and clapped the other to his forehead. He stayed like that for a long time. Then he sighed and walked out of the room.
Have you been unkind to him lately?
No, my good lord. I only refused to see him or answer his letters, as you commanded.
I had feared that his love for you was not genuine, but perhaps I was wrong.
Come, we must tell the King.

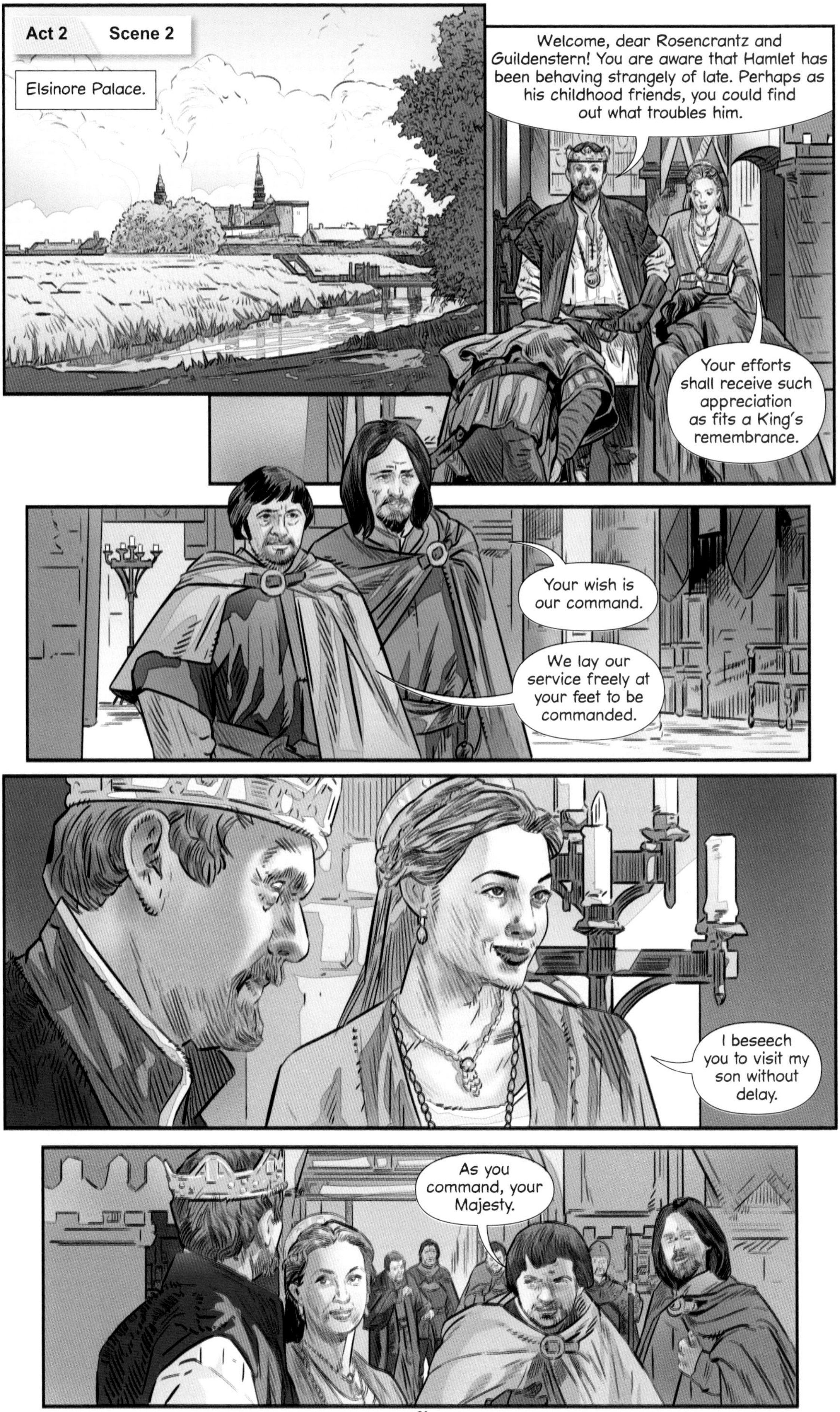
Act 2 Scene 2
Elsinore Palace.
Welcome, dear Rosencrantz and Guildenstern! You are aware that Hamlet has been behaving strangely of late. Perhaps as his childhood friends, you could find out what troubles him.
Your efforts shall receive such appreciation as fits a King's remembrance.
Your wish is our command.
We lay our service freely at your feet to be commanded.
I beseech you to visit my son without delay.
As you command, your Majesty.

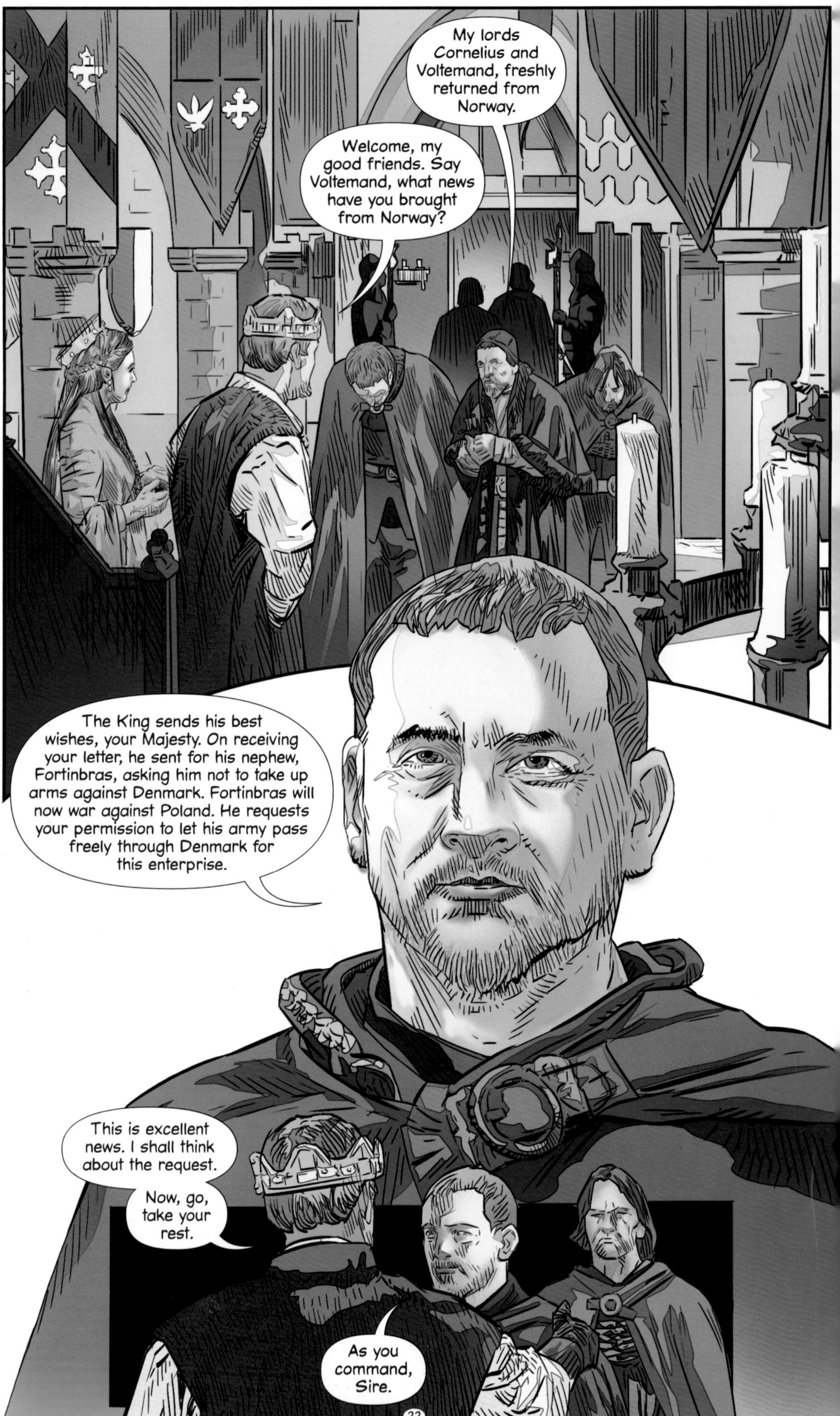
My lords Cornelius and Voltemand, freshly returned from Norway.
Welcome, my good friends. Say Voltemand, what news have you brought from Norway?
The King sends his best wishes, your Majesty. On receiving your letter, he sent for his nephew, Fortinbras, asking him not to take up arms against Denmark. Fortinbras will now war against Poland. He requests your permission to let his army pass freely through Denmark for this enterprise.
This is excellent news. I shall think about the request.
Now, go, take your rest.
As you command, Sire.

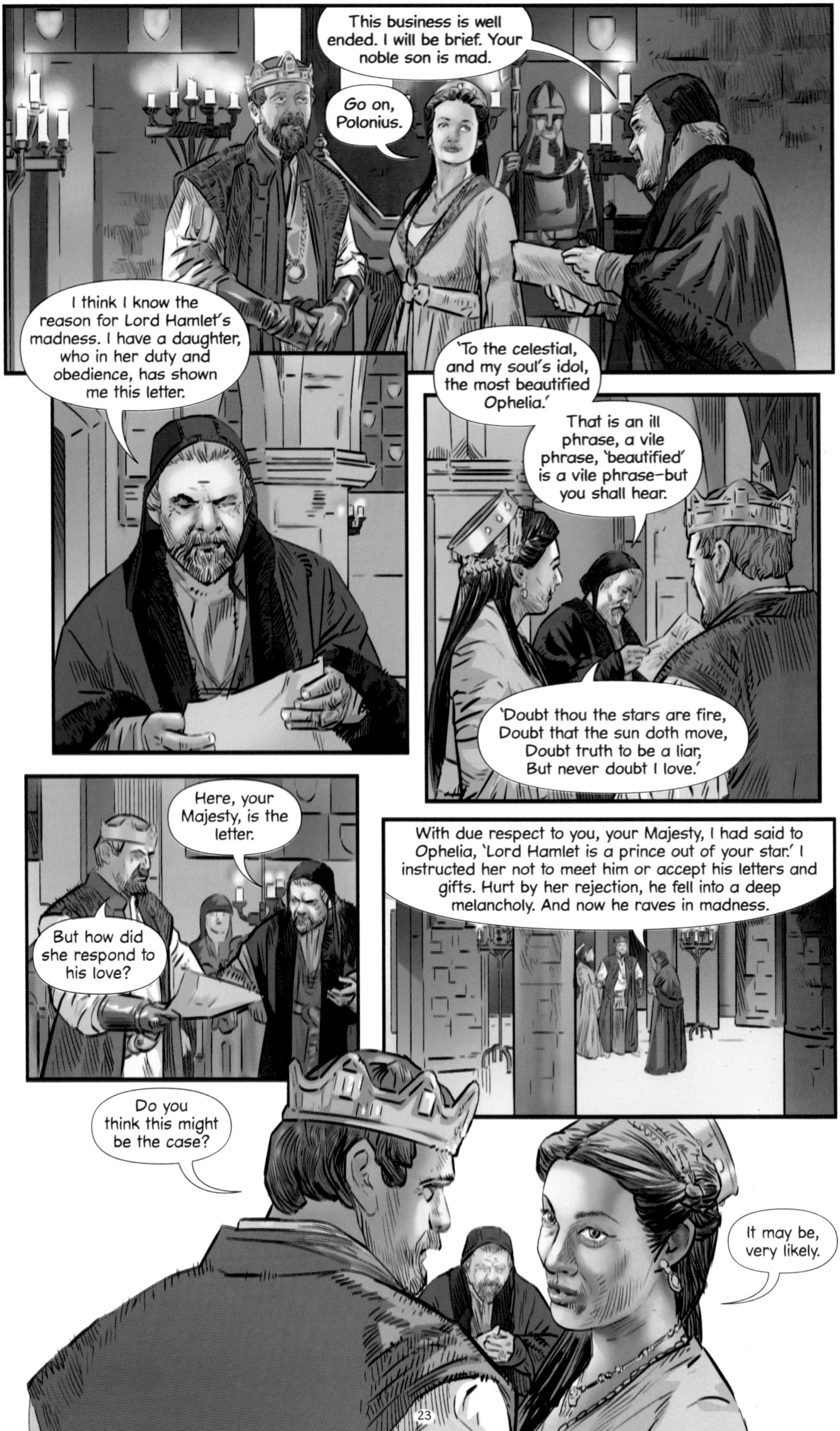
This business is well ended. I will be brief. Your noble son is mad.
Go on, Polonius.
I think I know the reason for Lord Hamlet's madness. I have a daughter, who in her duty and obedience, has shown me this letter.
'To the celestial, and my soul's idol, the most beautified Ophelia.'
That is an ill phrase, a vile phrase, 'beautified' is a vile phrase–but you shall hear.
'Doubt thou the stars are fire, Doubt that the sun doth move, Doubt truth to be a liar, But never doubt I love.'
Here, your Majesty, is the letter.
But how did she respond to his love?
With due respect to you, your Majesty, I had said to Ophelia, 'Lord Hamlet is a prince out of your star.' I instructed her not to meet him or accept his letters and gifts. Hurt by her rejection, he fell into a deep melancholy. And now he raves in madness.
Do you think this might be the case?
It may be, very likely.

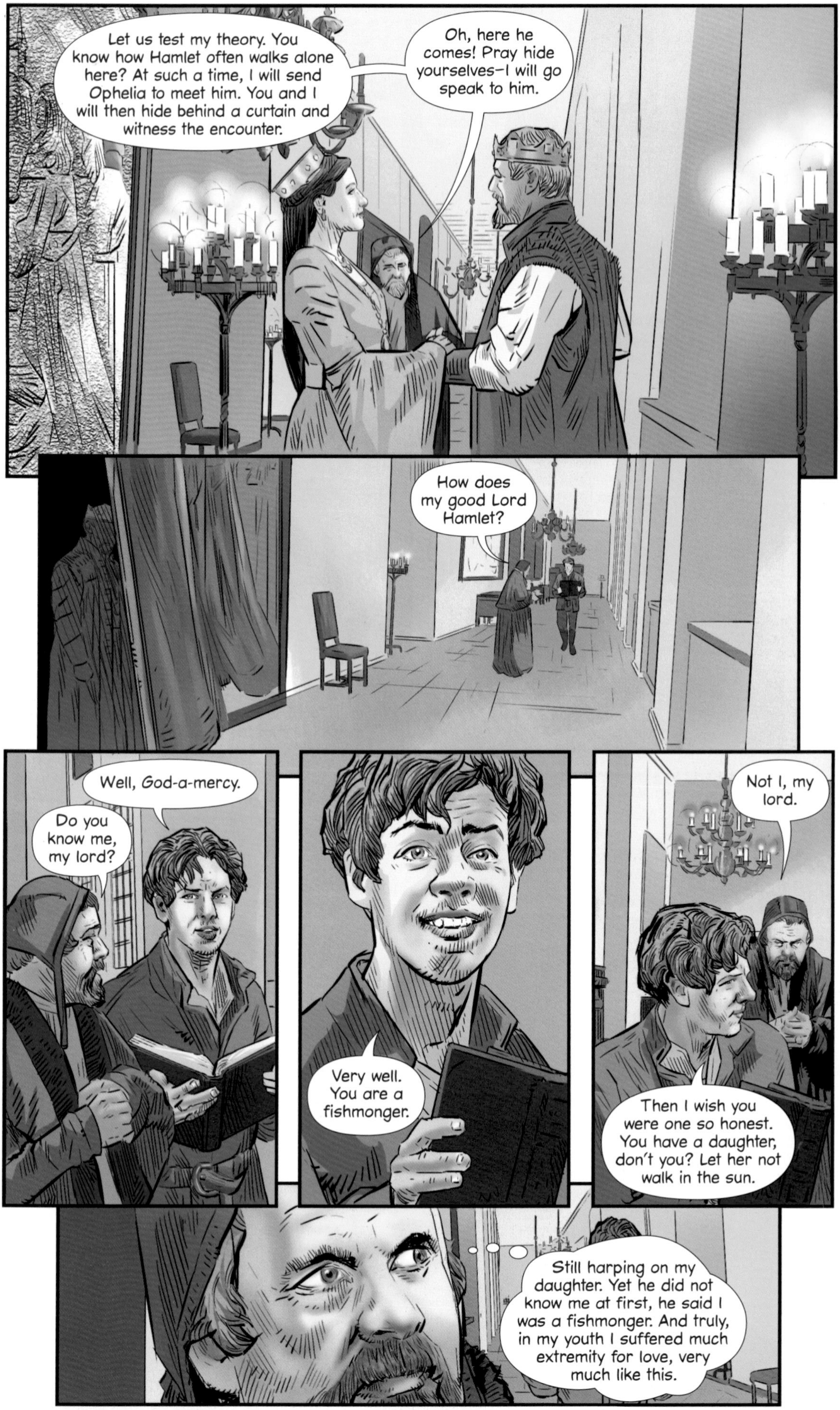
Let us test my theory. You know how Hamlet often walks alone here? At such a time, I will send Ophelia to meet him. You and I will then hide behind a curtain and witness the encounter.
Oh, here he comes! Pray hide yourselves—I will go speak to him.
How does my good Lord Hamlet?
Well, God-a-mercy.
Do you know me, my lord?
Very well. You are a fishmonger.
Not I, my lord.
Then I wish you were one so honest. You have a daughter, don't you? Let her not walk in the sun.
Still harping on my daughter. Yet he did not know me at first, he said I was a fishmonger. And truly, in my youth I suffered much extremity for love, very much like this.

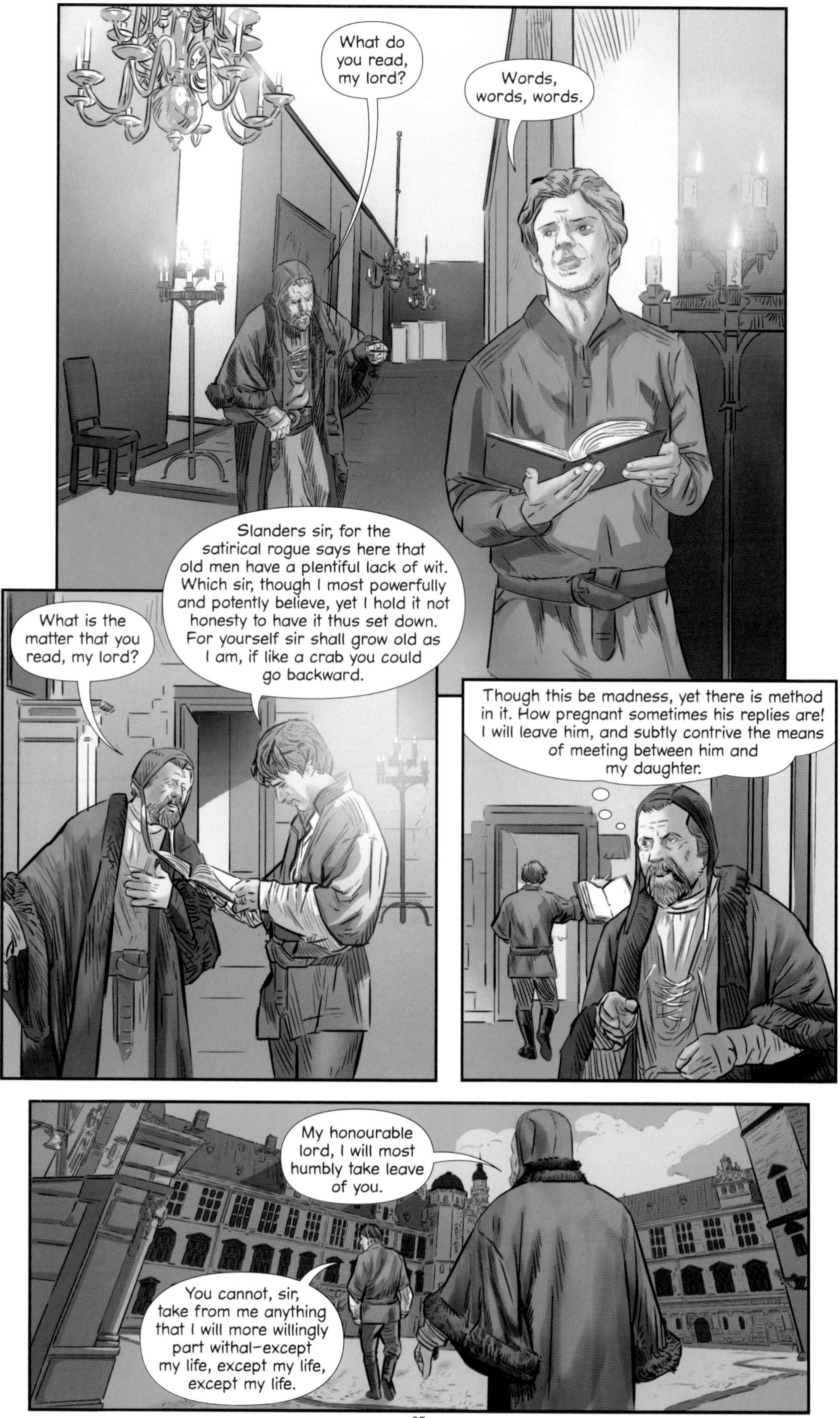
What do you read, my lord?
Words, words, words.
What is the matter that you read, my lord?
Slanders sir, for the satirical rogue says here that old men have a plentiful lack of wit. Which sir, though I most powerfully and potently believe, yet I hold it not honesty to have it thus set down. For yourself sir shall grow old as I am, if like a crab you could go backward.
Though this be madness, yet there is method in it. How pregnant sometimes his replies are! I will leave him, and subtly contrive the means of meeting between him and my daughter.
My honourable lord, I will most humbly take leave of you.
You cannot, sir, take from me anything that I will more willingly part withal—except my life, except my life, except my life.

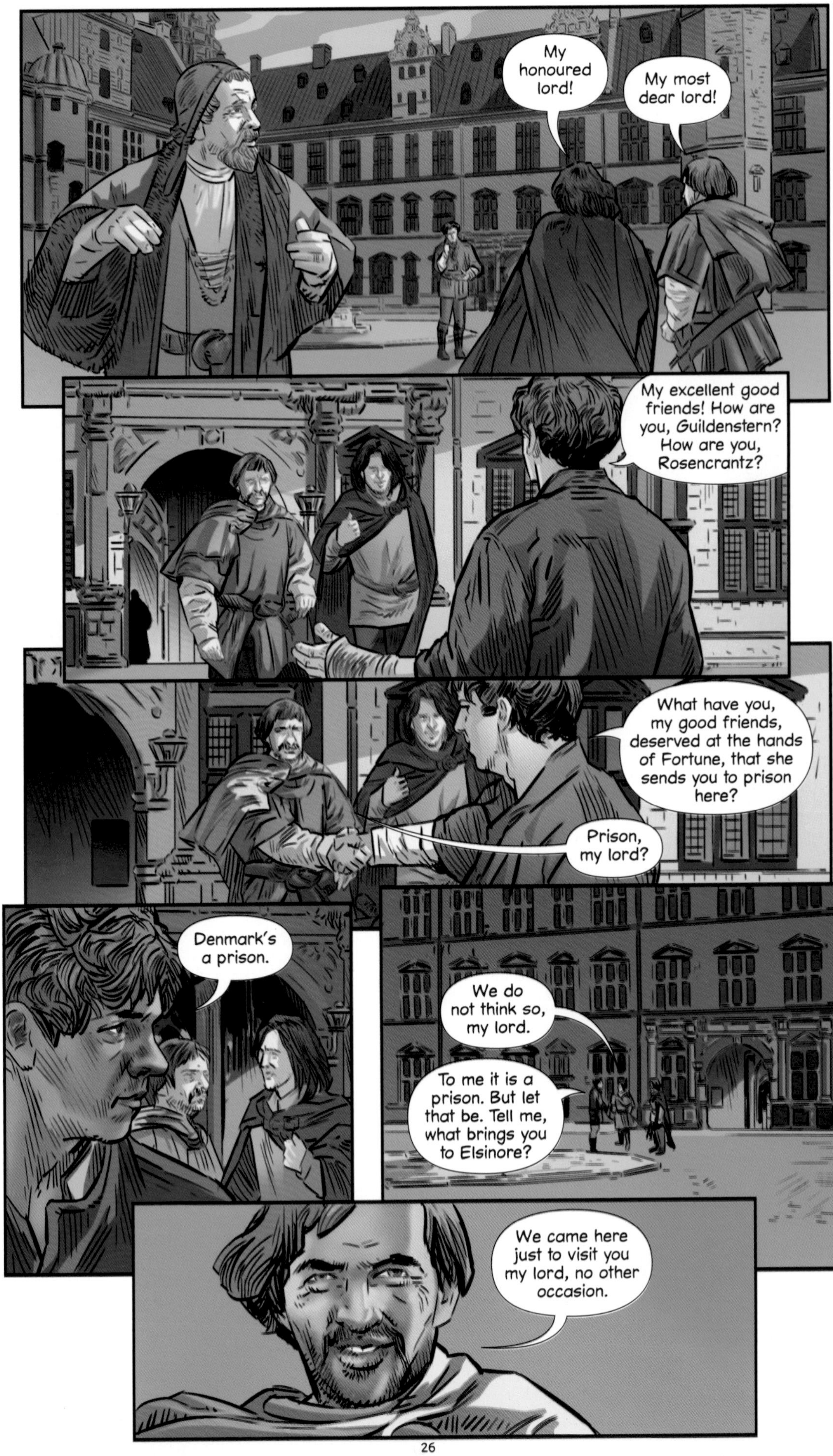
My honoured lord!
My most dear lord!
My excellent good friends! How are you, Guildenstern? How are you, Rosencrantz?
What have you, my good friends, deserved at the hands of Fortune, that she sends you to prison here?
Prison, my lord?
Denmark's a prison.
We do not think so, my lord.
To me it is a prison. But let that be. Tell me, what brings you to Elsinore?
We came here just to visit you my lord, no other occasion.

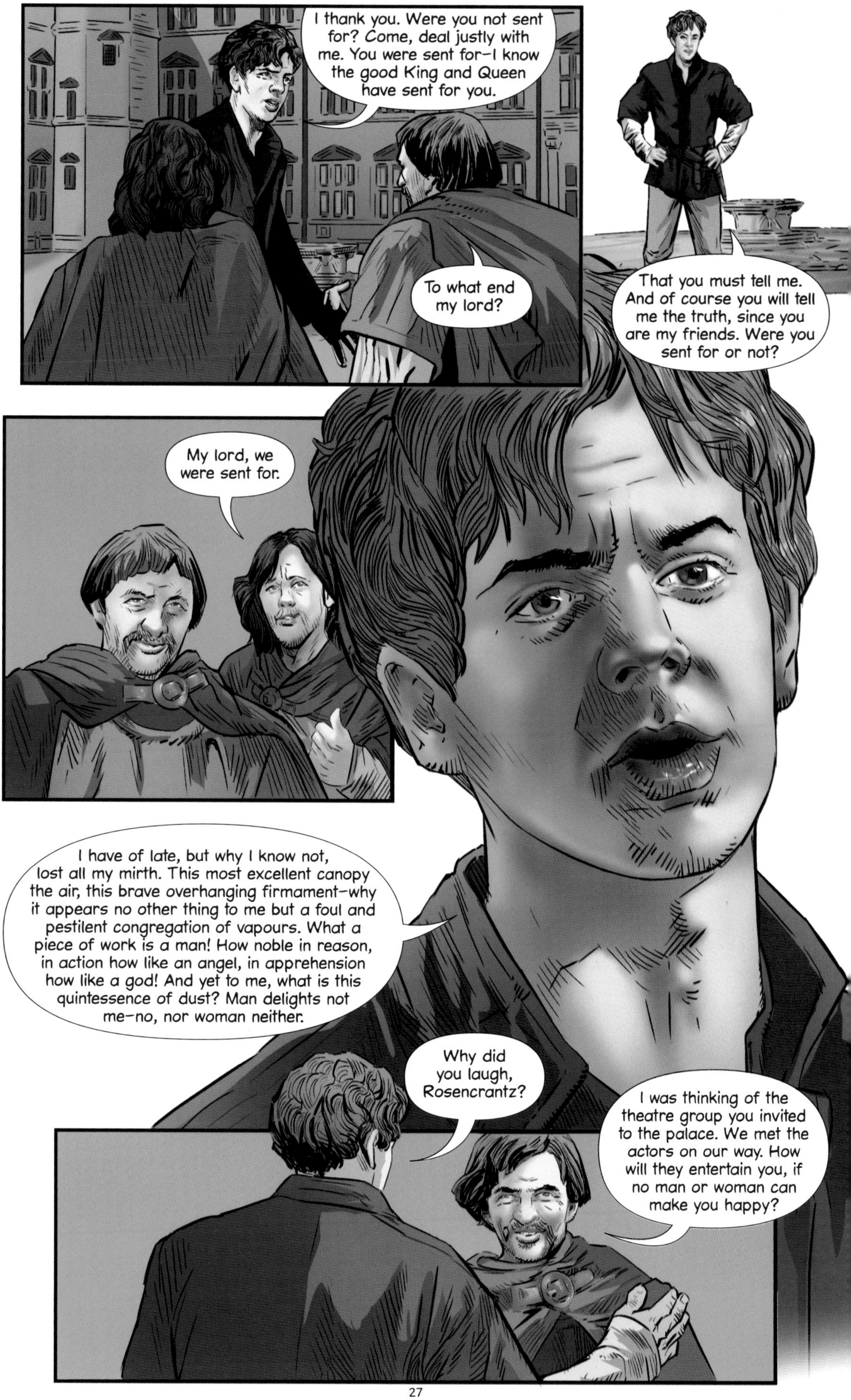

I thank you. Were you not sent for? Come, deal justly with me. You were sent for—I know the good King and Queen have sent for you.
To what end my lord?
That you must tell me. And of course you will tell me the truth, since you are my friends. Were you sent for or not?
My lord, we were sent for.
I have of late, but why I know not, lost all my mirth. This most excellent canopy the air, this brave overhanging firmament—why it appears no other thing to me but a foul and pestilent congregation of vapours. What a piece of work is a man! How noble in reason, in action how like an angel, in apprehension how like a god! And yet to me, what is this quintessence of dust? Man delights not me—no, nor woman neither.
Why did you laugh, Rosencrantz?
I was thinking of the theatre group you invited to the palace. We met the actors on our way. How will they entertain you, if no man or woman can make you happy?

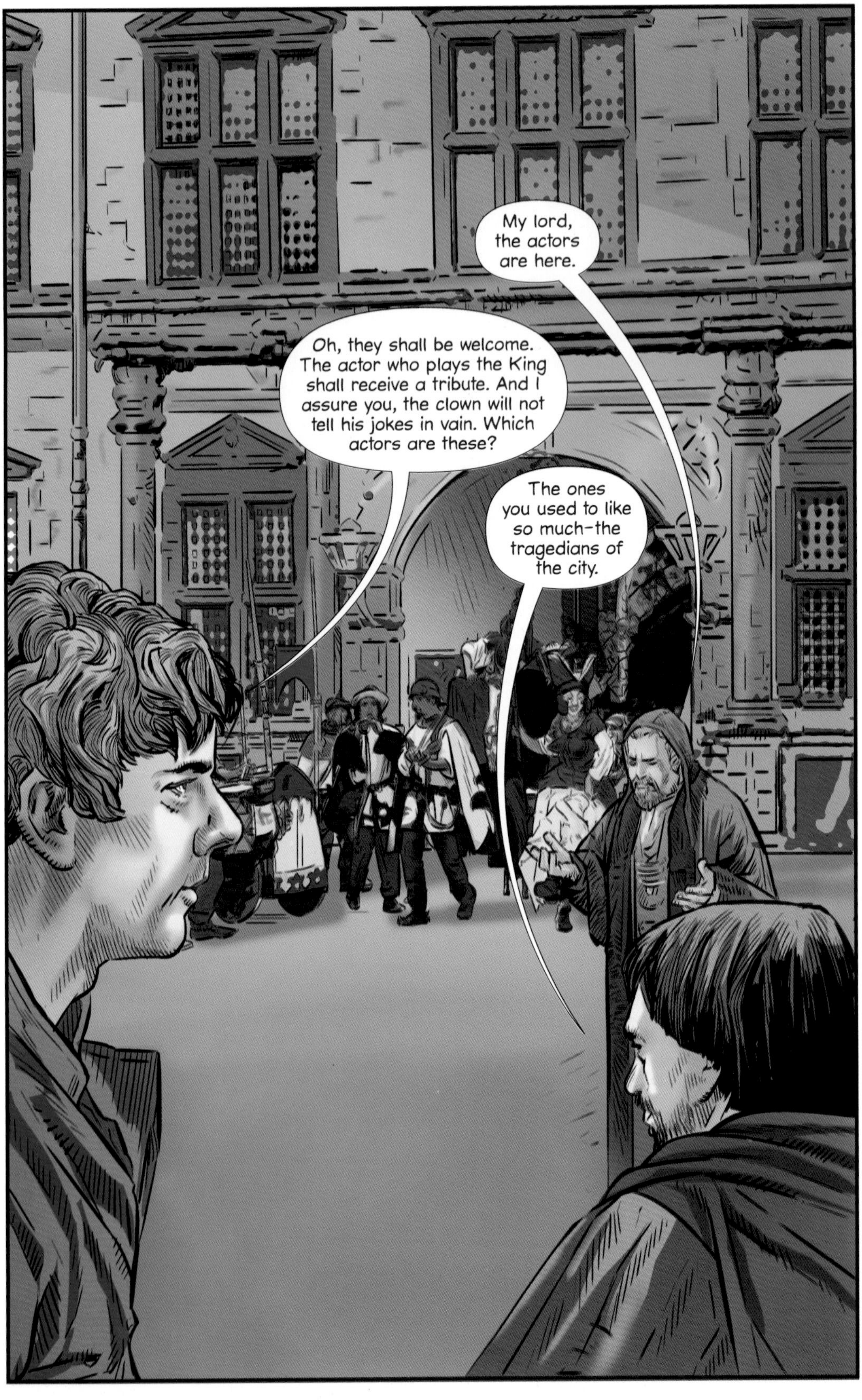
My lord, the actors are here.
Oh, they shall be welcome. The actor who plays the King shall receive a tribute. And I assure you, the clown will not tell his jokes in vain. Which actors are these?
The ones you used to like so much–the tragedians of the city.

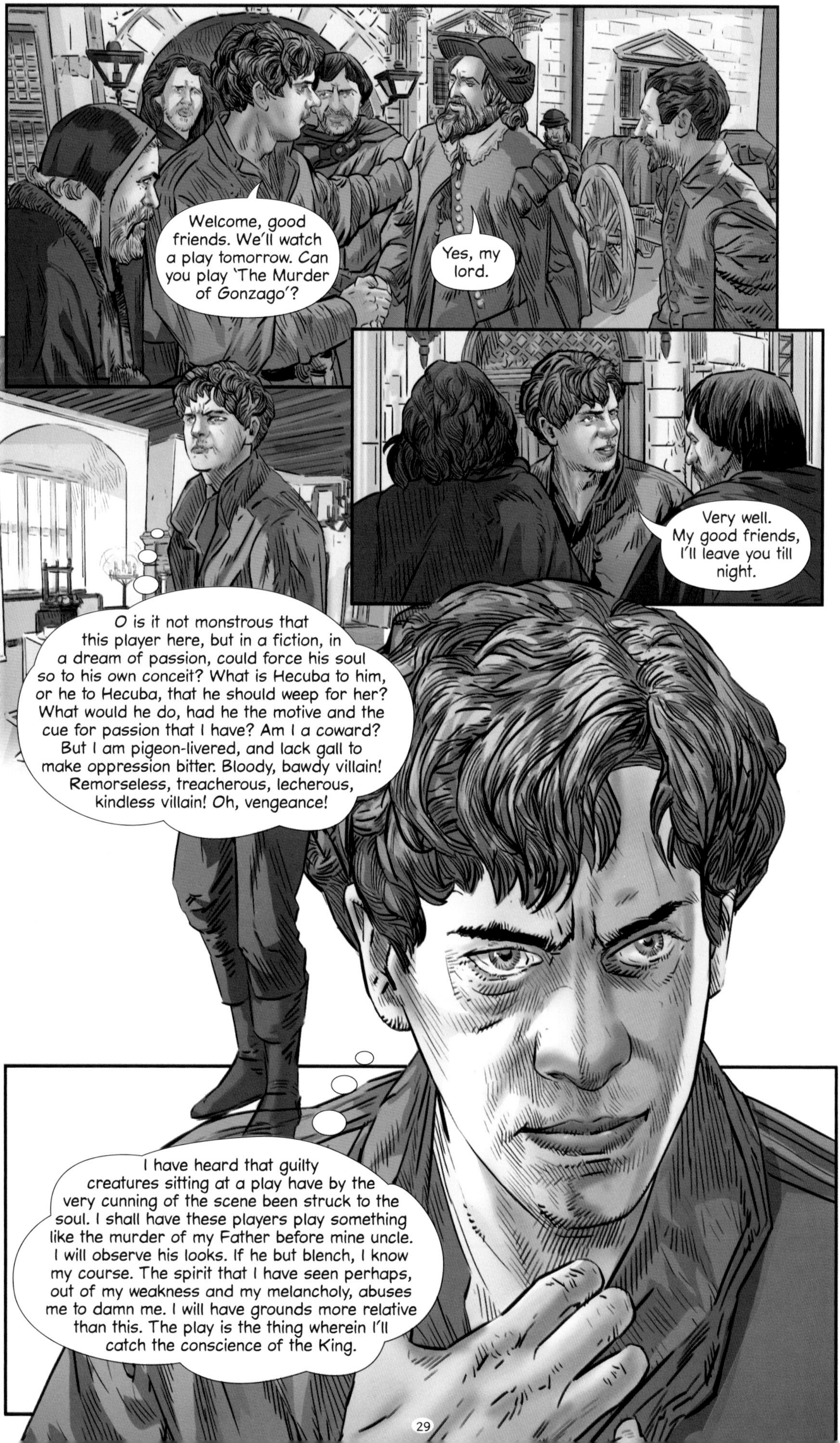
Welcome, good friends. We'll watch a play tomorrow. Can you play 'The Murder of Gonzago'?
Yes, my lord.
Very well. My good friends, I'll leave you till night.
O is it not monstrous that this player here, but in a fiction, in a dream of passion, could force his soul so to his own conceit? What is Hecuba to him, or he to Hecuba, that he should weep for her? What would he do, had he the motive and the cue for passion that I have? Am I a coward? But I am pigeon-livered, and lack gall to make oppression bitter. Bloody, bawdy villain! Remorseless, treacherous, lecherous, kindless villain! Oh, vengeance!
I have heard that guilty creatures sitting at a play have by the very cunning of the scene been struck to the soul. I shall have these players play something like the murder of my Father before mine uncle. I will observe his looks. If he but blench, I know my course. The spirit that I have seen perhaps, out of my weakness and my melancholy, abuses me to damn me. I will have grounds more relative than this. The play is the thing wherein I'll catch the conscience of the King.

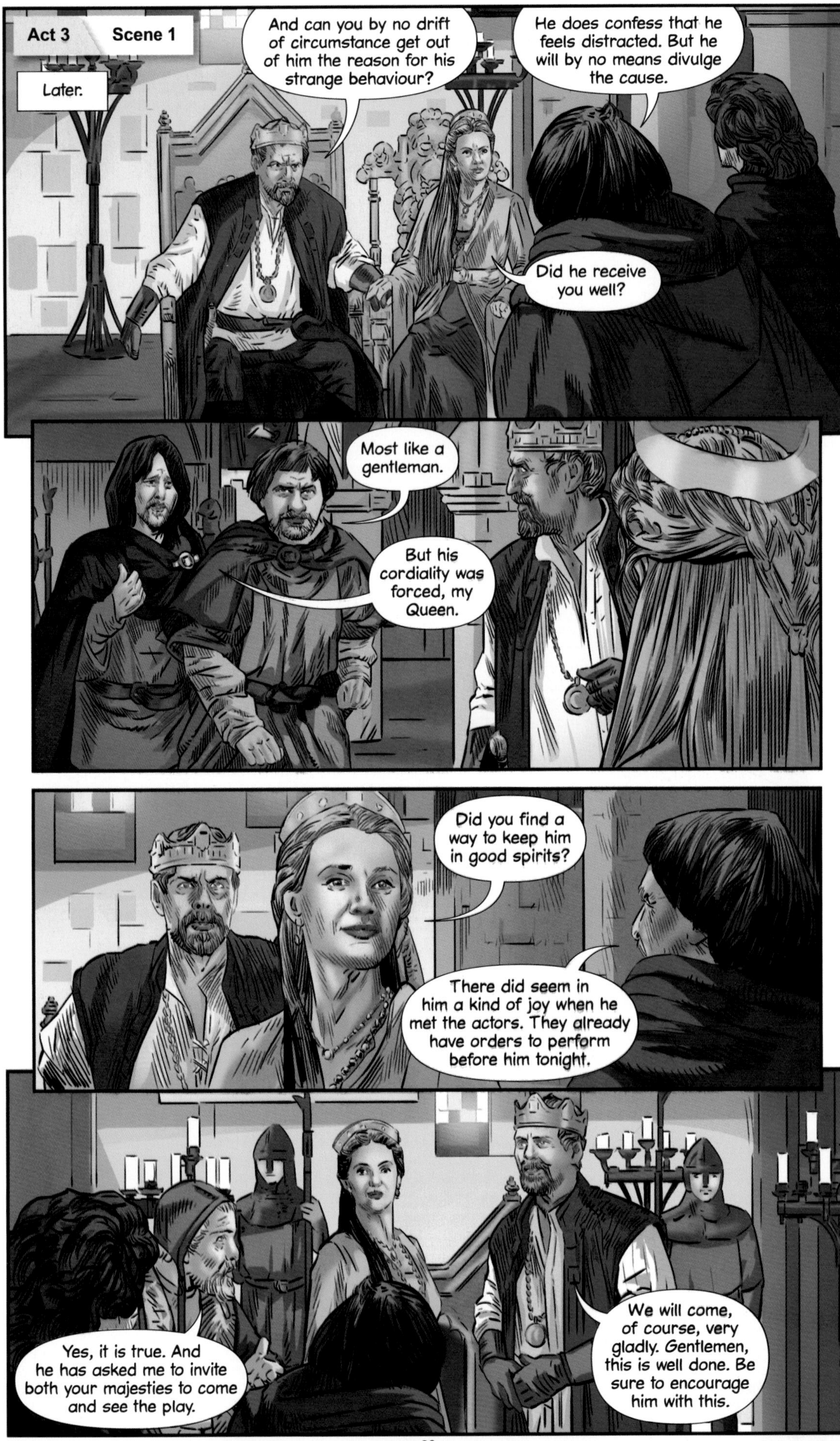

Act 3 Scene 1
Later.
And can you by no drift of circumstance get out of him the reason for his strange behaviour?
He does confess that he feels distracted. But he will by no means divulge the cause.
Did he receive you well?
Most like a gentleman.
But his cordiality was forced, my Queen.
Did you find a way to keep him in good spirits?
There did seem in him a kind of joy when he met the actors. They already have orders to perform before him tonight.
Yes, it is true. And he has asked me to invite both your majesties to come and see the play.
We will come, of course, very gladly. Gentlemen, this is well done. Be sure to encourage him with this.

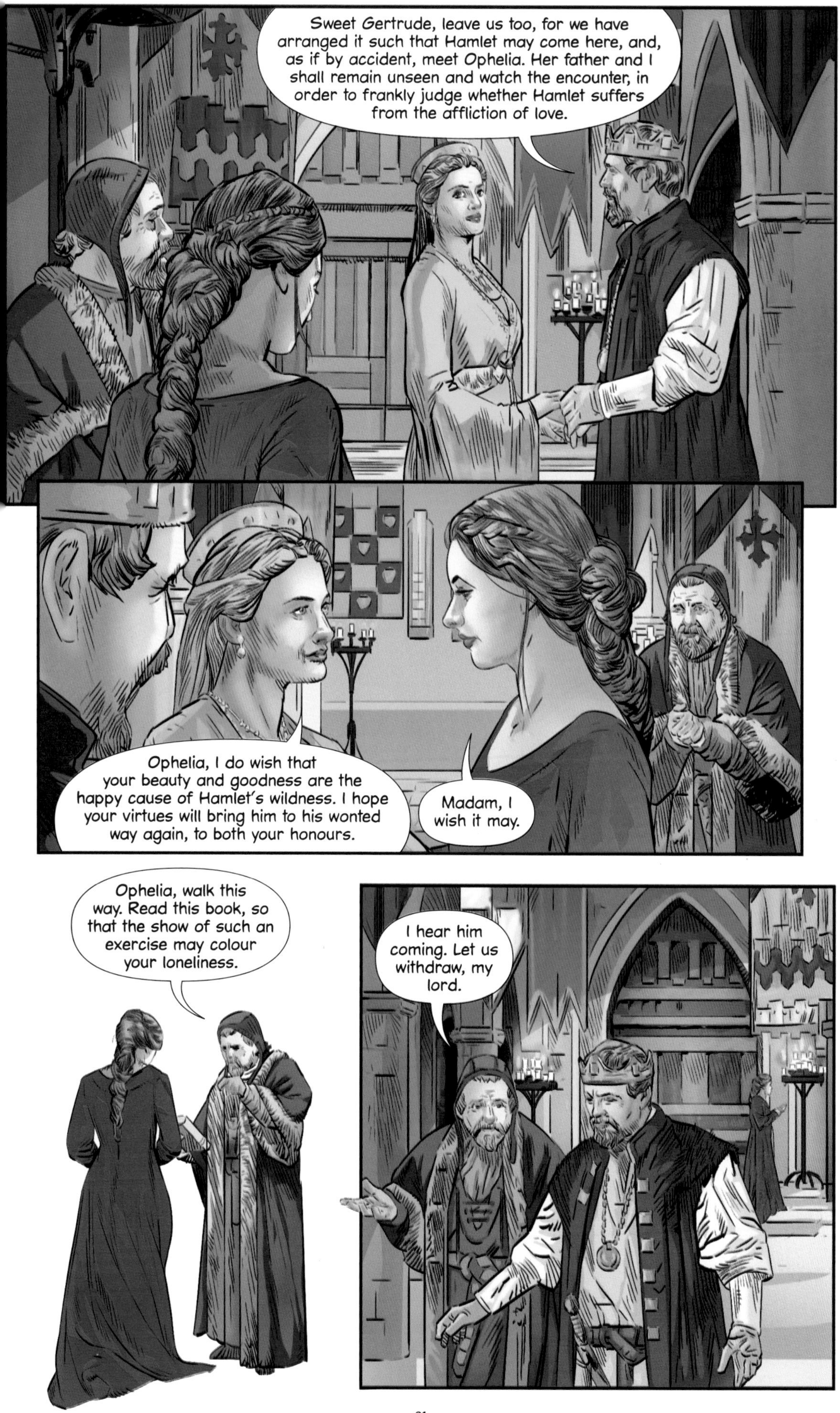

Sweet Gertrude, leave us too, for we have arranged it such that Hamlet may come here, and, as if by accident, meet Ophelia. Her father and I shall remain unseen and watch the encounter, in order to frankly judge whether Hamlet suffers from the affliction of love.
Ophelia, I do wish that your beauty and goodness are the happy cause of Hamlet's wildness. I hope your virtues will bring him to his wonted way again, to both your honours.
Madam, I wish it may.
Ophelia, walk this way. Read this book, so that the show of such an exercise may colour your loneliness.
I hear him coming. Let us withdraw, my lord.

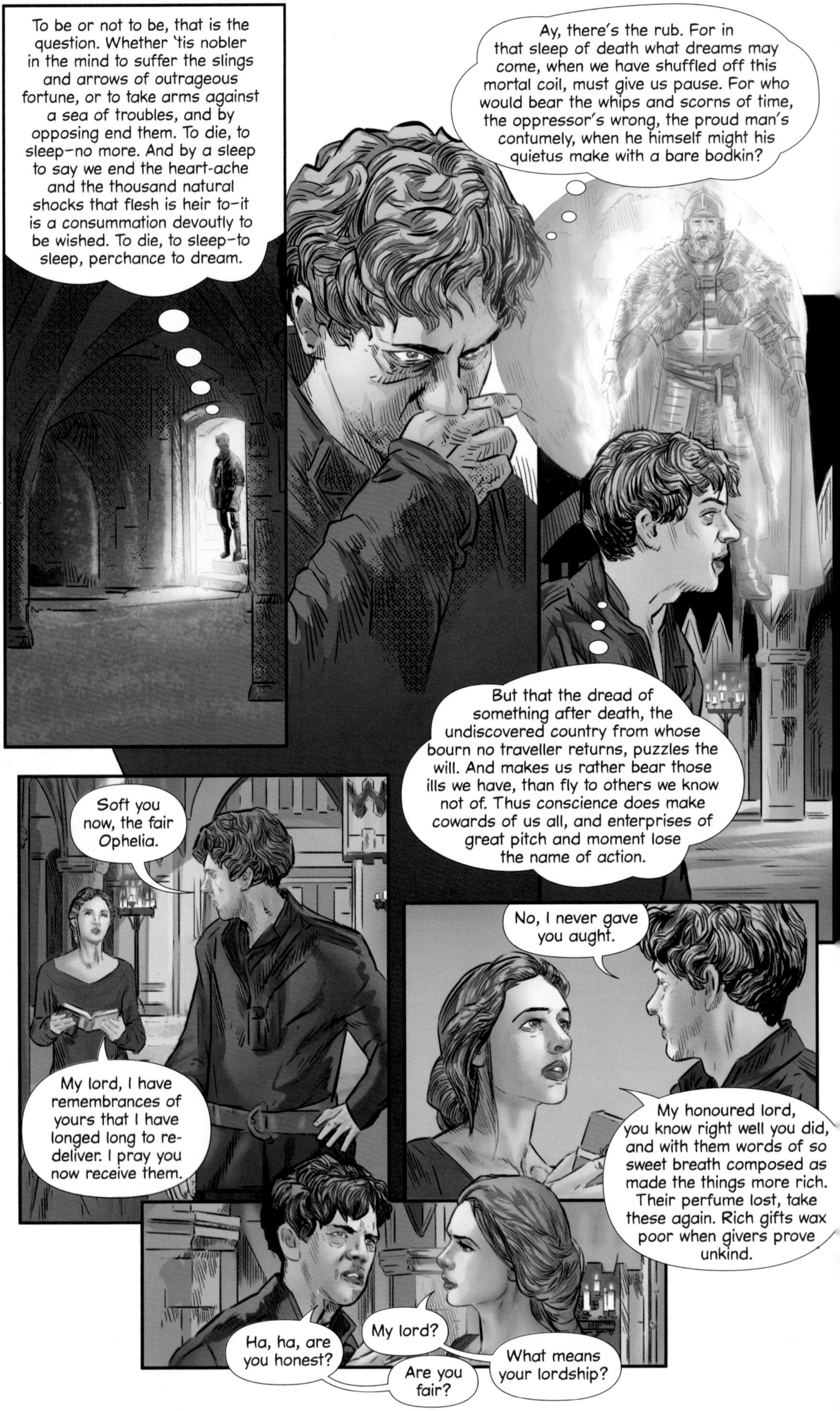

To be or not to be, that is the question. Whether 'tis nobler in the mind to suffer the slings and arrows of outrageous fortune, or to take arms against a sea of troubles, and by opposing end them. To die, to sleep—no more. And by a sleep to say we end the heart-ache and the thousand natural shocks that flesh is heir to—it is a consummation devoutly to be wished. To die, to sleep—to sleep, perchance to dream.
Ay, there's the rub. For in that sleep of death what dreams may come, when we have shuffled off this mortal coil, must give us pause. For who would bear the whips and scorns of time, the oppressor's wrong, the proud man's contumely, when he himself might his quietus make with a bare bodkin?
But that the dread of something after death, the undiscovered country from whose bourn no traveller returns, puzzles the will. And makes us rather bear those ills we have, than fly to others we know not of. Thus conscience does make cowards of us all, and enterprises of great pitch and moment lose the name of action.
Soft you now, the fair Ophelia.
My lord, I have remembrances of yours that I have longed long to re-deliver. I pray you now receive them.
No, I never gave you aught.
My honoured lord, you know right well you did, and with them words of so sweet breath composed as made the things more rich. Their perfume lost, take these again. Rich gifts wax poor when givers prove unkind.
Ha, ha, are you honest?
My lord?
Are you fair?
What means your lordship?

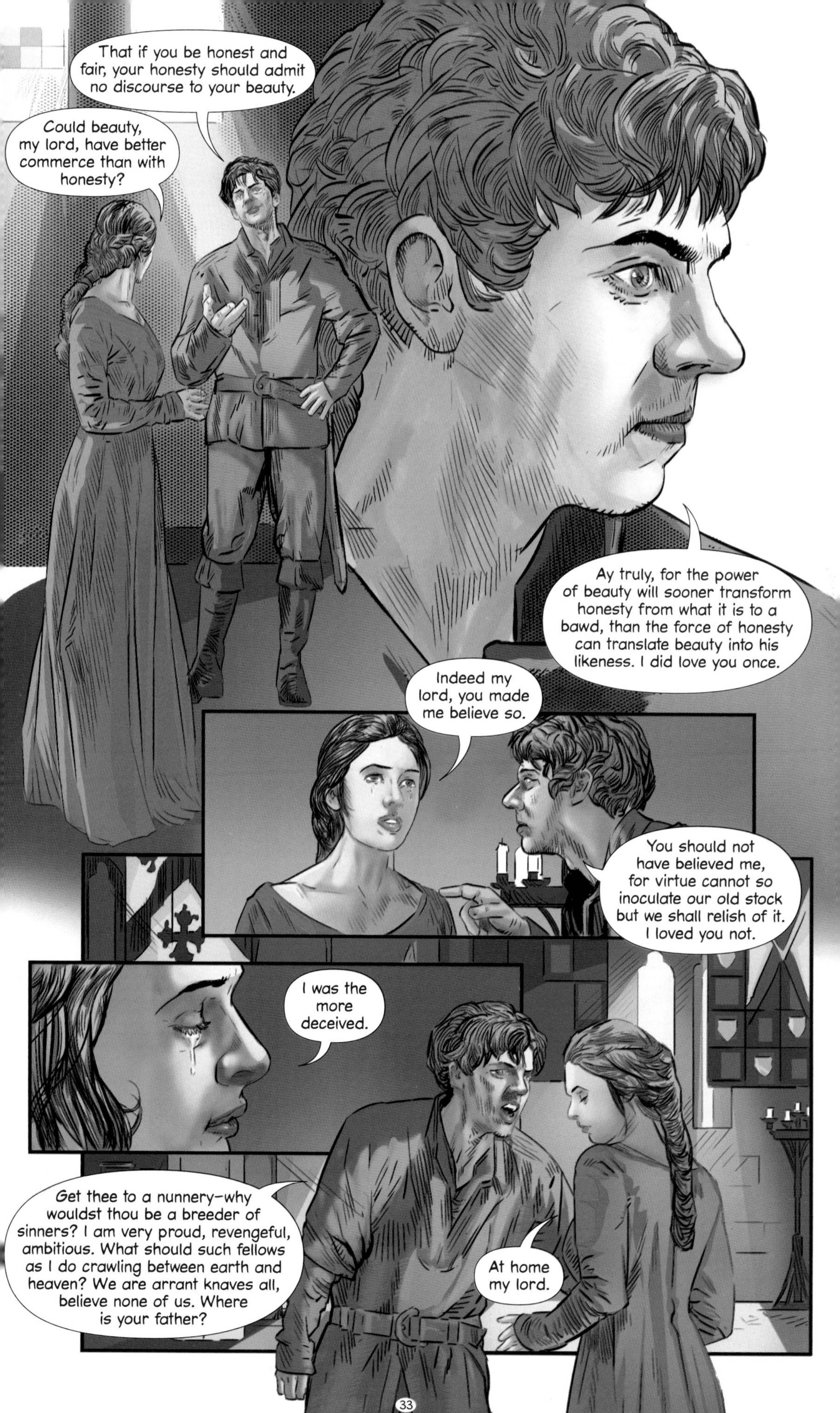

That if you be honest and fair, your honesty should admit no discourse to your beauty.
Could beauty, my lord, have better commerce than with honesty?
Ay truly, for the power of beauty will sooner transform honesty from what it is to a bawd, than the force of honesty can translate beauty into his likeness. I did love you once.
Indeed my lord, you made me believe so.
You should not have believed me, for virtue cannot so inoculate our old stock but we shall relish of it. I loved you not.
I was the more deceived.
Get thee to a nunnery–why wouldst thou be a breeder of sinners? I am very proud, revengeful, ambitious. What should such fellows as I do crawling between earth and heaven? We are arrant knaves all, believe none of us. Where is your father?
At home my lord.

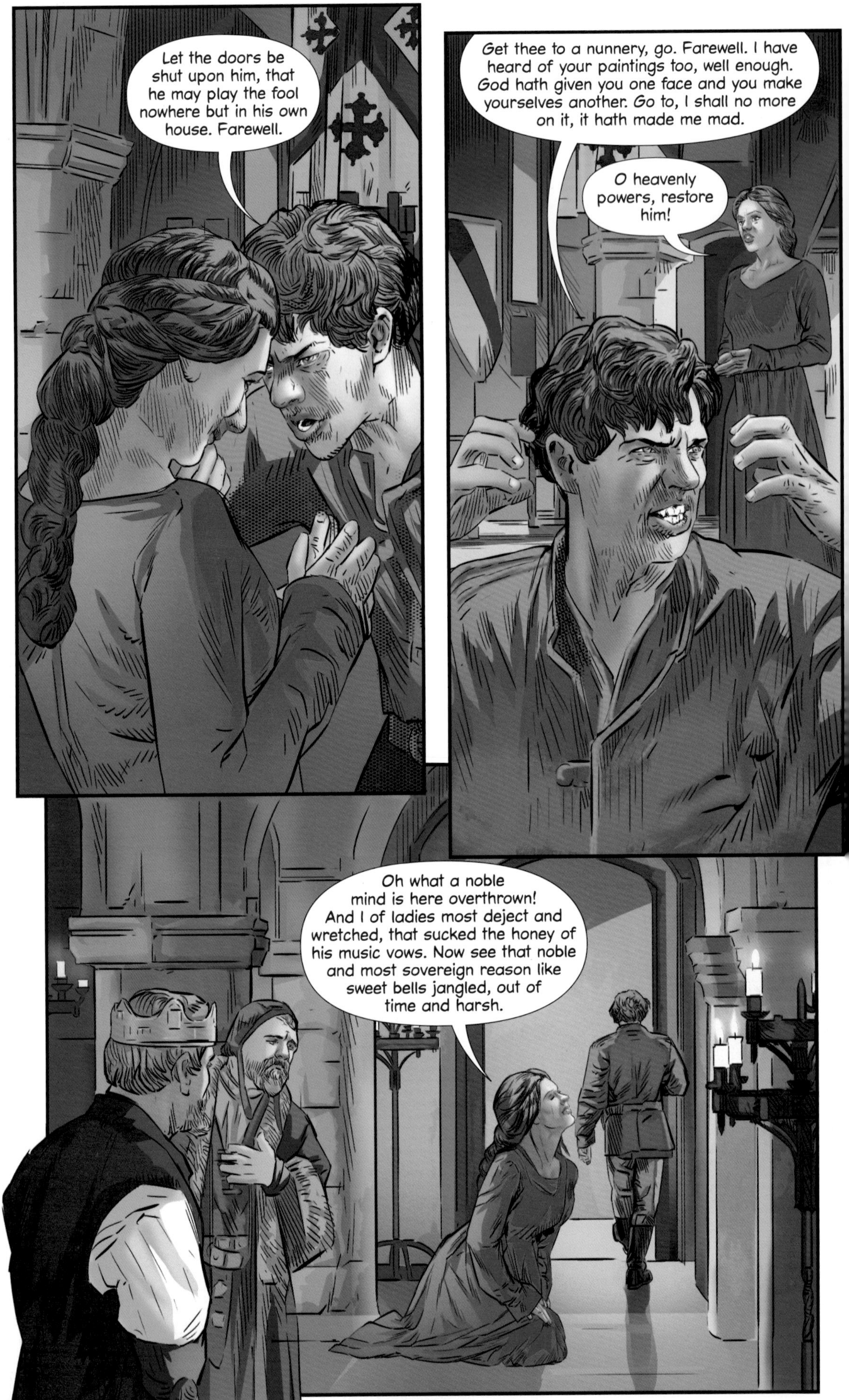
Let the doors be shut upon him, that he may play the fool nowhere but in his own house. Farewell.
Get thee to a nunnery, go. Farewell. I have heard of your paintings too, well enough. God hath given you one face and you make yourselves another. Go to, I shall no more on it, it hath made me mad.
O heavenly powers, restore him!
Oh what a noble mind is here overthrown! And I of ladies most deject and wretched, that sucked the honey of his music vows. Now see that noble and most sovereign reason like sweet bells jangled, out of time and harsh.

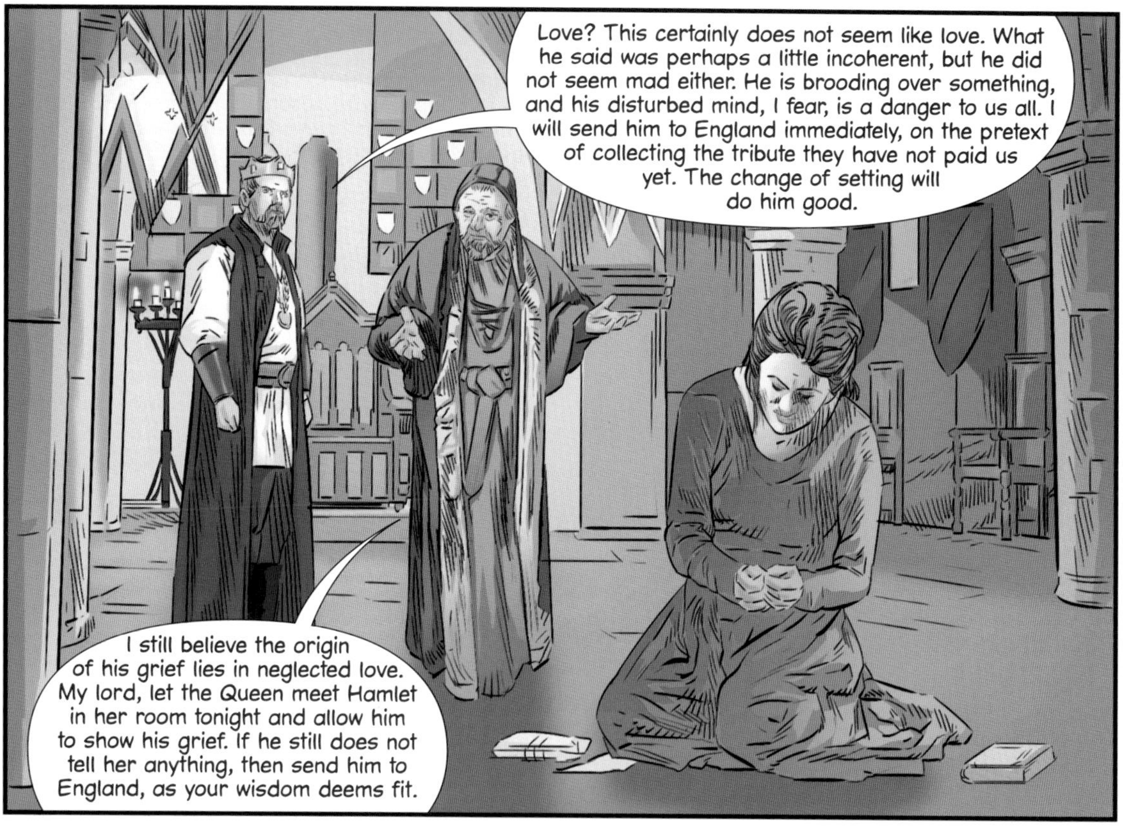
Love? This certainly does not seem like love. What he said was perhaps a little incoherent, but he did not seem mad either. He is brooding over something, and his disturbed mind, I fear, is a danger to us all. I will send him to England immediately, on the pretext of collecting the tribute they have not paid us yet. The change of setting will do him good.
I still believe the origin of his grief lies in neglected love. My lord, let the Queen meet Hamlet in her room tonight and allow him to show his grief. If he still does not tell her anything, then send him to England, as your wisdom deems fit.

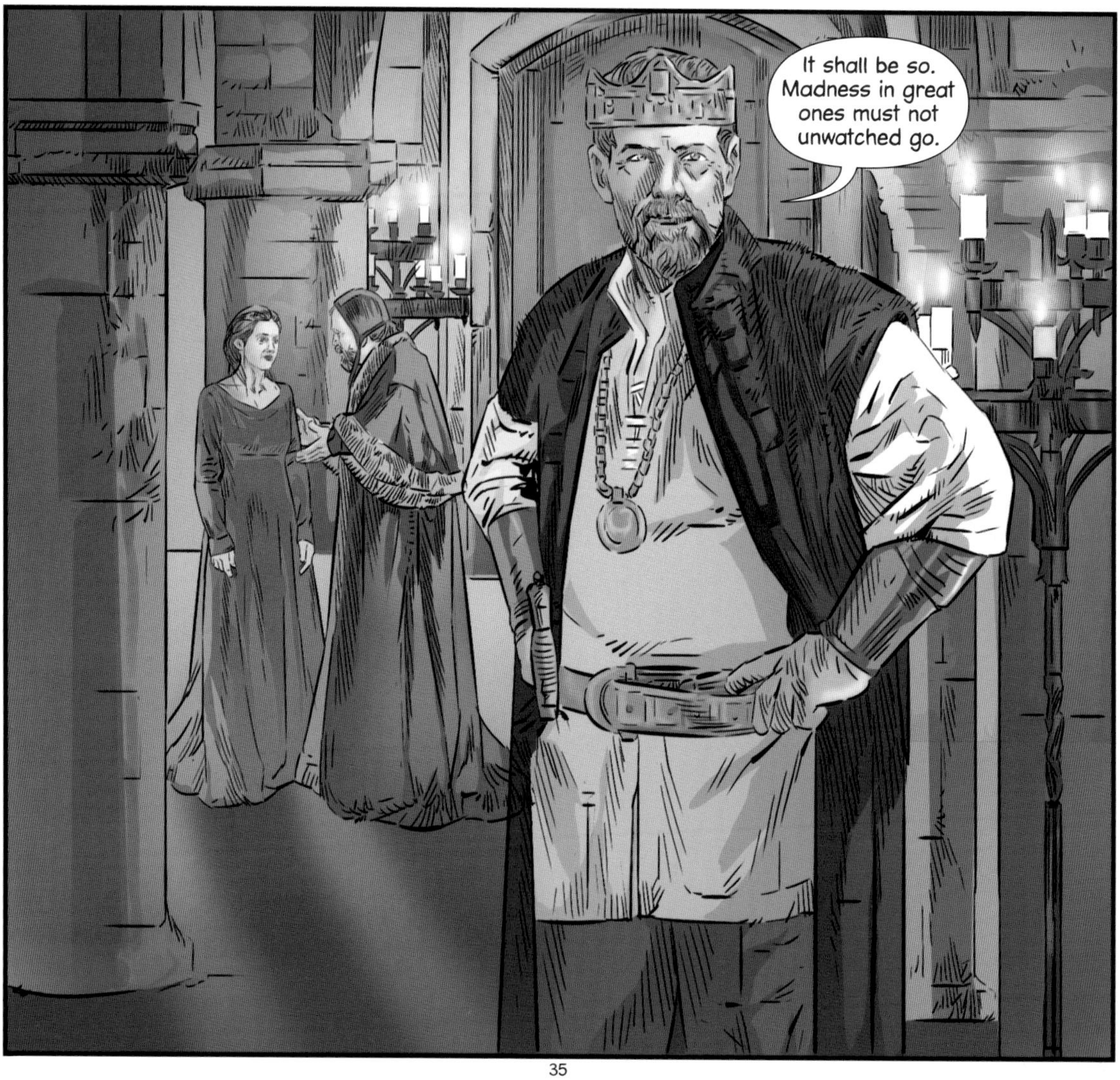
It shall be so. Madness in great ones must not unwatched go.

Later in the day, Hamlet watches the actors prepare for the play.

Do not saw the air too much with your hand thus; use your limbs gently. Nor is there a need to be too tame. Let your own discretion be your tutor. Suit the action to the word and the word to the action, with this special observance that you do not overstep the modesty of nature. Anything so overdone defeats the purpose of acting, whose end is to hold the mirror up to nature.

What news do you bring, my lord? Will the King see this piece of work?

Yes, and the Queen will see it too. They will be here shortly.

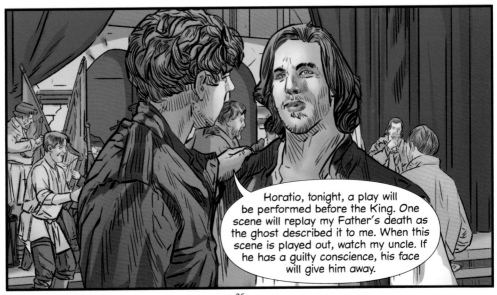

Horatio, tonight, a play will be performed before the King. One scene will replay my Father's death as the ghost described it to me. When this scene is played out, watch my uncle. If he has a guilty conscience, his face will give him away.

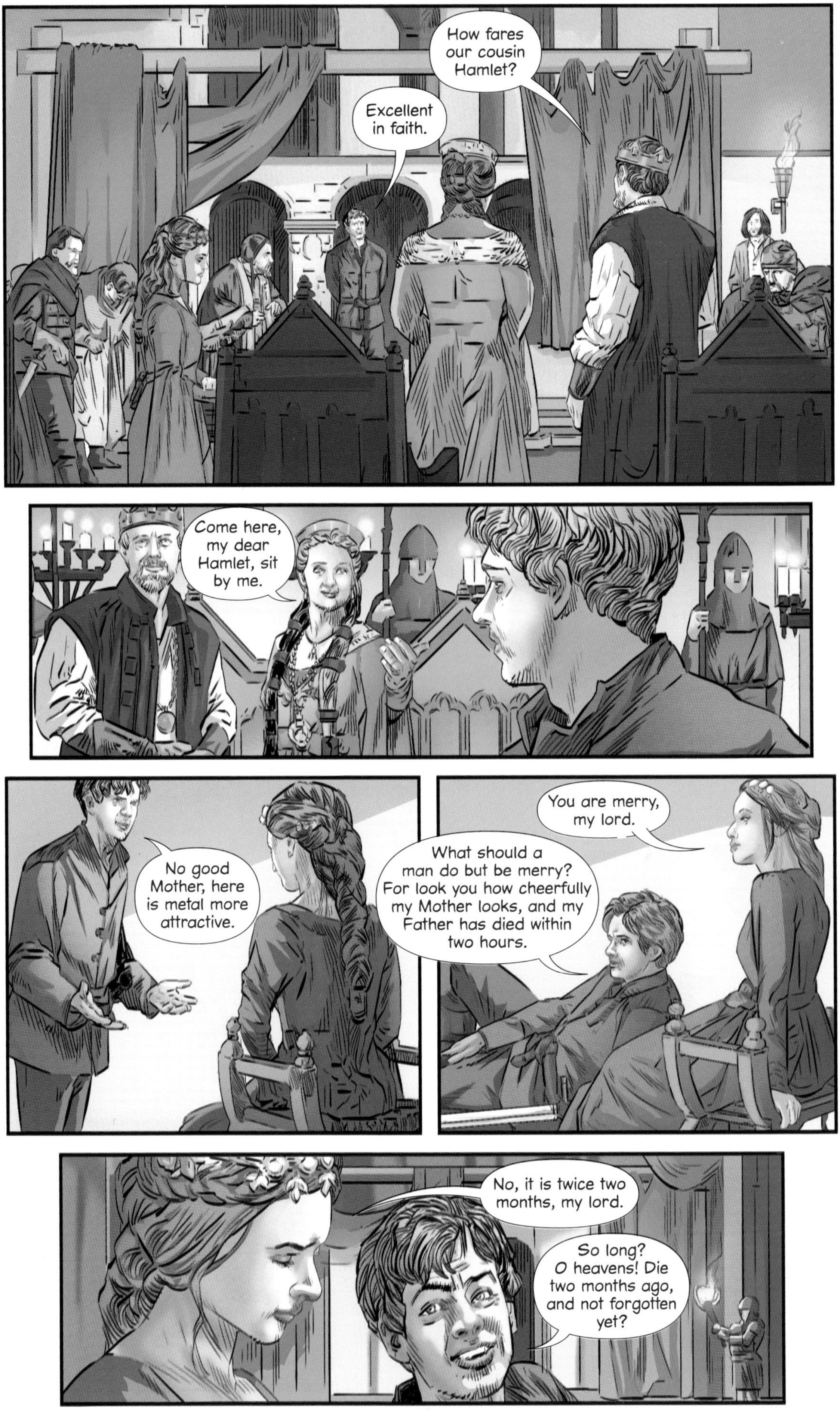

How fares our cousin Hamlet?
Excellent in faith.
Come here, my dear Hamlet, sit by me.
No good Mother, here is metal more attractive.
What should a man do but be merry? For look you how cheerfully my Mother looks, and my Father has died within two hours.
You are merry, my lord.
No, it is twice two months, my lord.
So long? O heavens! Die two months ago, and not forgotten yet?

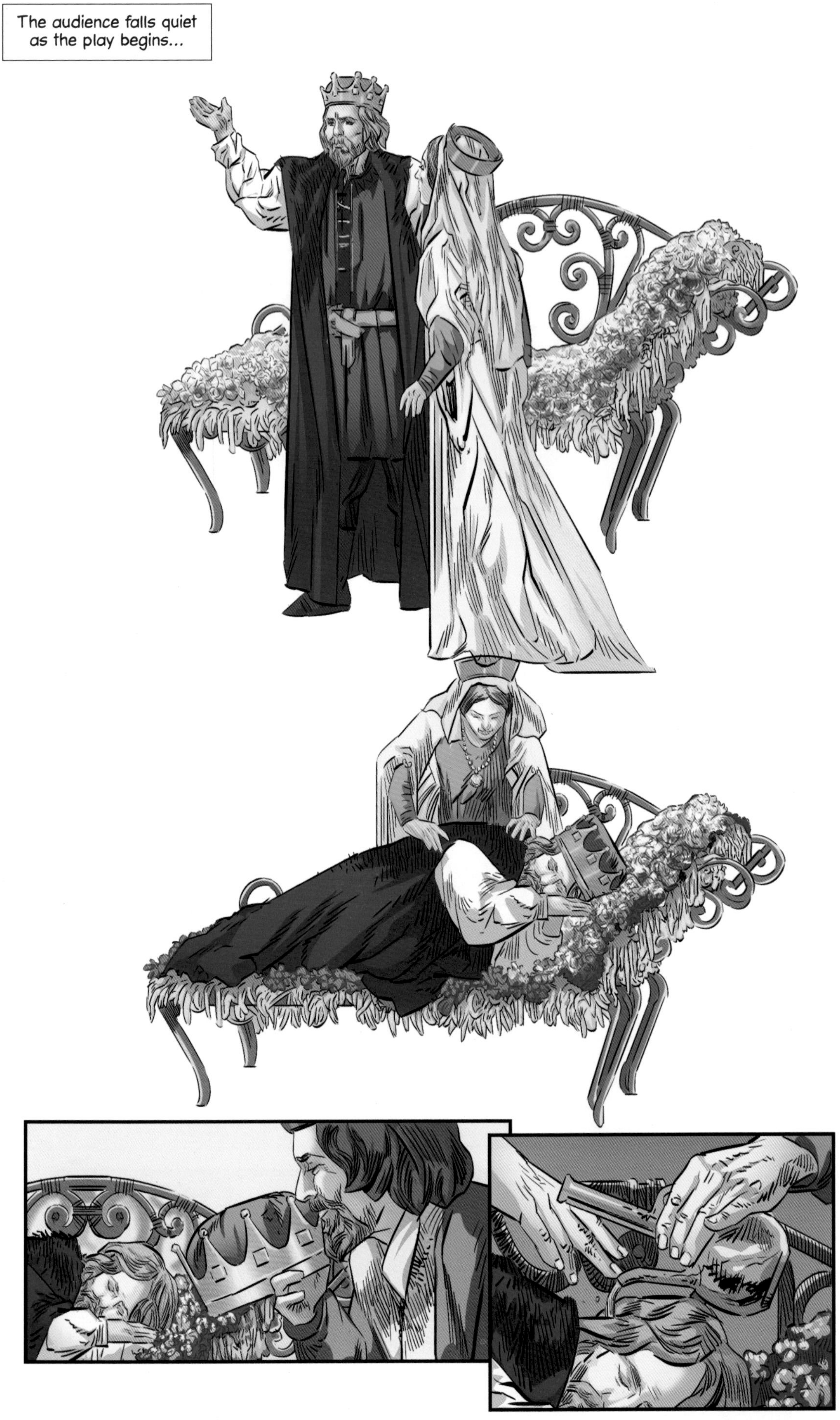
The audience falls quiet as the play begins...

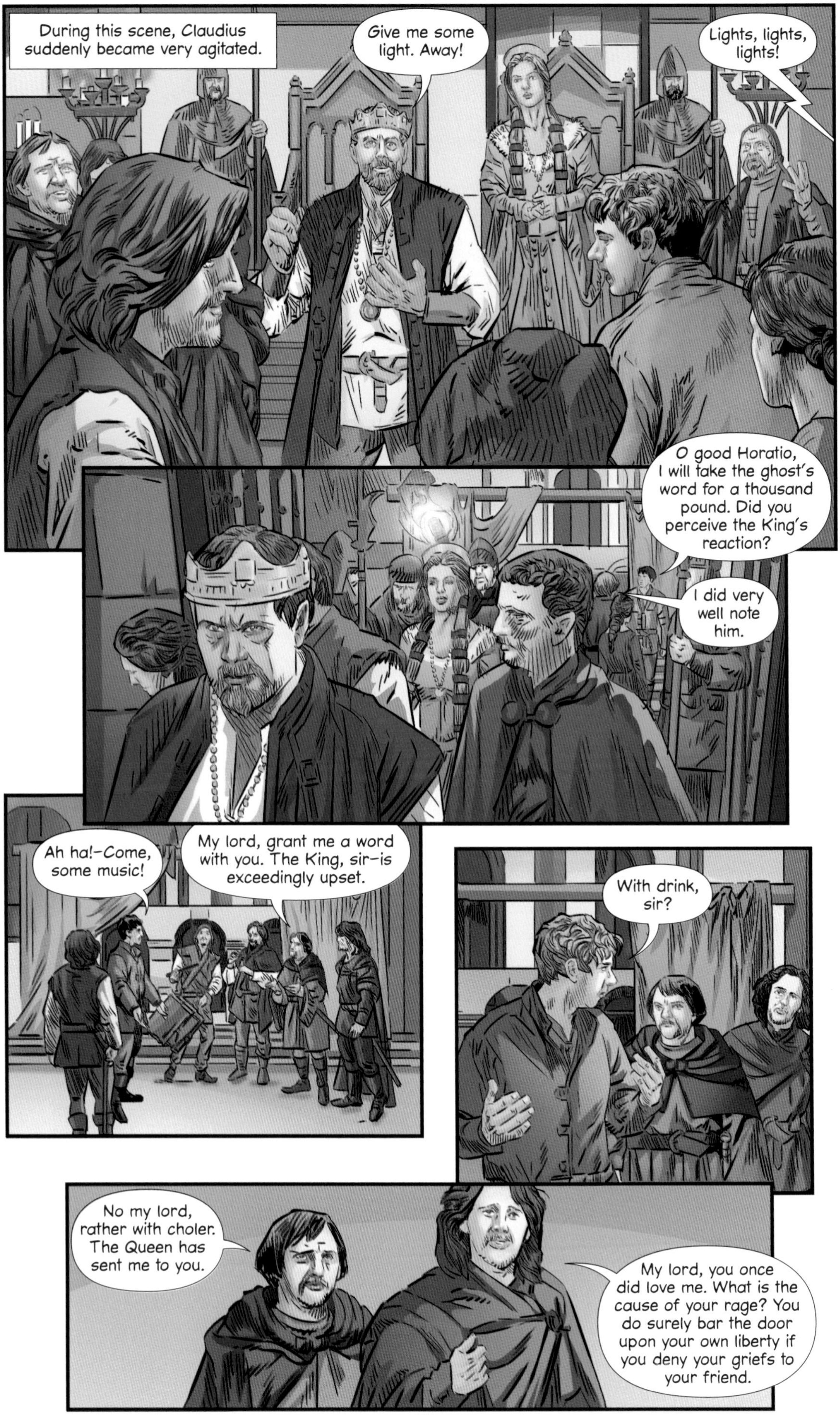
During this scene, Claudius suddenly became very agitated.
Give me some light. Away!
Lights, lights, lights!
O good Horatio, I will take the ghost's word for a thousand pound. Did you perceive the King's reaction?
I did very well note him.
Ah ha!–Come, some music!
My lord, grant me a word with you. The King, sir–is exceedingly upset.
With drink, sir?
No my lord, rather with choler. The Queen has sent me to you.
My lord, you once did love me. What is the cause of your rage? You do surely bar the door upon your own liberty if you deny your griefs to your friend.

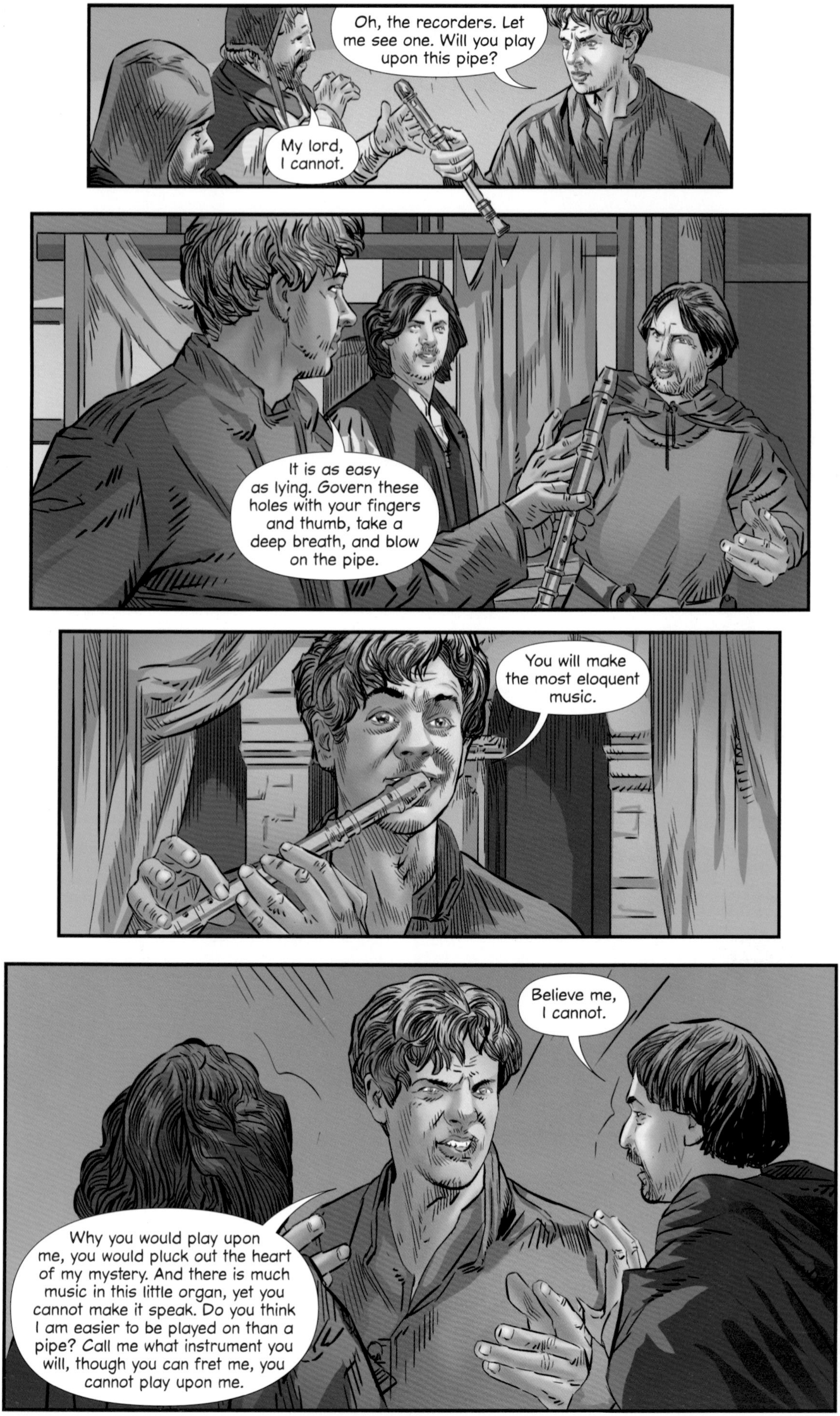
Oh, the recorders. Let me see one. Will you play upon this pipe?
My lord, I cannot.
It is as easy as lying. Govern these holes with your fingers and thumb, take a deep breath, and blow on the pipe.
You will make the most eloquent music.
Believe me, I cannot.
Why you would play upon me, you would pluck out the heart of my mystery. And there is much music in this little organ, yet you cannot make it speak. Do you think I am easier to be played on than a pipe? Call me what instrument you will, though you can fret me, you cannot play upon me.

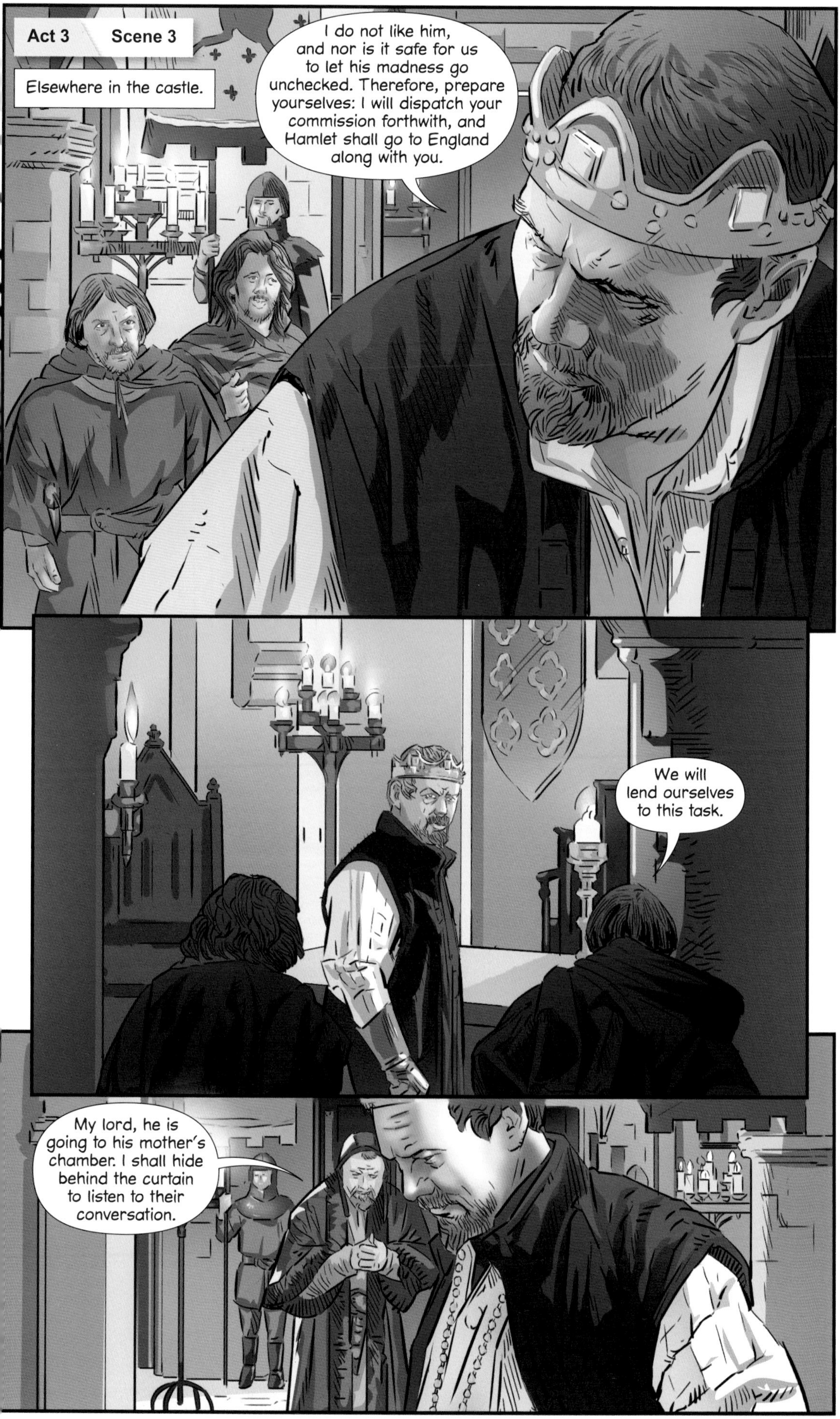
Act 3 Scene 3
Elsewhere in the castle.
I do not like him, and nor is it safe for us to let his madness go unchecked. Therefore, prepare yourselves: I will dispatch your commission forthwith, and Hamlet shall go to England along with you.
We will lend ourselves to this task.
My lord, he is going to his mother's chamber. I shall hide behind the curtain to listen to their conversation.

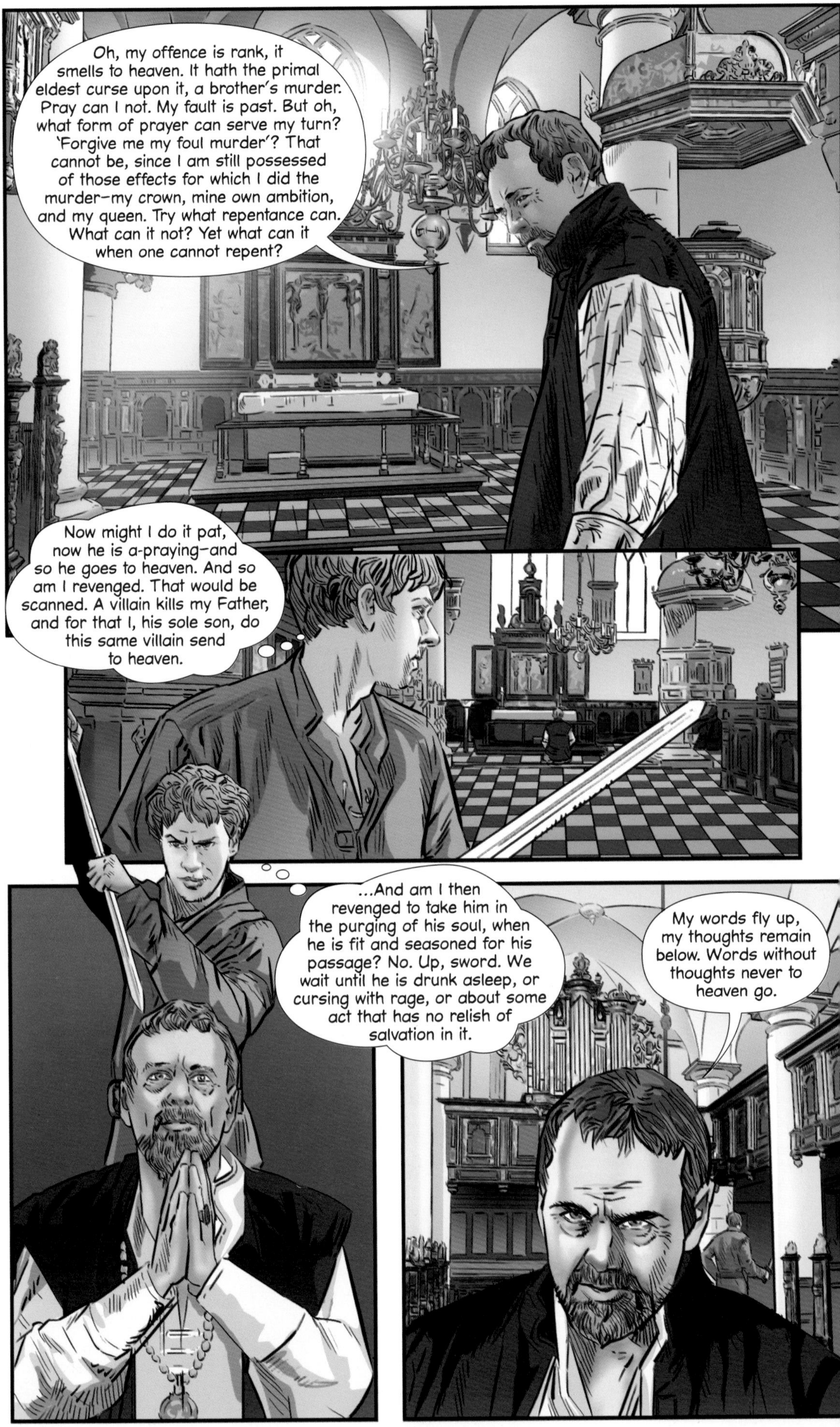
Oh, my offence is rank, it smells to heaven. It hath the primal eldest curse upon it, a brother's murder. Pray can I not. My fault is past. But oh, what form of prayer can serve my turn? 'Forgive me my foul murder'? That cannot be, since I am still possessed of those effects for which I did the murder–my crown, mine own ambition, and my queen. Try what repentance can. What can it not? Yet what can it when one cannot repent?
Now might I do it pat, now he is a-praying–and so he goes to heaven. And so am I revenged. That would be scanned. A villain kills my Father, and for that I, his sole son, do this same villain send to heaven.
...And am I then revenged to take him in the purging of his soul, when he is fit and seasoned for his passage? No. Up, sword. We wait until he is drunk asleep, or cursing with rage, or about some act that has no relish of salvation in it.
My words fly up, my thoughts remain below. Words without thoughts never to heaven go.

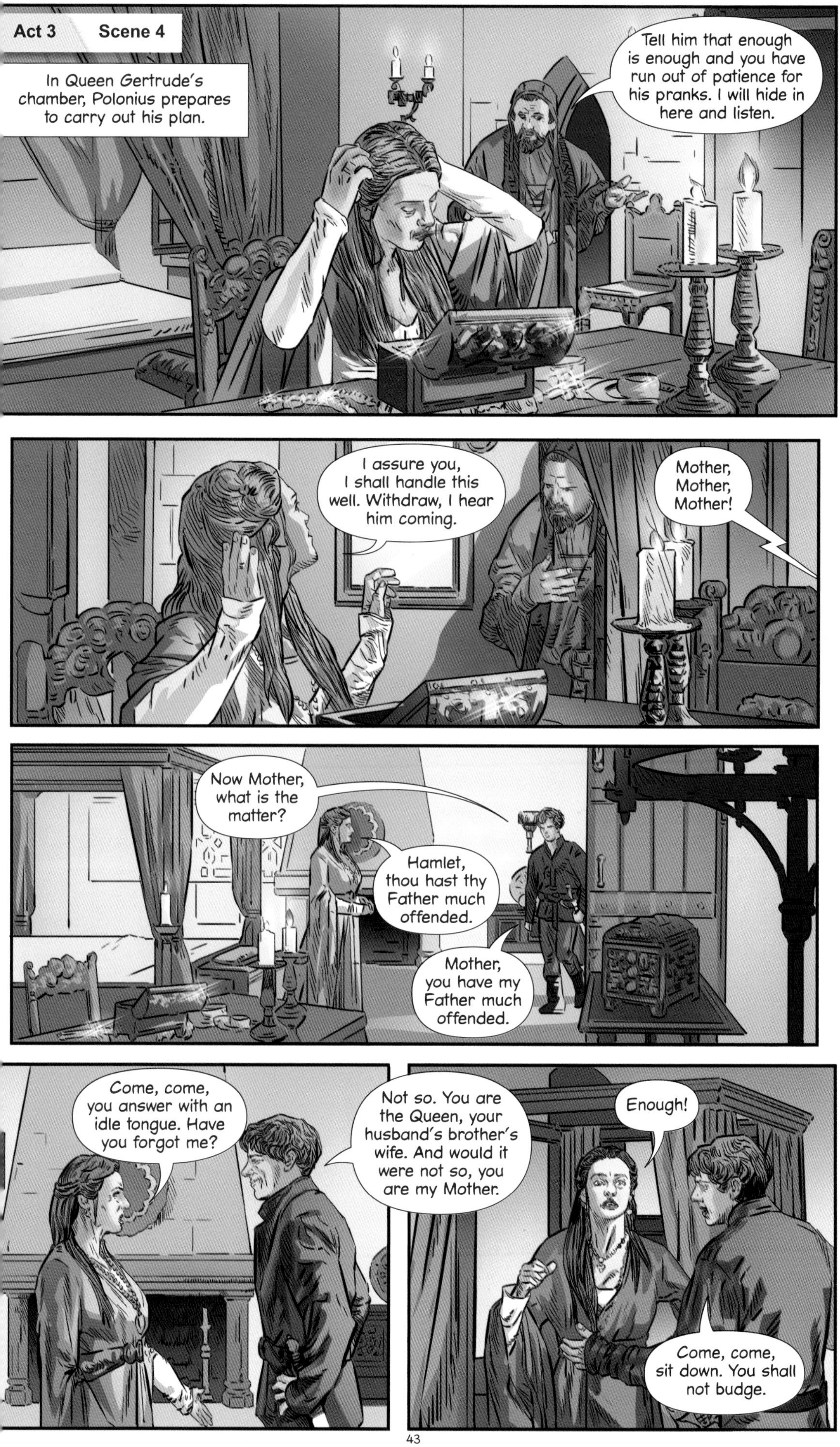
Act 3 Scene 4
In Queen Gertrude's chamber, Polonius prepares to carry out his plan.
Tell him that enough is enough and you have run out of patience for his pranks. I will hide in here and listen.
I assure you, I shall handle this well. Withdraw, I hear him coming.
Mother, Mother, Mother!
Now Mother, what is the matter?
Hamlet, thou hast thy Father much offended.
Mother, you have my Father much offended.
Come, come, you answer with an idle tongue. Have you forgot me?
Not so. You are the Queen, your husband's brother's wife. And would it were not so, you are my Mother.
Enough!
Come, come, sit down. You shall not budge.

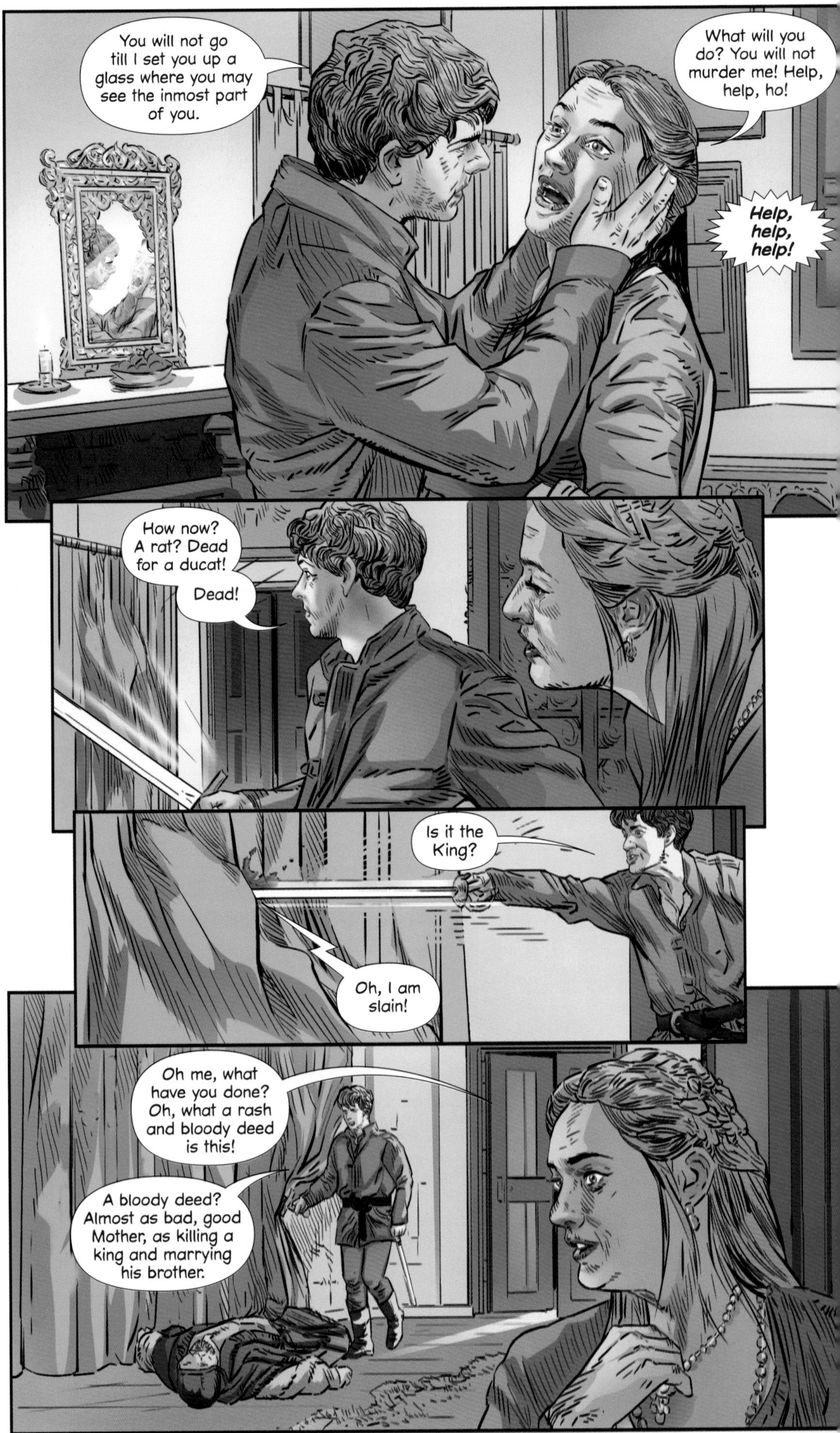
You will not go till I set you up a glass where you may see the inmost part of you.
What will you do? You will not murder me! Help, help, ho!
Help, help, help!
How now? A rat? Dead for a ducat!
Dead!
Is it the King?
Oh, I am slain!
Oh me, what have you done? Oh, what a rash and bloody deed is this!
A bloody deed? Almost as bad, good Mother, as killing a king and marrying his brother.

As killing a King?

Yes lady, that was my word. Stop wringing your hands. Peace! Sit down and let me wring your heart, for so I shall. Look here upon this picture, and on this.

See what a grace was seated on this brow. An eye like Mars, to threaten and command. A combination and a form indeed, where every god did seem to set his seal to give the world assurance of a man. This was your husband.

Here is your husband, like a mildewed ear blasting his wholesome brother. Have you eyes? You cannot call it love, for at your age the heyday in the blood is tame, it is humble, and waits upon the judgement. And what judgement would step from this to this?

O Hamlet, speak no more. You turn my eyes into my very soul.

A murderer and a villain, a cutpurse of the empire and rule, that from a shelf the precious diadem stole and put it in his pocket!

Oh speak to me no more. These words like daggers enter in my ears. No more, sweet Hamlet.

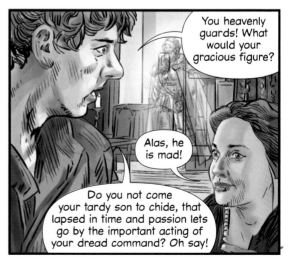

You heavenly guards! What would your gracious figure?

Alas, he is mad!

Do you not come your tardy son to chide, that lapsed in time and passion lets go by the important acting of your dread command? Oh say!

Look, amazement on thy Mother sits. Speak to her, Hamlet.

How is it with you lady?

Alas, how is it with you my son, that you speak with the air? What are you looking at?

Look you, how pale he glares. Do you see nothing there?

No, nothing.

He is leaving us.

Confess yourself to heaven. Repent what is past, avoid what is to come. Good night—but go not to my uncle's bed. I must be cruel only to be kind. One word more, good lady.

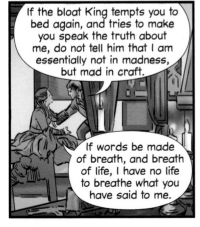

If the bloat King tempts you to bed again, and tries to make you speak the truth about me, do not tell him that I am essentially not in madness, but mad in craft.

If words be made of breath, and breath of life, I have no life to breathe what you have said to me.

I must go to England, do you know that? The letters are sealed, and my two schoolfellows, whom I will trust as I will trust fanged snakes, bear the mandate.

Good night, Mother.

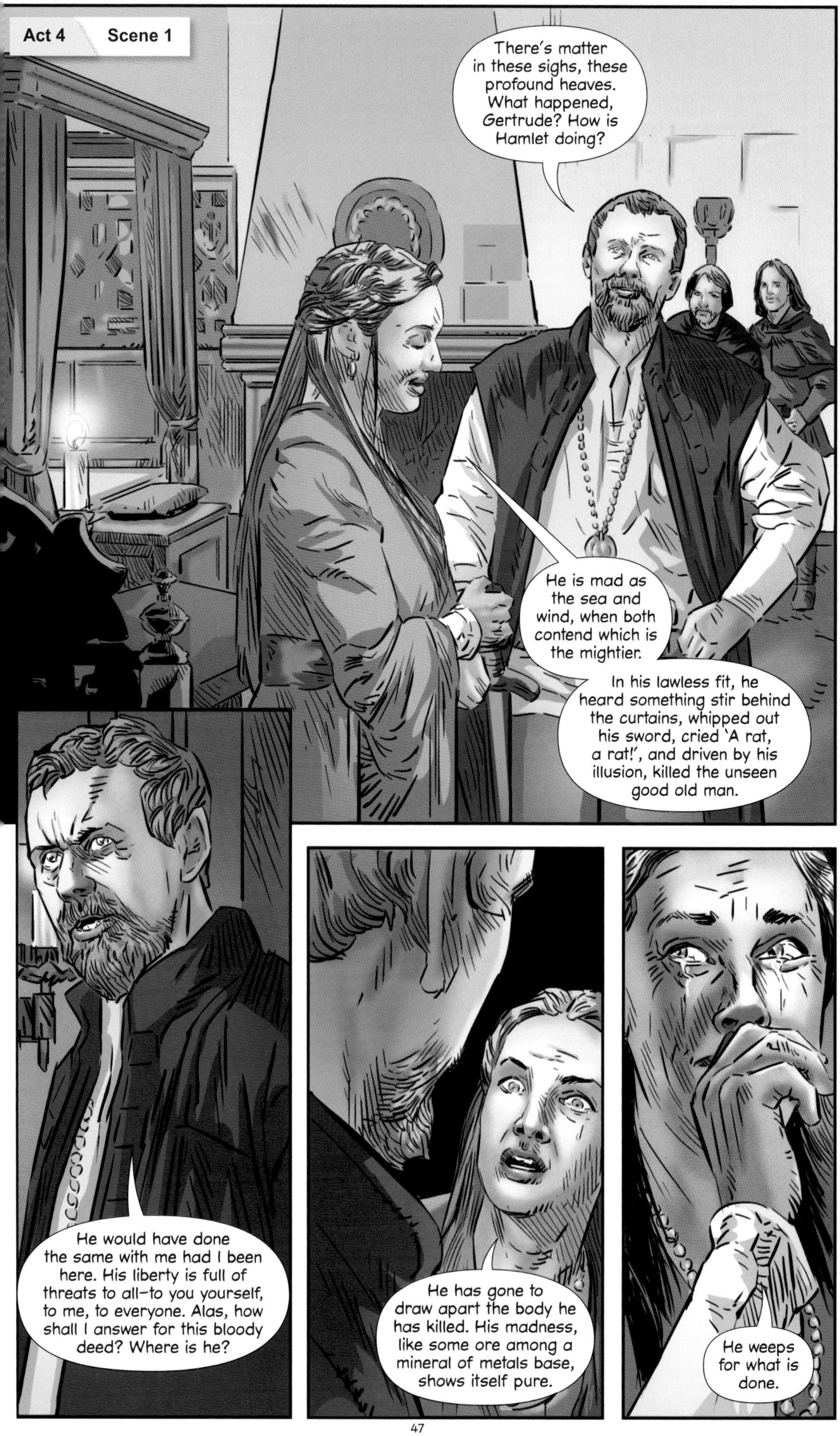
Act 4 Scene 1
There's matter in these sighs, these profound heaves. What happened, Gertrude? How is Hamlet doing?
He is mad as the sea and wind, when both contend which is the mightier.
In his lawless fit, he heard something stir behind the curtains, whipped out his sword, cried 'A rat, a rat!', and driven by his illusion, killed the unseen good old man.
He would have done the same with me had I been here. His liberty is full of threats to all–to you yourself, to me, to everyone. Alas, how shall I answer for this bloody deed? Where is he?
He has gone to draw apart the body he has killed. His madness, like some ore among a mineral of metals base, shows itself pure.
He weeps for what is done.

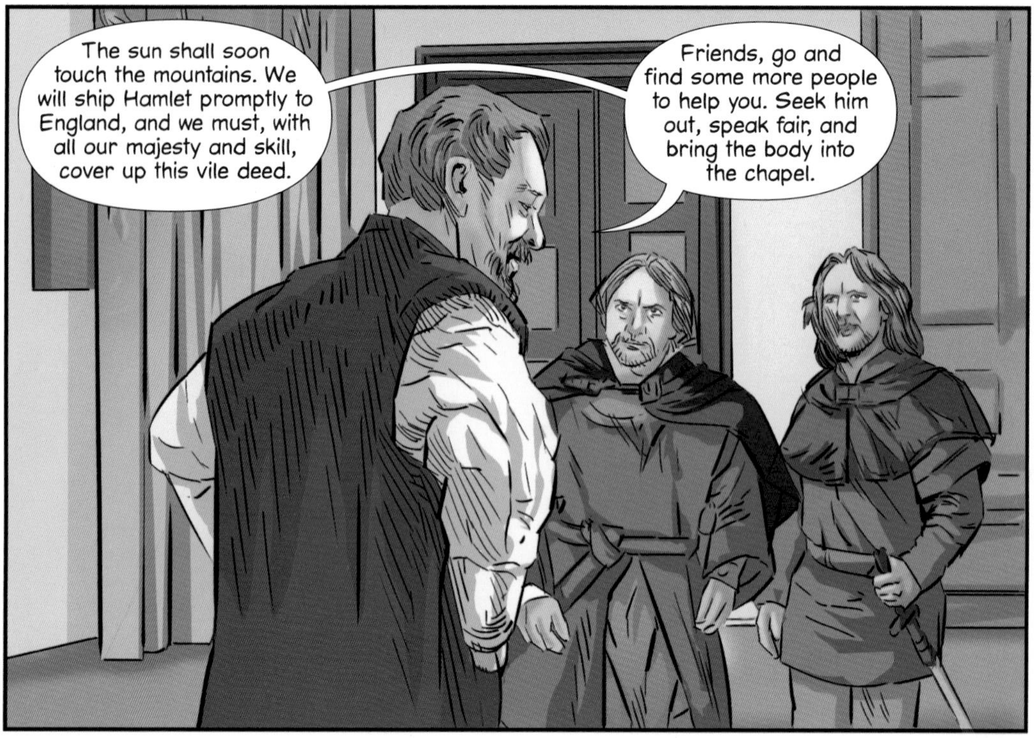
The sun shall soon touch the mountains. We will ship Hamlet promptly to England, and we must, with all our majesty and skill, cover up this vile deed.
Friends, go and find some more people to help you. Seek him out, speak fair, and bring the body into the chapel.

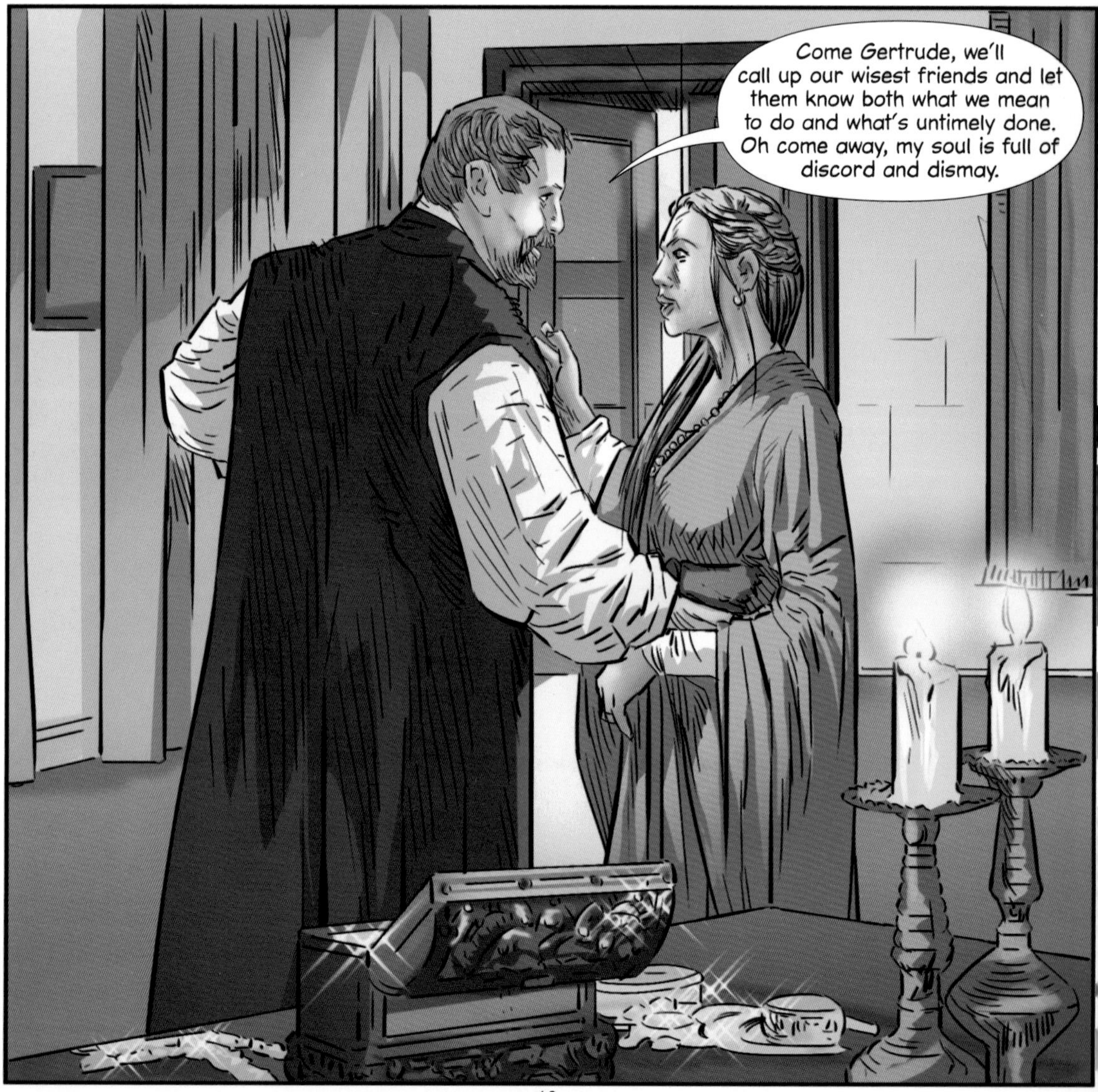
Come Gertrude, we'll call up our wisest friends and let them know both what we mean to do and what's untimely done. Oh come away, my soul is full of discord and dismay.

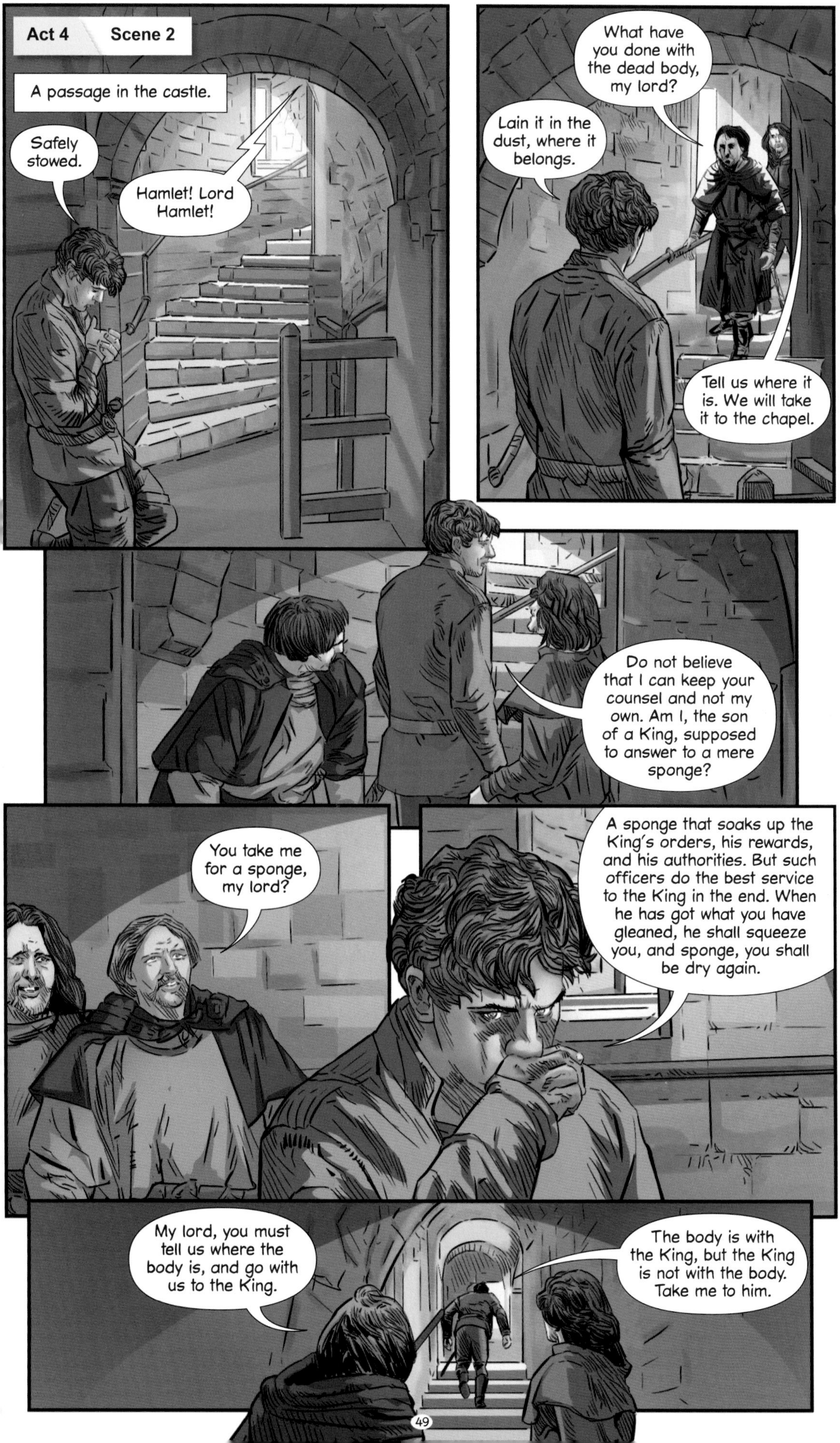

Act 4 Scene 2
A passage in the castle.
Safely stowed.
Hamlet! Lord Hamlet!
What have you done with the dead body, my lord?
Lain it in the dust, where it belongs.
Tell us where it is. We will take it to the chapel.
Do not believe that I can keep your counsel and not my own. Am I, the son of a King, supposed to answer to a mere sponge?
You take me for a sponge, my lord?
A sponge that soaks up the King's orders, his rewards, and his authorities. But such officers do the best service to the King in the end. When he has got what you have gleaned, he shall squeeze you, and sponge, you shall be dry again.
My lord, you must tell us where the body is, and go with us to the King.
The body is with the King, but the King is not with the body. Take me to him.

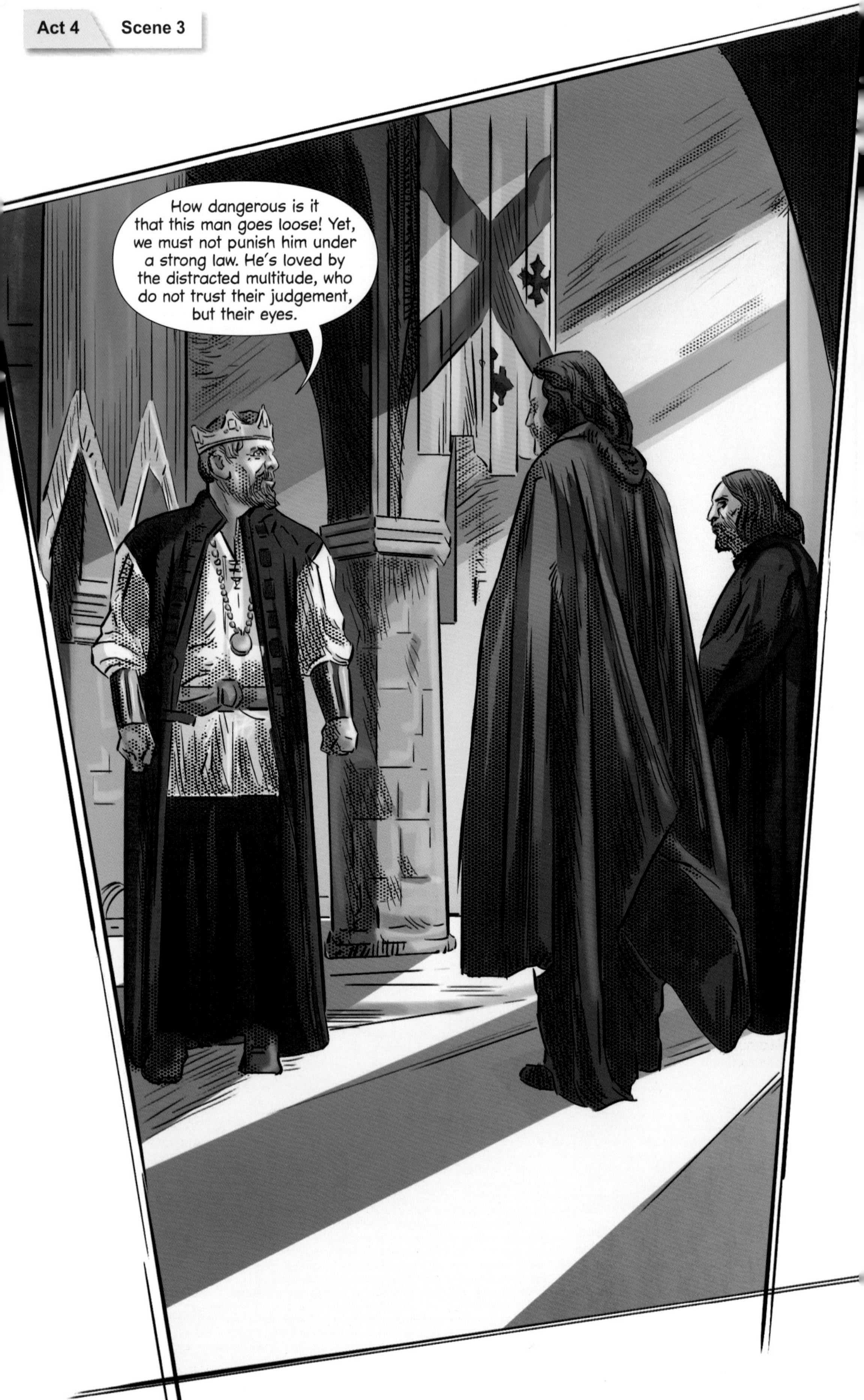
How dangerous is it that this man goes loose! Yet, we must not punish him under a strong law. He's loved by the distracted multitude, who do not trust their judgement, but their eyes.

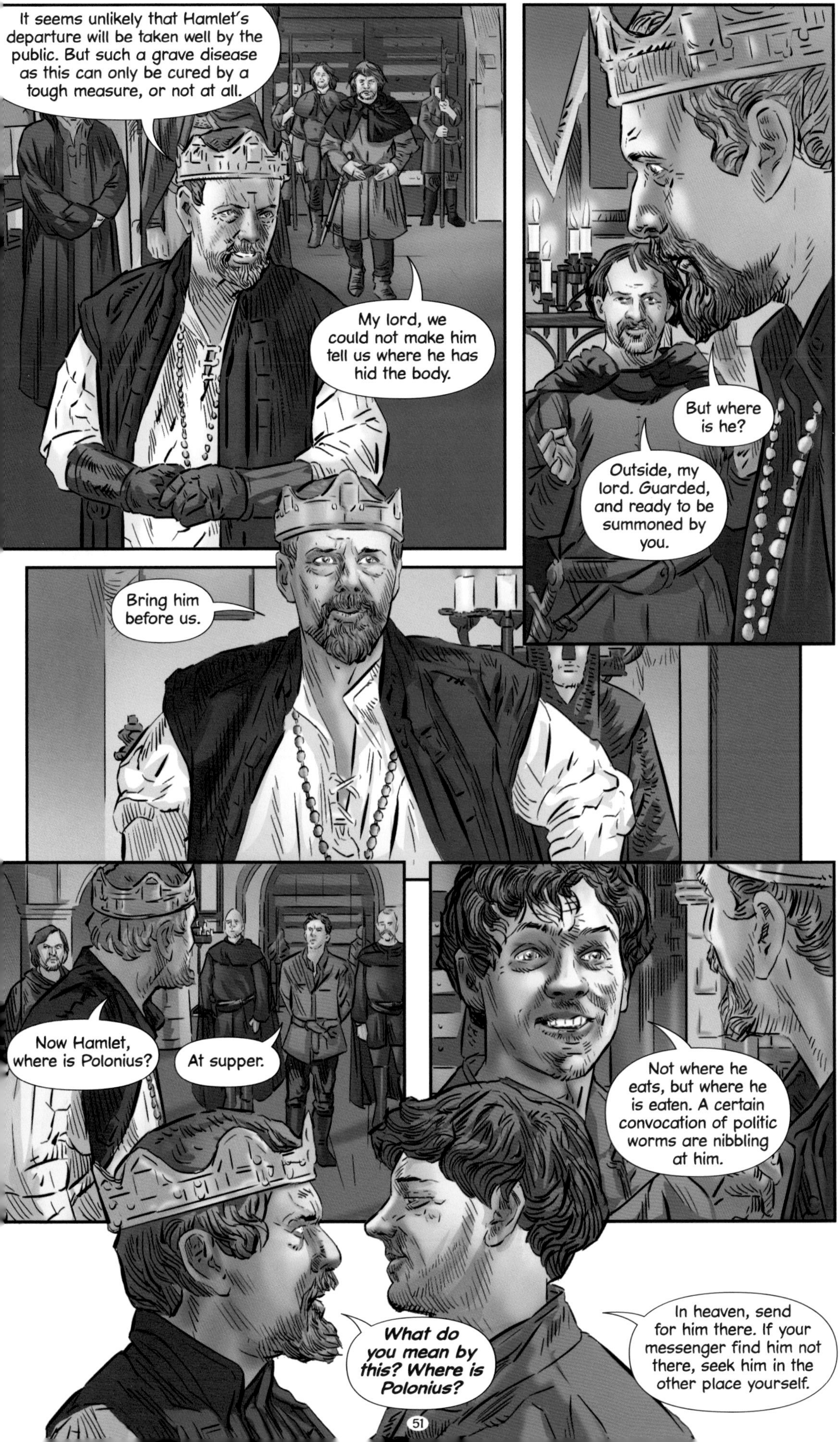
It seems unlikely that Hamlet's departure will be taken well by the public. But such a grave disease as this can only be cured by a tough measure, or not at all.
My lord, we could not make him tell us where he has hid the body.
But where is he?
Outside, my lord. Guarded, and ready to be summoned by you.
Bring him before us.
Now Hamlet, where is Polonius?
At supper.
Not where he eats, but where he is eaten. A certain convocation of politic worms are nibbling at him.
What do you mean by this? Where is Polonius?
In heaven, send for him there. If your messenger find him not there, seek him in the other place yourself.

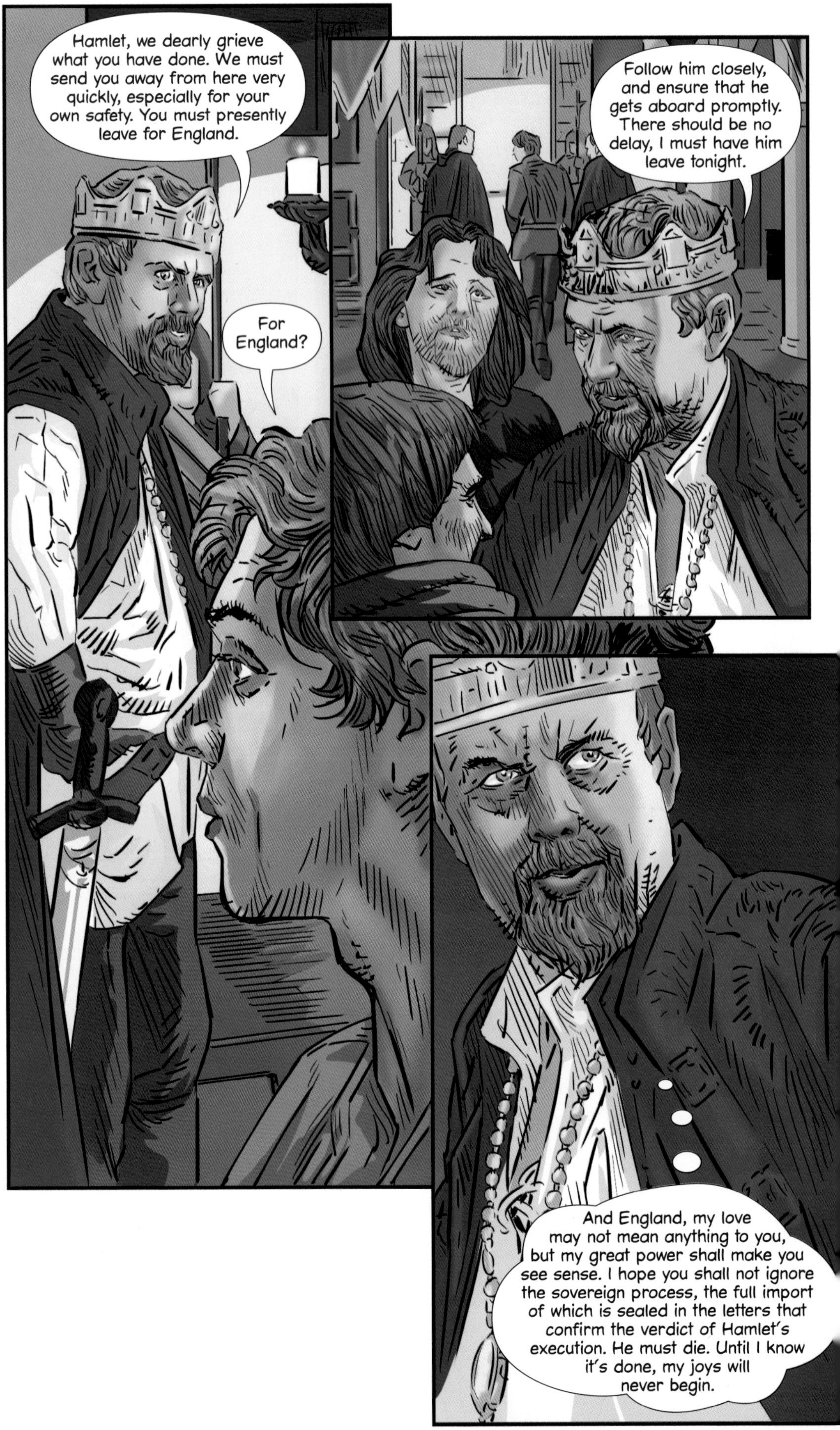

Hamlet, we dearly grieve what you have done. We must send you away from here very quickly, especially for your own safety. You must presently leave for England.
For England?
Follow him closely, and ensure that he gets aboard promptly. There should be no delay, I must have him leave tonight.
And England, my love may not mean anything to you, but my great power shall make you see sense. I hope you shall not ignore the sovereign process, the full import of which is sealed in the letters that confirm the verdict of Hamlet's execution. He must die. Until I know it's done, my joys will never begin.

Near the castle of Elsinore.

Go captain, offer my greetings to the Danish king. Tell him that by his licence, Fortinbras asks for the passage of his army through his kingdom, as promised.

Yes, my lord.

Good sir, whose forces are these? Who commands them, sir? Where are they headed?

The King of Norway, sir. His nephew Fortinbras commands us. We are off to attack Poland.

The army charges against the main of Poland, sir, or for some frontier?

To speak the truth, we stand to gain only a small patch of land that has no profit in it, only the name. The soil is so fallow that I would not pay five ducats to farm it.

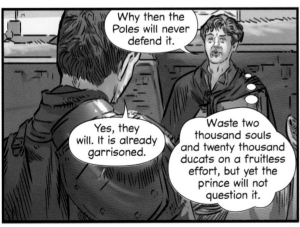

Why then the Poles will never defend it.

Yes, they will. It is already garrisoned.

Waste two thousand souls and twenty thousand ducats on a fruitless effort, but yet the prince will not question it.

Wealth and peace has wrongly convinced him; he is dead inside, and yet, on the outside, no one can see what caused his malady.

I humbly thank you, sir.

God be with you, sir.

Shall we go, my lord?

How all occasions do inform against me, and spur my dull revenge!

Oh, from this time forth, my thoughts be bloody or be nothing worth.

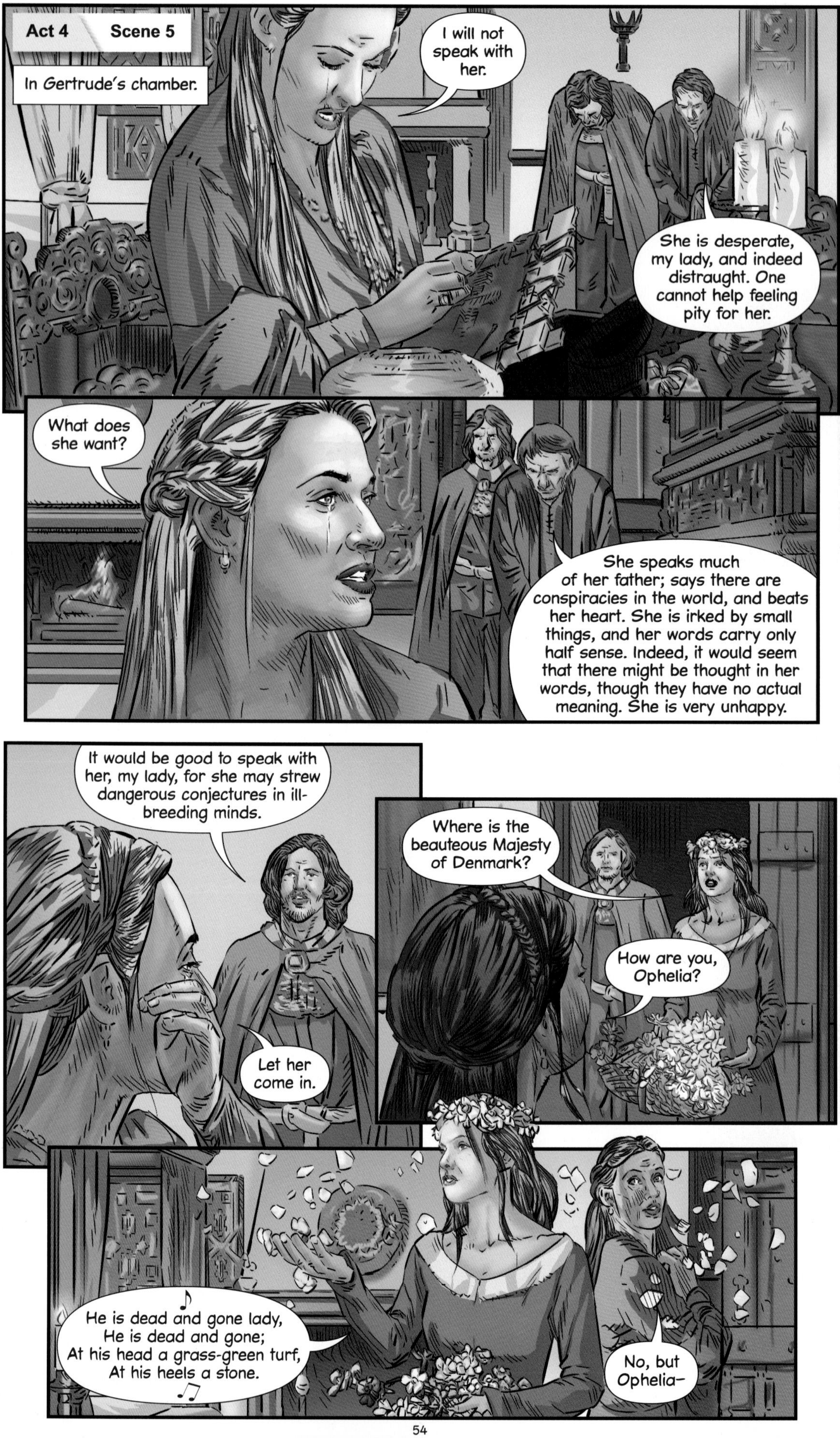

Act 4 Scene 5
In Gertrude's chamber.
I will not speak with her.
She is desperate, my lady, and indeed distraught. One cannot help feeling pity for her.
What does she want?
She speaks much of her father; says there are conspiracies in the world, and beats her heart. She is irked by small things, and her words carry only half sense. Indeed, it would seem that there might be thought in her words, though they have no actual meaning. She is very unhappy.
It would be good to speak with her, my lady, for she may strew dangerous conjectures in ill-breeding minds.
Let her come in.
Where is the beauteous Majesty of Denmark?
How are you, Ophelia?
He is dead and gone lady,
He is dead and gone;
At his head a grass-green turf,
At his heels a stone.
No, but Ophelia–

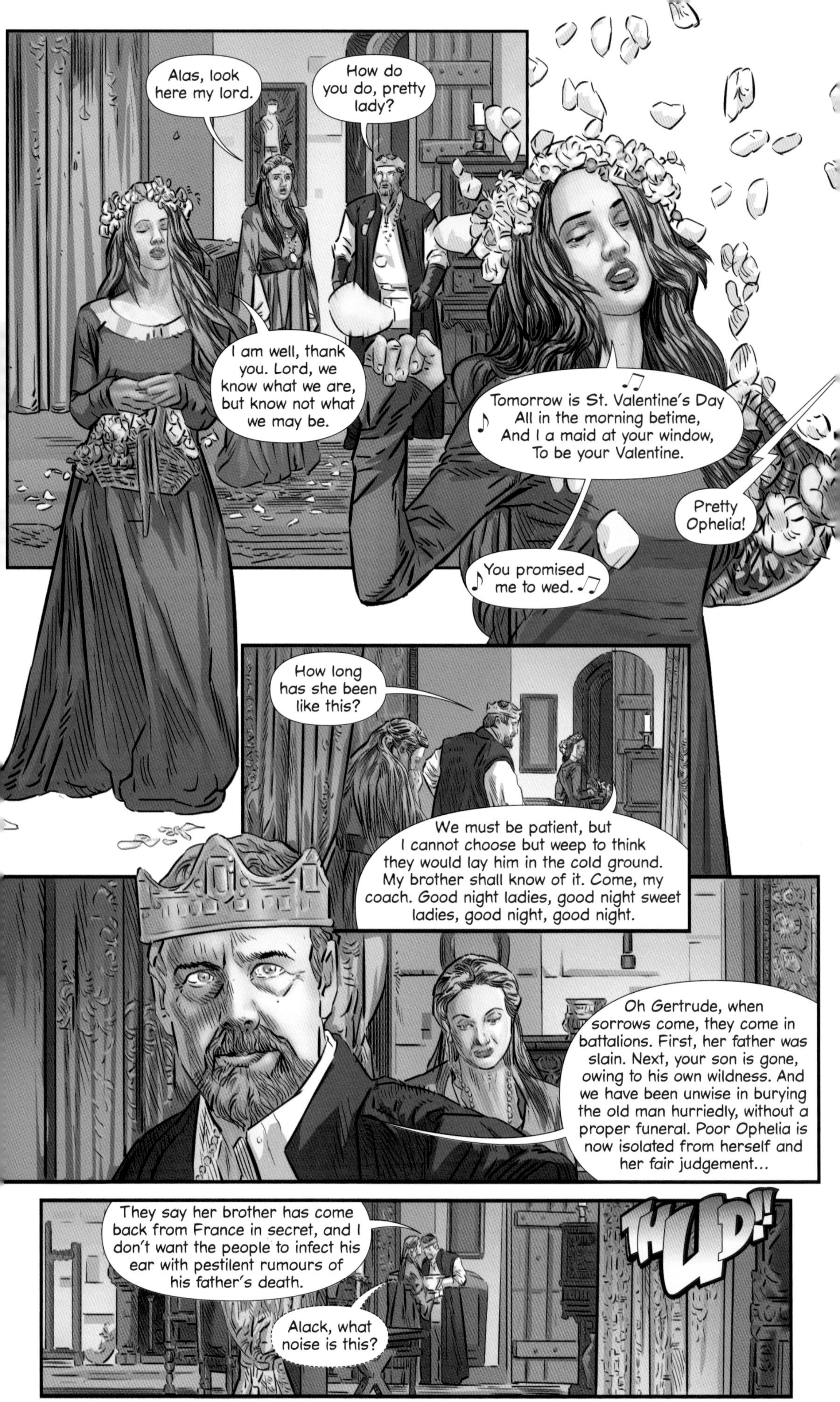
Alas, look here my lord.
How do you do, pretty lady?
I am well, thank you. Lord, we know what we are, but know not what we may be.
♪ Tomorrow is St. Valentine's Day All in the morning betime, And I a maid at your window, To be your Valentine. ♫
Pretty Ophelia!
♪ You promised me to wed. ♫
How long has she been like this?
We must be patient, but I cannot choose but weep to think they would lay him in the cold ground. My brother shall know of it. Come, my coach. Good night ladies, good night sweet ladies, good night, good night.
Oh Gertrude, when sorrows come, they come in battalions. First, her father was slain. Next, your son is gone, owing to his own wildness. And we have been unwise in burying the old man hurriedly, without a proper funeral. Poor Ophelia is now isolated from herself and her fair judgement...
They say her brother has come back from France in secret, and I don't want the people to infect his ear with pestilent rumours of his father's death.
THUD!
Alack, what noise is this?

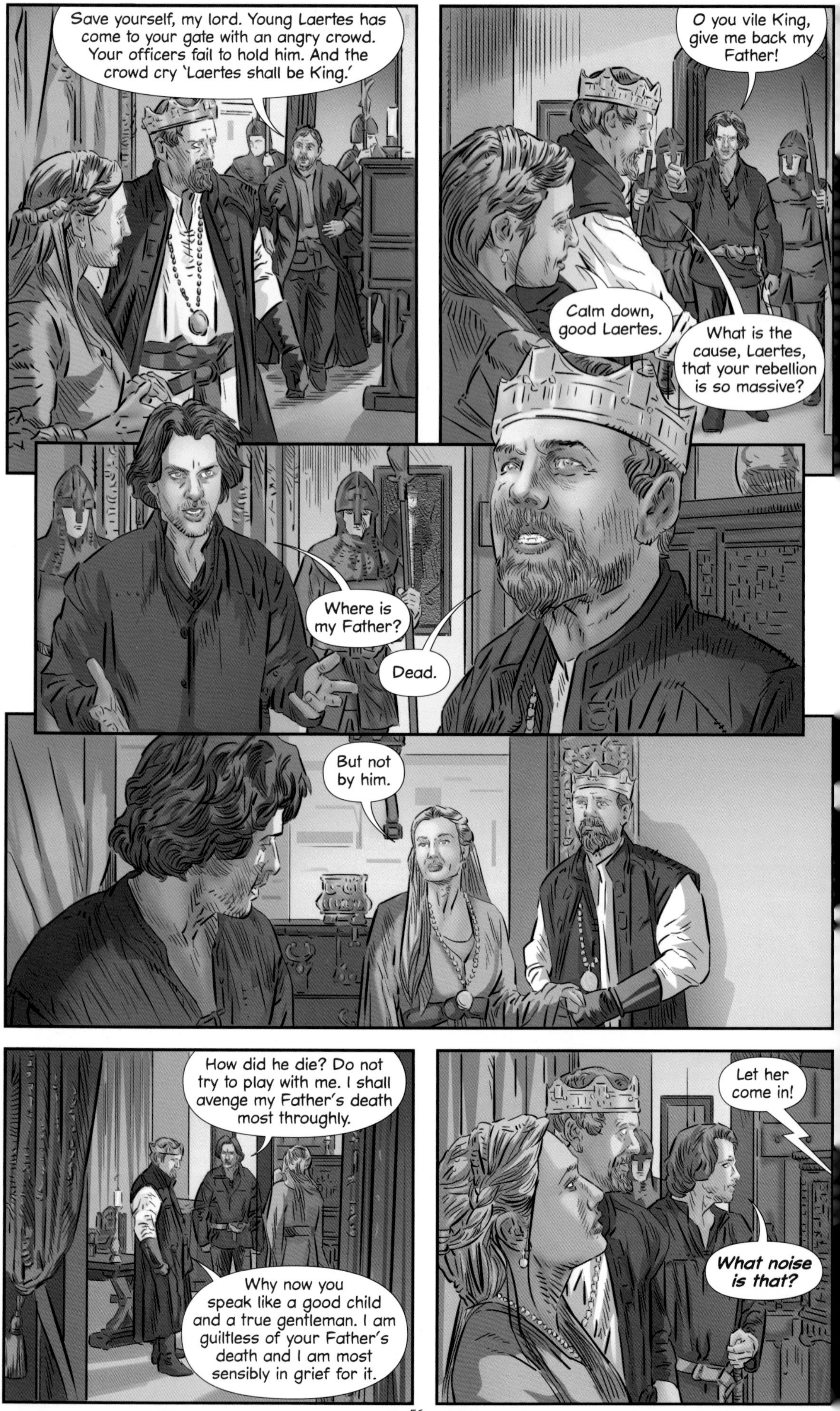
Save yourself, my lord. Young Laertes has come to your gate with an angry crowd. Your officers fail to hold him. And the crowd cry 'Laertes shall be King.'
O you vile King, give me back my Father!
Calm down, good Laertes.
What is the cause, Laertes, that your rebellion is so massive?
Where is my Father?
Dead.
But not by him.
How did he die? Do not try to play with me. I shall avenge my Father's death most throughly.
Why now you speak like a good child and a true gentleman. I am guiltless of your Father's death and I am most sensibly in grief for it.
Let her come in!
What noise is that?

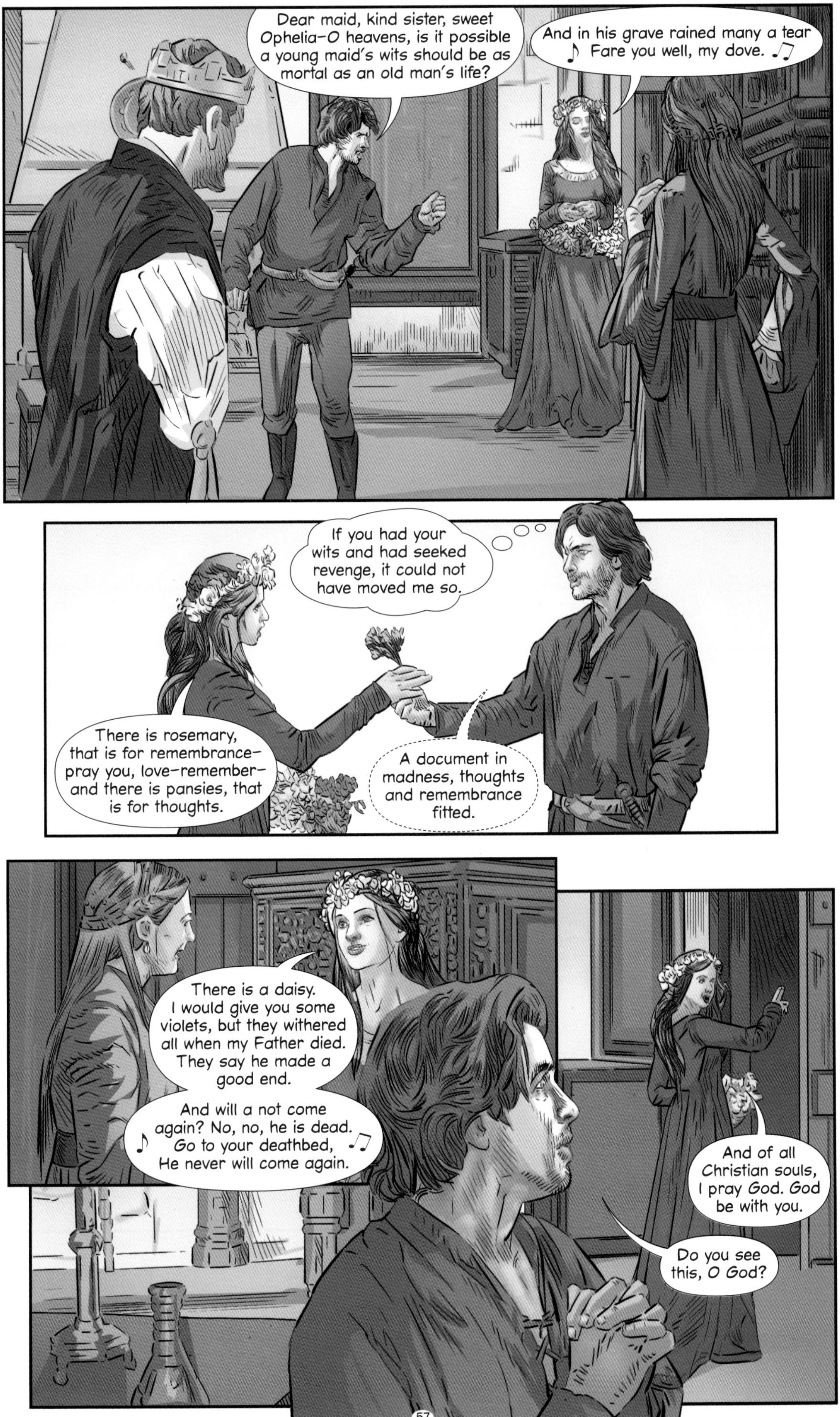
Dear maid, kind sister, sweet Ophelia–O heavens, is it possible a young maid's wits should be as mortal as an old man's life?
And in his grave rained many a tear ♪ Fare you well, my dove. ♫
If you had your wits and had seeked revenge, it could not have moved me so.
There is rosemary, that is for remembrance– pray you, love–remember– and there is pansies, that is for thoughts.
A document in madness, thoughts and remembrance fitted.
There is a daisy. I would give you some violets, but they withered all when my Father died. They say he made a good end.
And will a not come again? No, no, he is dead. ♪ Go to your deathbed, ♫ He never will come again.
And of all Christian souls, I pray God. God be with you.
Do you see this, O God?

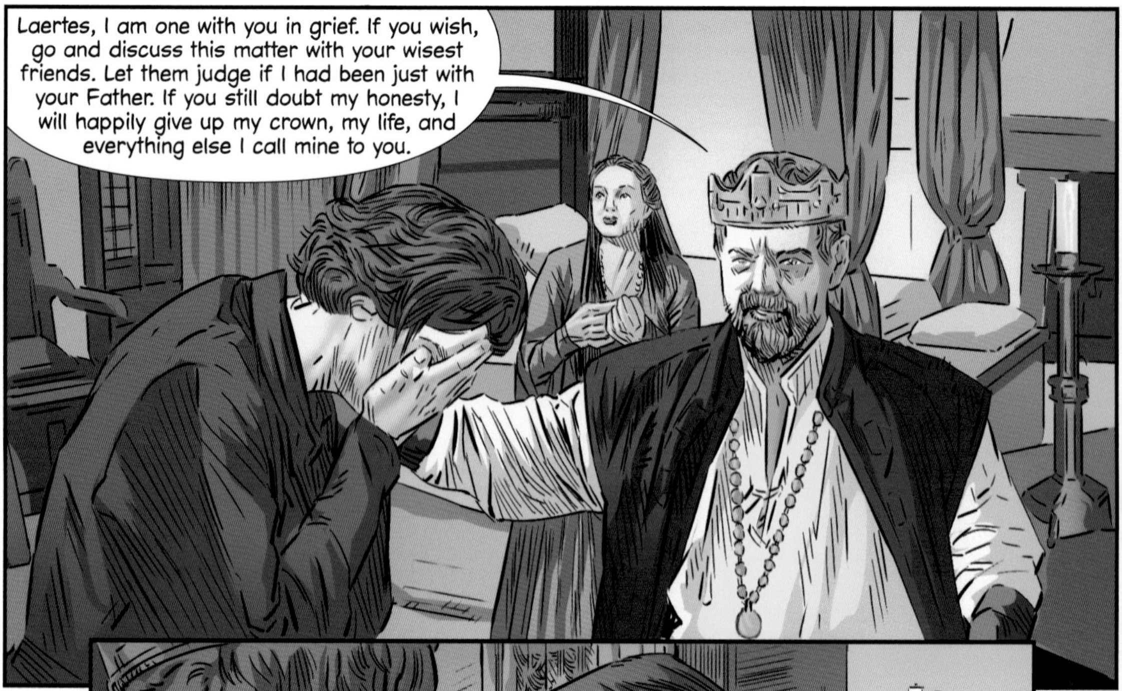
Laertes, I am one with you in grief. If you wish, go and discuss this matter with your wisest friends. Let them judge if I had been just with your Father. If you still doubt my honesty, I will happily give up my crown, my life, and everything else I call mine to you.

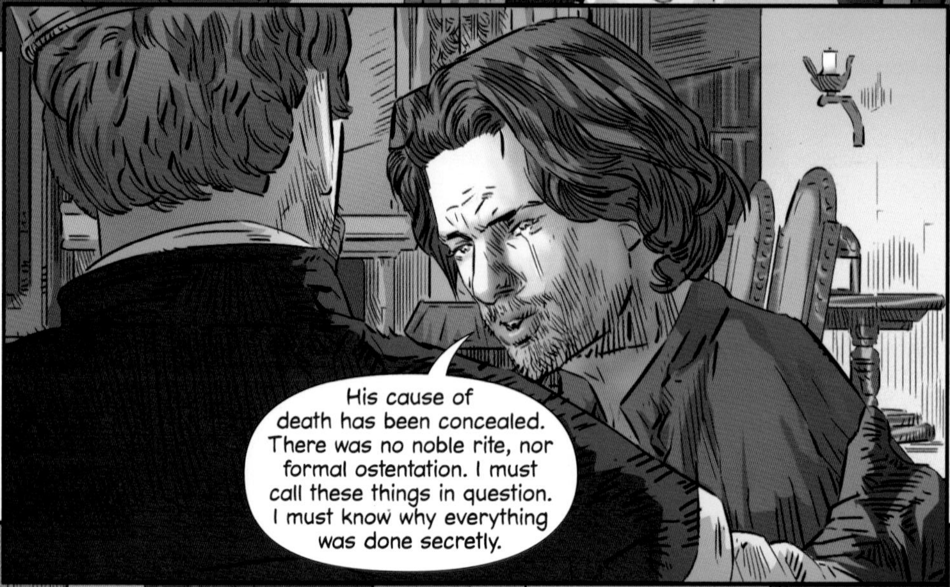
His cause of death has been concealed. There was no noble rite, nor formal ostentation. I must call these things in question. I must know why everything was done secretly.

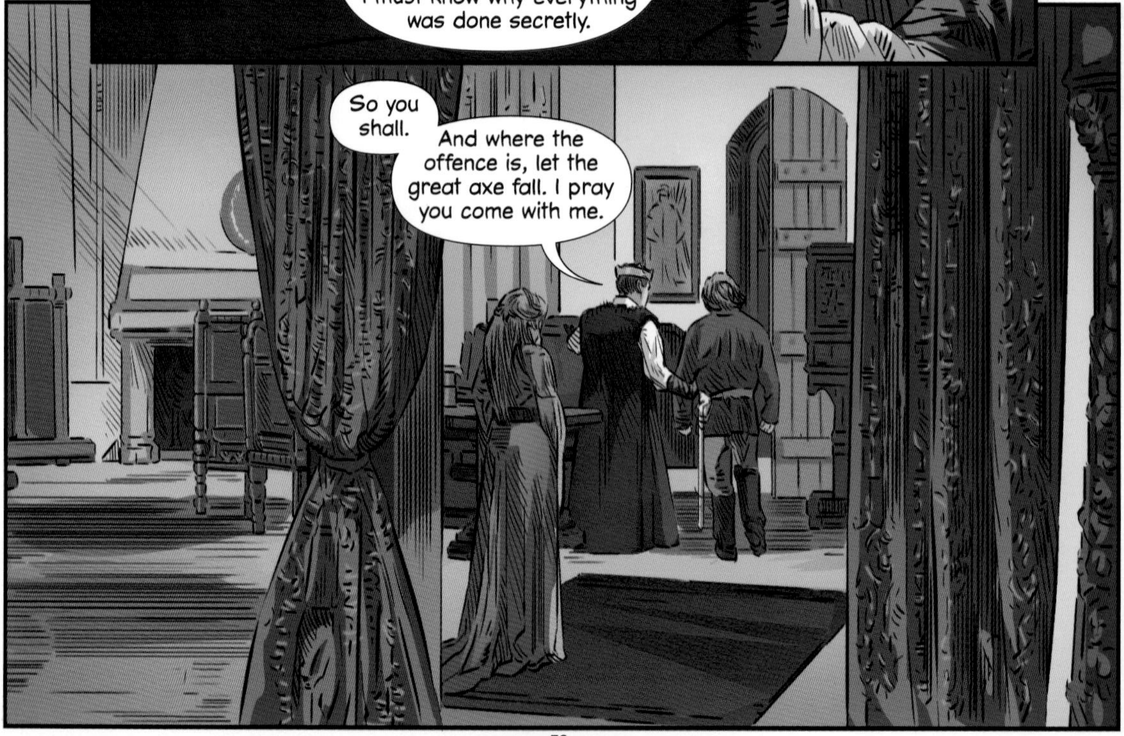
So you shall.
And where the offence is, let the great axe fall. I pray you come with me.

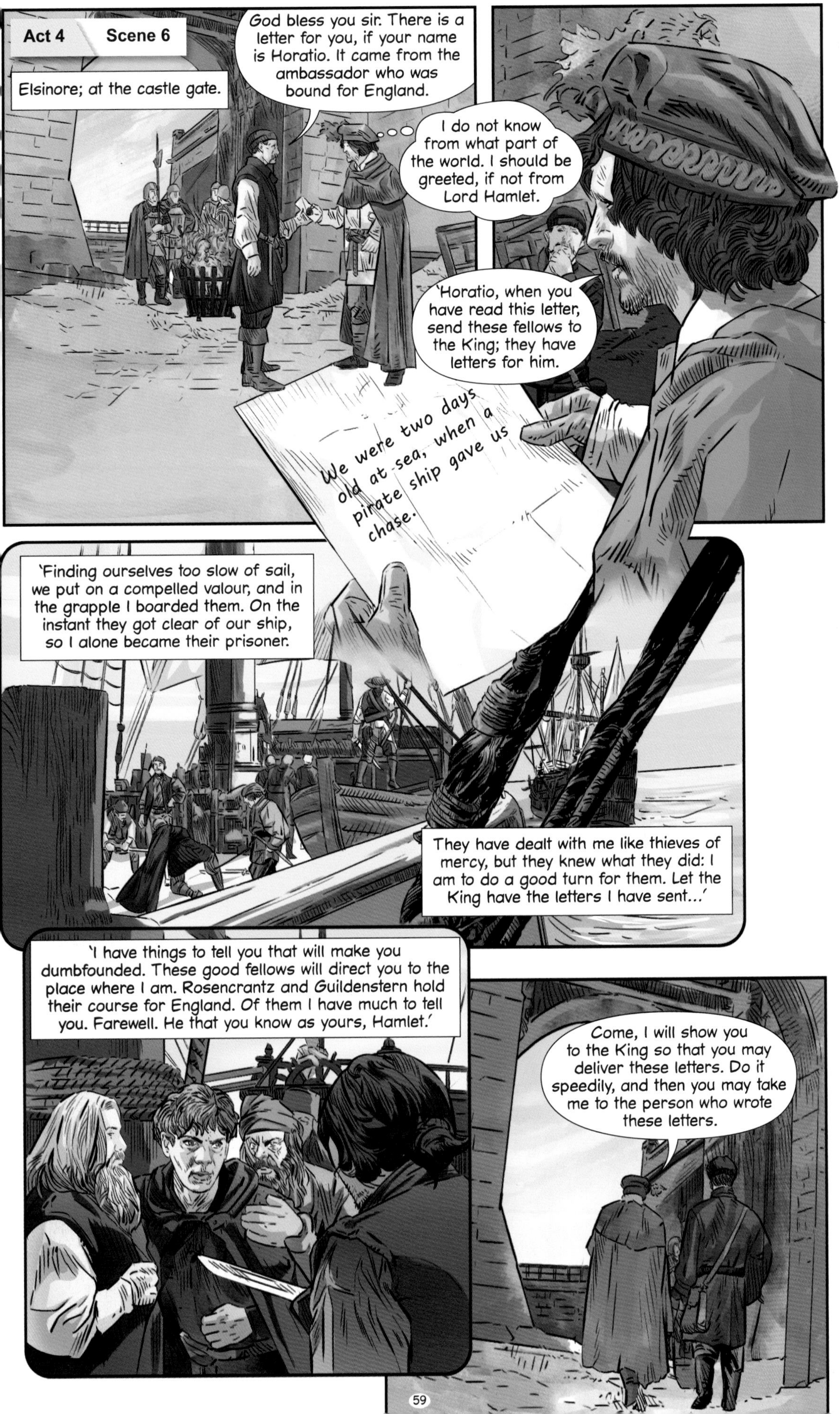

Act 4 Scene 6
Elsinore; at the castle gate.
God bless you sir. There is a letter for you, if your name is Horatio. It came from the ambassador who was bound for England.
I do not know from what part of the world. I should be greeted, if not from Lord Hamlet.
'Horatio, when you have read this letter, send these fellows to the King; they have letters for him.
We were two days old at sea, when a pirate ship gave us chase.
'Finding ourselves too slow of sail, we put on a compelled valour, and in the grapple I boarded them. On the instant they got clear of our ship, so I alone became their prisoner.
They have dealt with me like thieves of mercy, but they knew what they did: I am to do a good turn for them. Let the King have the letters I have sent...'
'I have things to tell you that will make you dumbfounded. These good fellows will direct you to the place where I am. Rosencrantz and Guildenstern hold their course for England. Of them I have much to tell you. Farewell. He that you know as yours, Hamlet.'
Come, I will show you to the King so that you may deliver these letters. Do it speedily, and then you may take me to the person who wrote these letters.

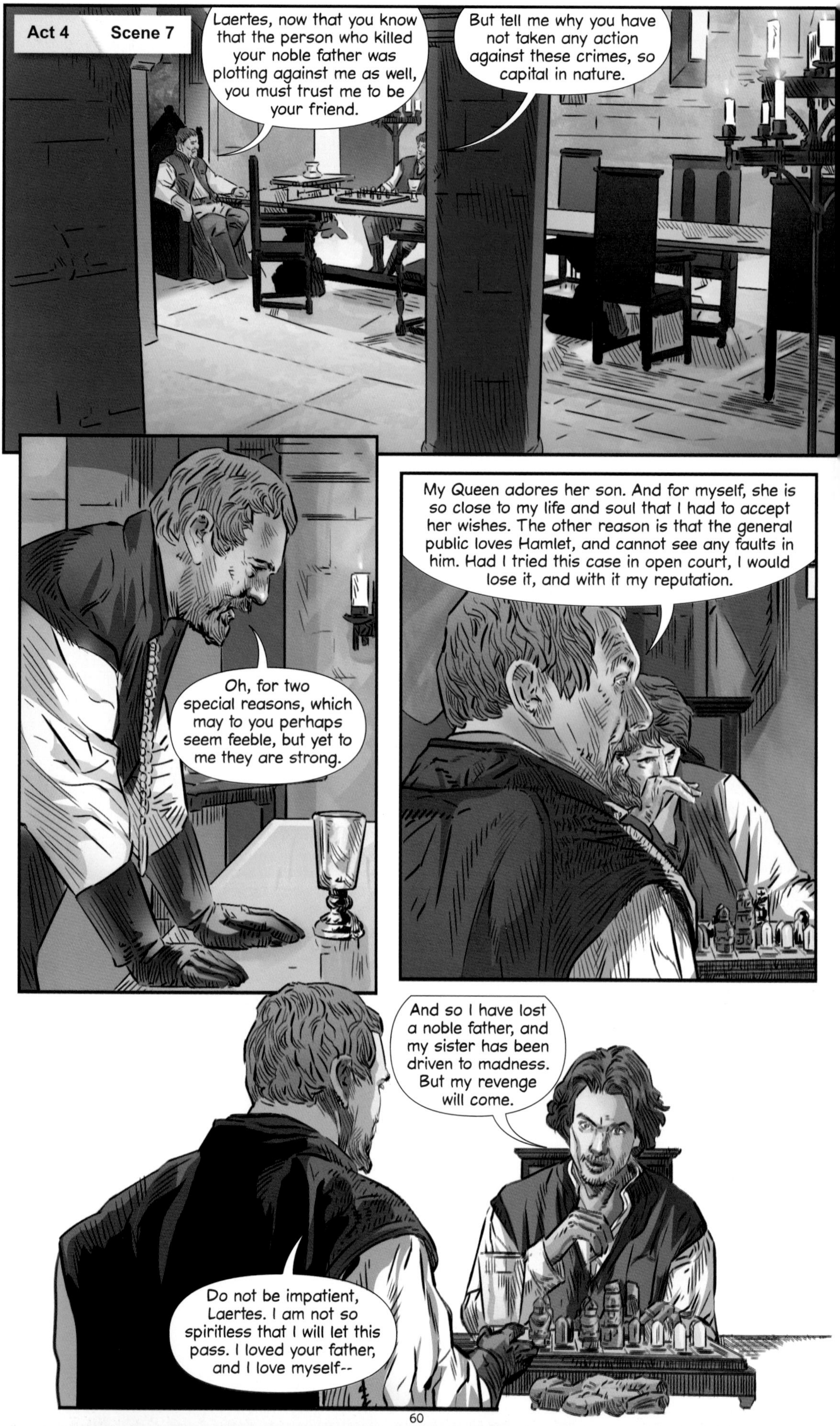
Act 4 Scene 7
Laertes, now that you know that the person who killed your noble father was plotting against me as well, you must trust me to be your friend.
But tell me why you have not taken any action against these crimes, so capital in nature.
Oh, for two special reasons, which may to you perhaps seem feeble, but yet to me they are strong.
My Queen adores her son. And for myself, she is so close to my life and soul that I had to accept her wishes. The other reason is that the general public loves Hamlet, and cannot see any faults in him. Had I tried this case in open court, I would lose it, and with it my reputation.
And so I have lost a noble father, and my sister has been driven to madness. But my revenge will come.
Do not be impatient, Laertes. I am not so spiritless that I will let this pass. I loved your father, and I love myself--

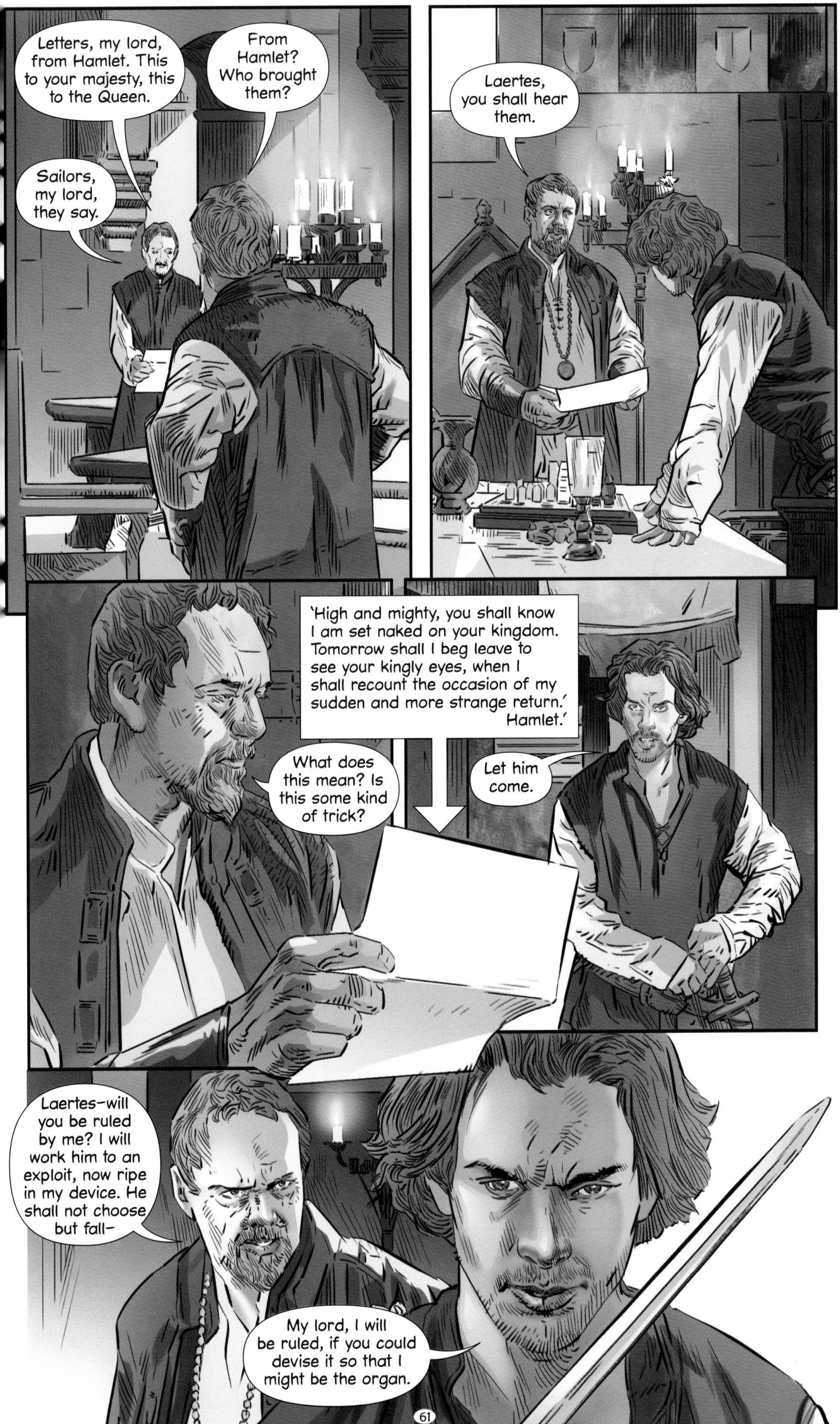

Letters, my lord, from Hamlet. This to your majesty, this to the Queen.
From Hamlet? Who brought them?
Sailors, my lord, they say.
Laertes, you shall hear them.
'High and mighty, you shall know I am set naked on your kingdom. Tomorrow shall I beg leave to see your kingly eyes, when I shall recount the occasion of my sudden and more strange return.' Hamlet.'
What does this mean? Is this some kind of trick?
Let him come.
Laertes–will you be ruled by me? I will work him to an exploit, now ripe in my device. He shall not choose but fall–
My lord, I will be ruled, if you could devise it so that I might be the organ.

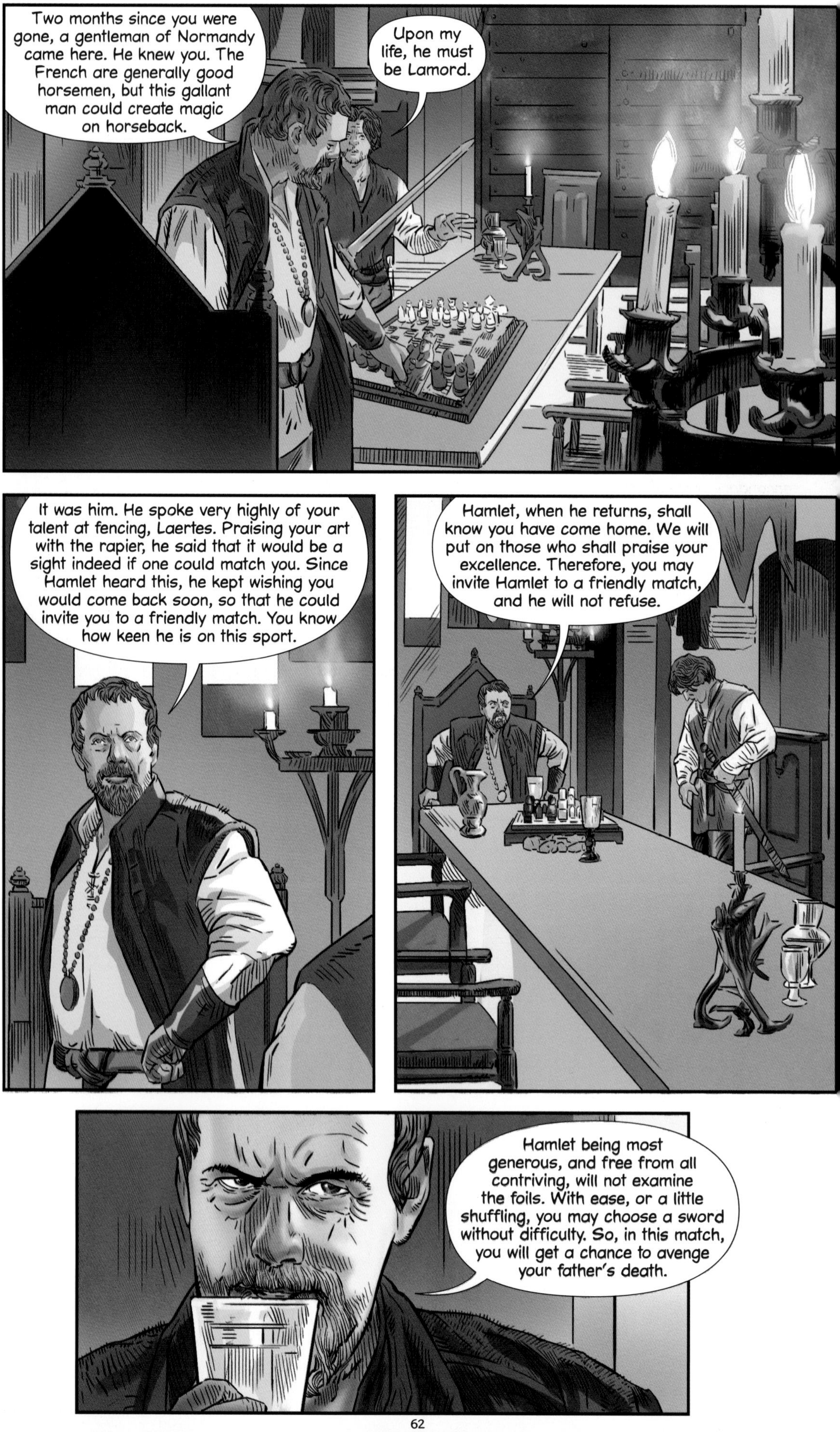
Two months since you were gone, a gentleman of Normandy came here. He knew you. The French are generally good horsemen, but this gallant man could create magic on horseback.
Upon my life, he must be Lamord.
It was him. He spoke very highly of your talent at fencing, Laertes. Praising your art with the rapier, he said that it would be a sight indeed if one could match you. Since Hamlet heard this, he kept wishing you would come back soon, so that he could invite you to a friendly match. You know how keen he is on this sport.
Hamlet, when he returns, shall know you have come home. We will put on those who shall praise your excellence. Therefore, you may invite Hamlet to a friendly match, and he will not refuse.
Hamlet being most generous, and free from all contriving, will not examine the foils. With ease, or a little shuffling, you may choose a sword without difficulty. So, in this match, you will get a chance to avenge your father's death.

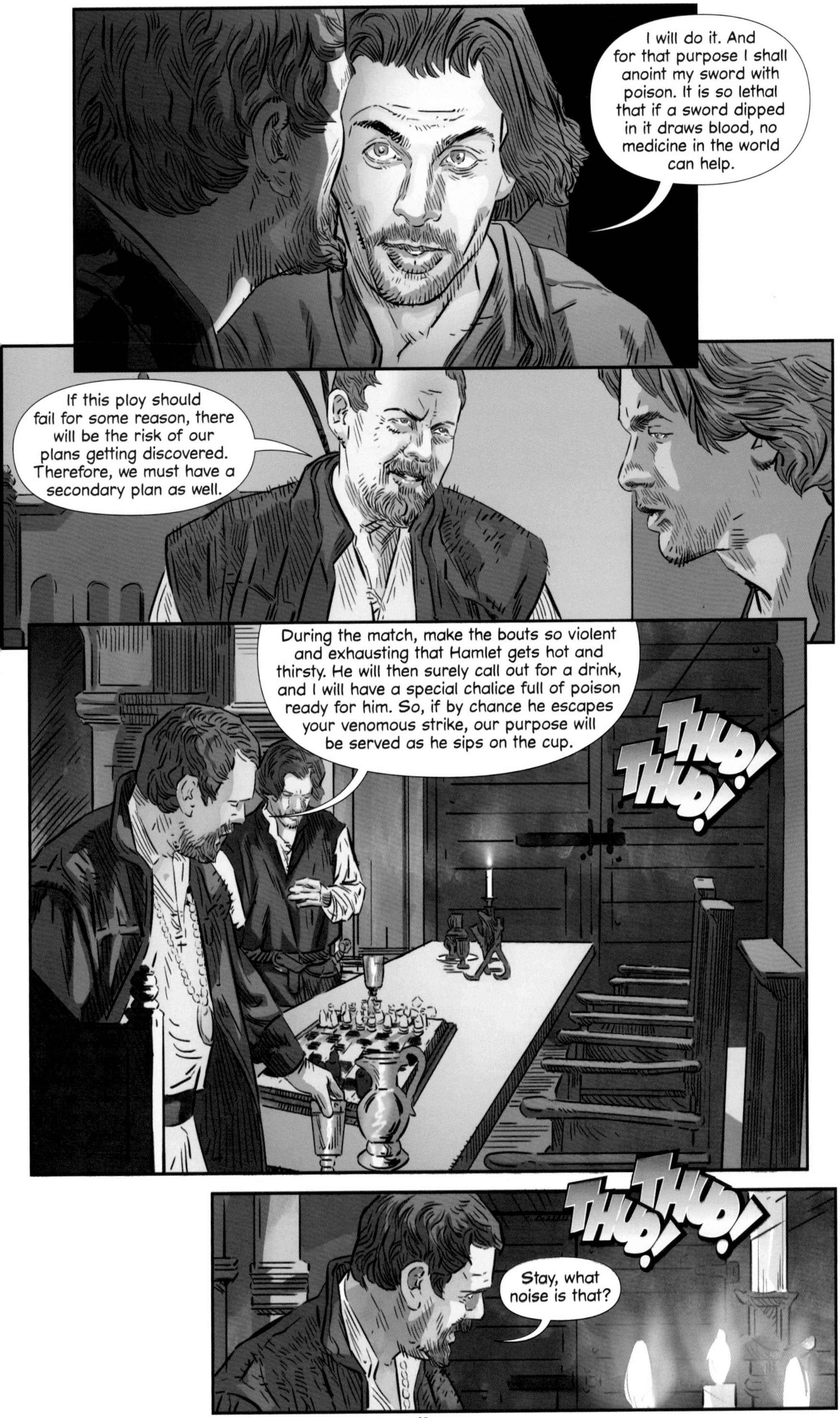
I will do it. And for that purpose I shall anoint my sword with poison. It is so lethal that if a sword dipped in it draws blood, no medicine in the world can help.
If this ploy should fail for some reason, there will be the risk of our plans getting discovered. Therefore, we must have a secondary plan as well.
During the match, make the bouts so violent and exhausting that Hamlet gets hot and thirsty. He will then surely call out for a drink, and I will have a special chalice full of poison ready for him. So, if by chance he escapes your venomous strike, our purpose will be served as he sips on the cup.
THUD! THUD!
THUD! THUD!
Stay, what noise is that?

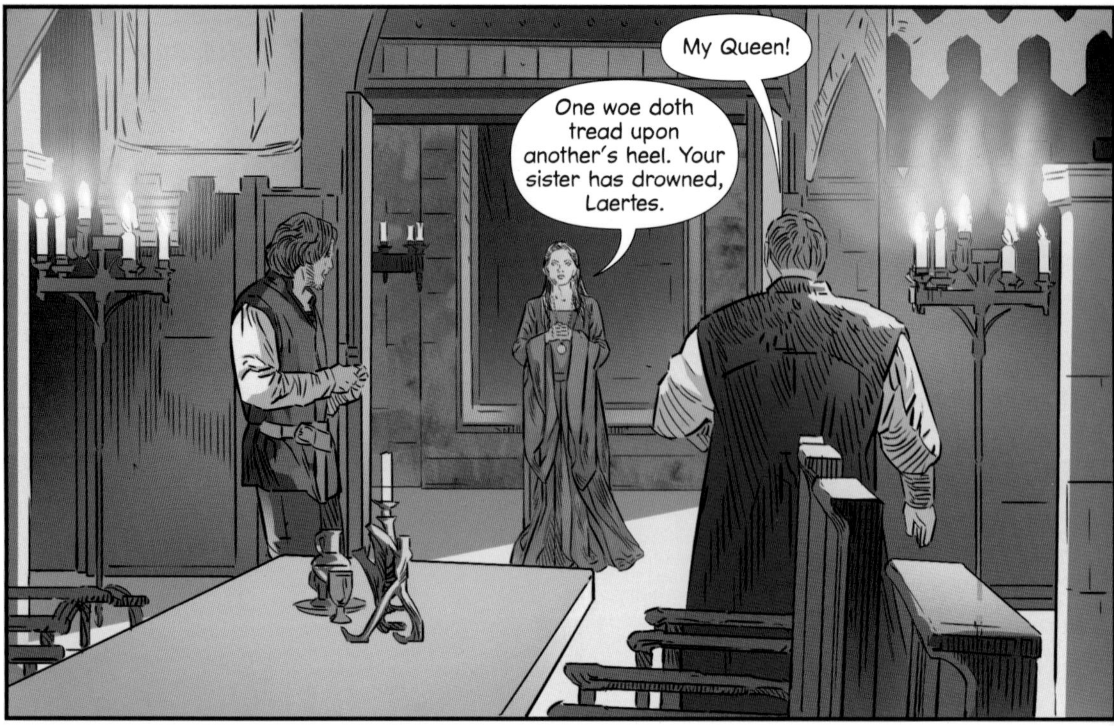
My Queen!
One woe doth tread upon another's heel. Your sister has drowned, Laertes.

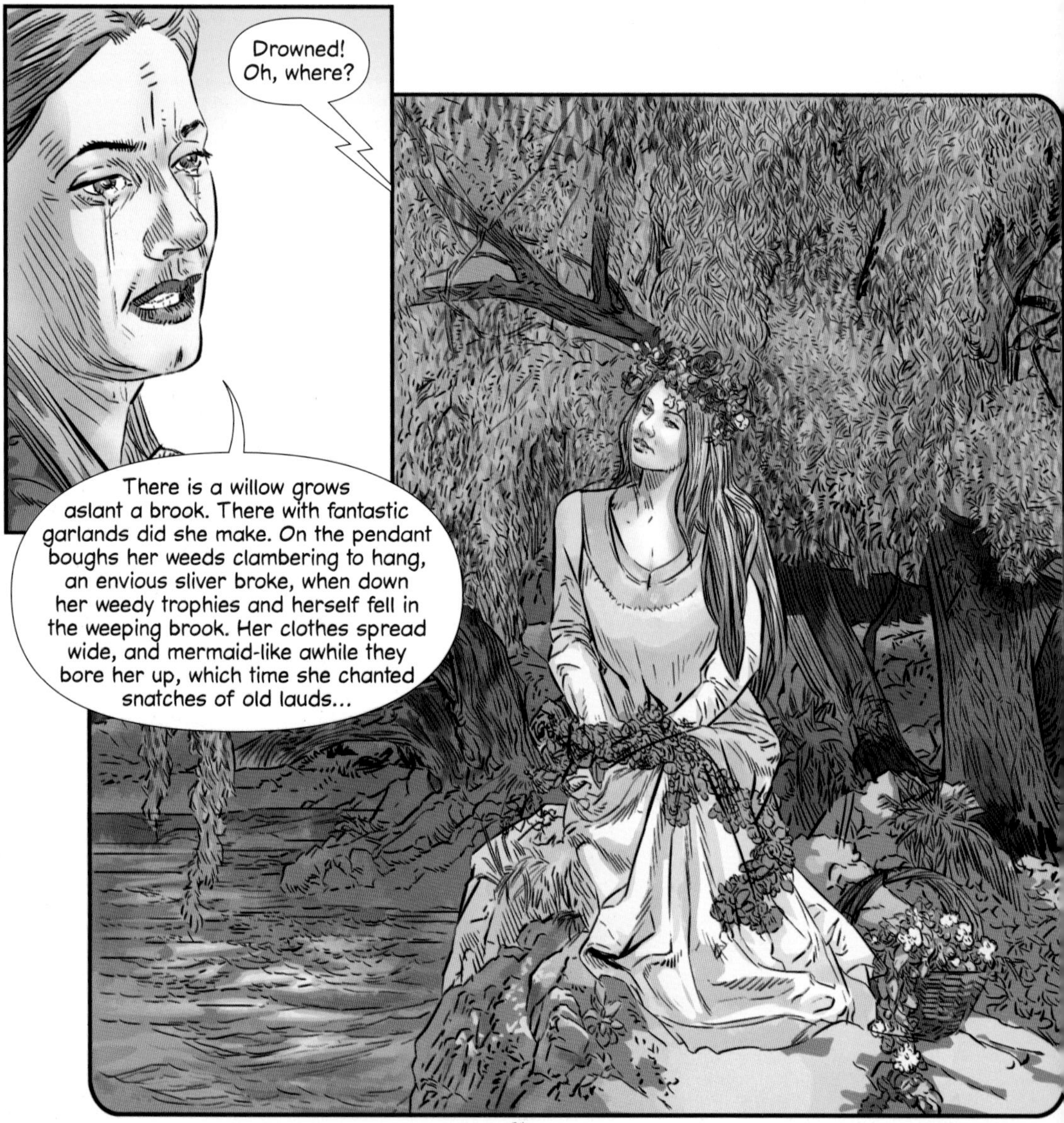
Drowned! Oh, where?
There is a willow grows aslant a brook. There with fantastic garlands did she make. On the pendant boughs her weeds clambering to hang, an envious sliver broke, when down her weedy trophies and herself fell in the weeping brook. Her clothes spread wide, and mermaid-like awhile they bore her up, which time she chanted snatches of old lauds...

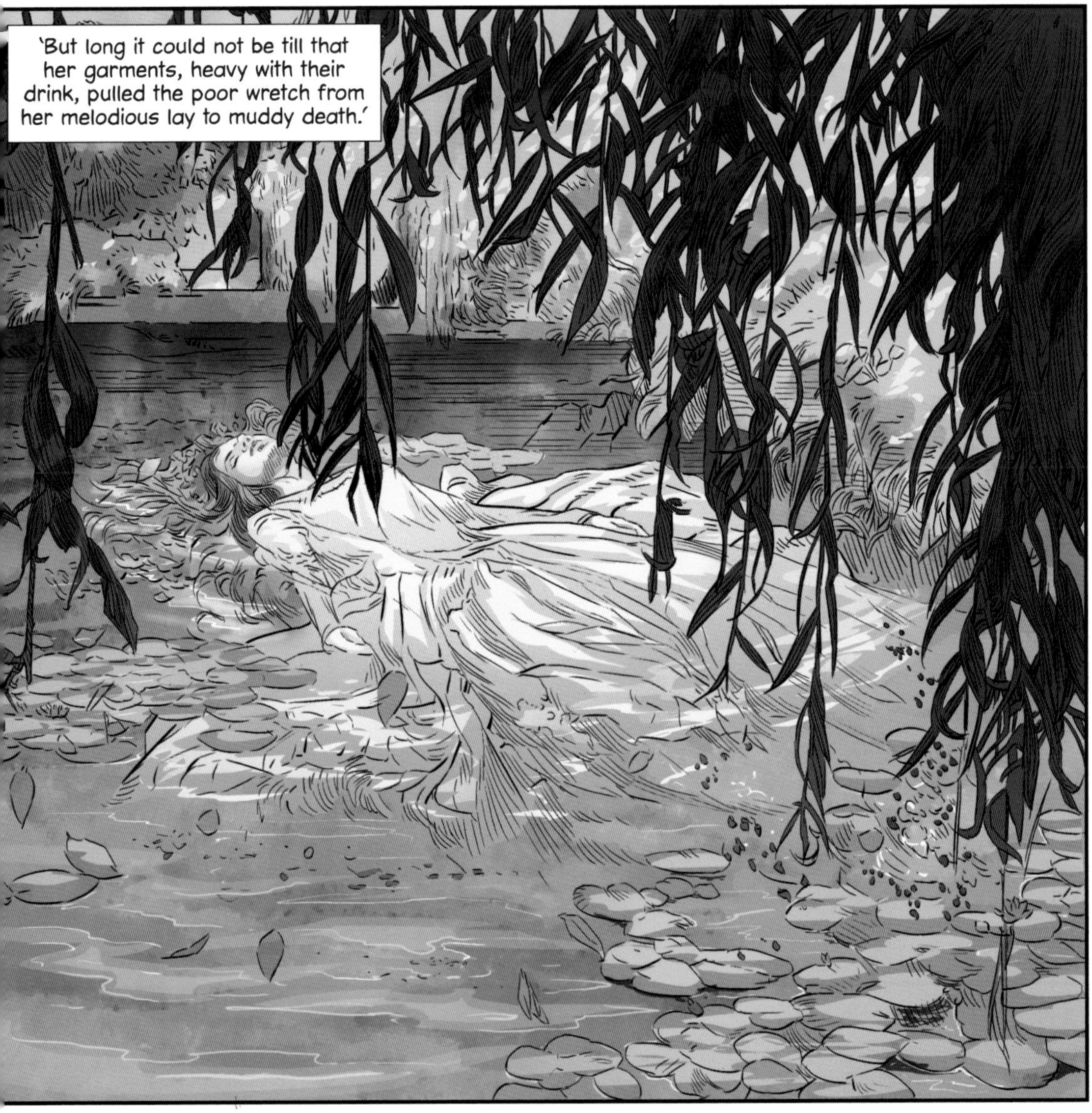
'But long it could not be till that her garments, heavy with their drink, pulled the poor wretch from her melodious lay to muddy death.'

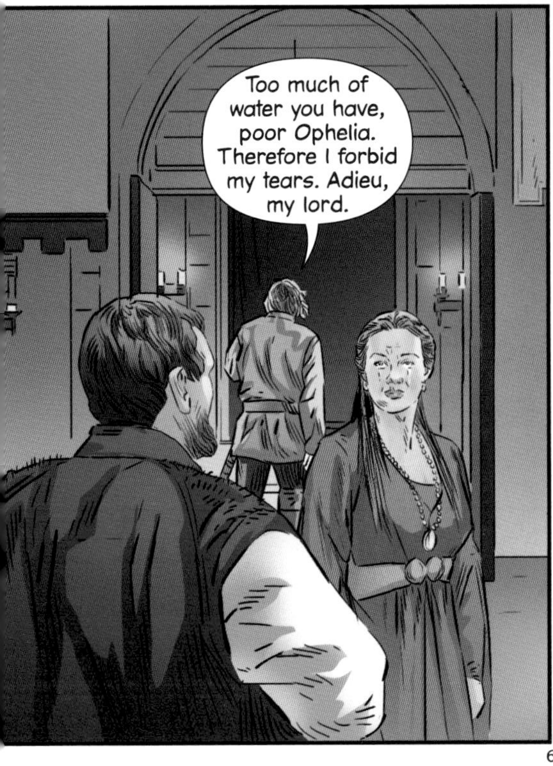
Too much of water you have, poor Ophelia. Therefore I forbid my tears. Adieu, my lord.

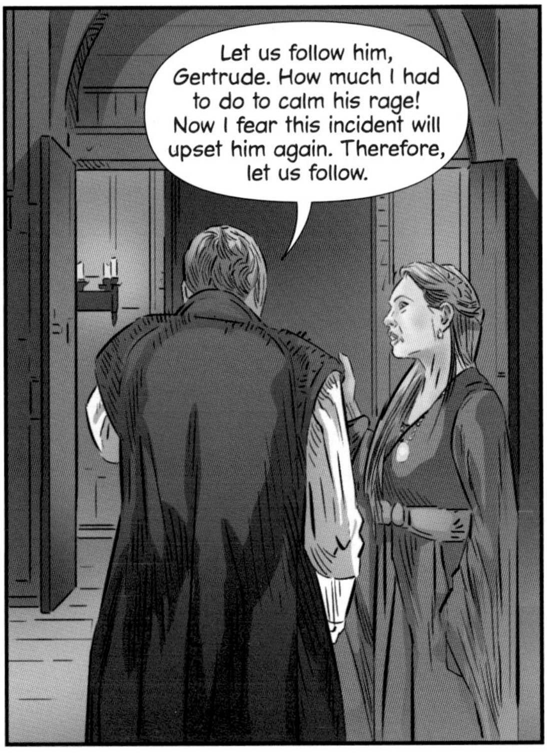
Let us follow him, Gertrude. How much I had to do to calm his rage! Now I fear this incident will upset him again. Therefore, let us follow.

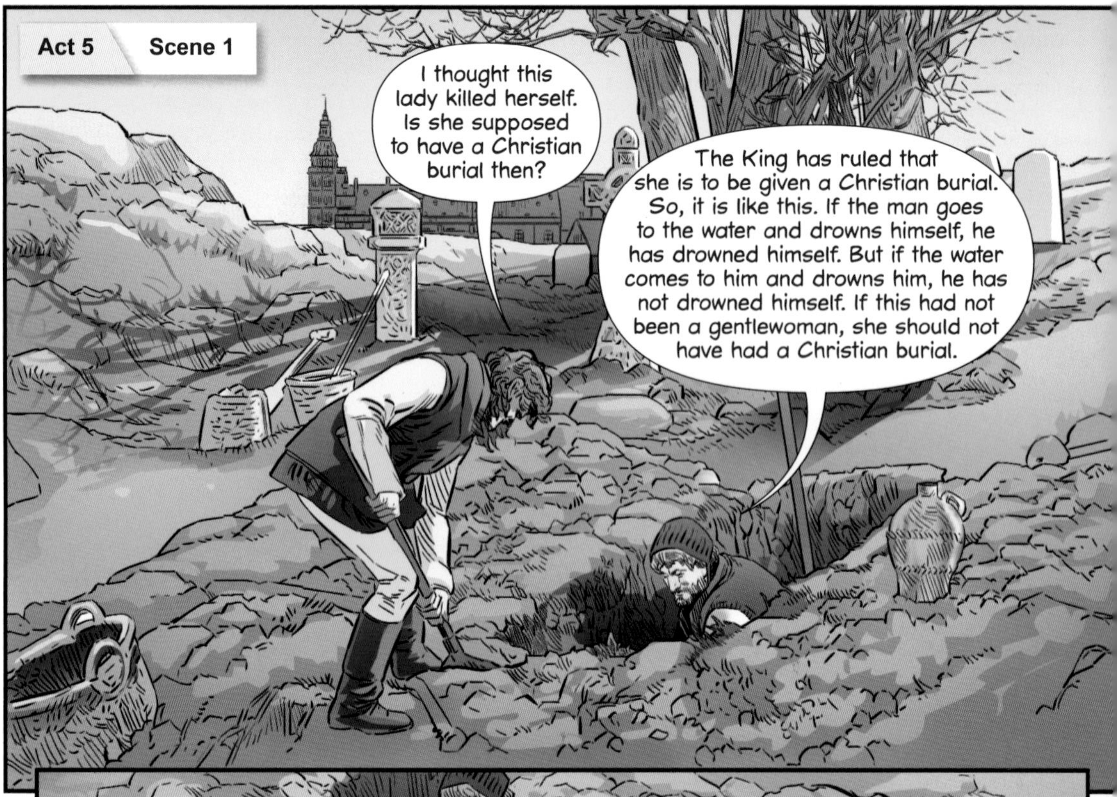
Act 5 Scene 1
I thought this lady killed herself. Is she supposed to have a Christian burial then?
The King has ruled that she is to be given a Christian burial. So, it is like this. If the man goes to the water and drowns himself, he has drowned himself. But if the water comes to him and drowns him, he has not drowned himself. If this had not been a gentlewoman, she should not have had a Christian burial.

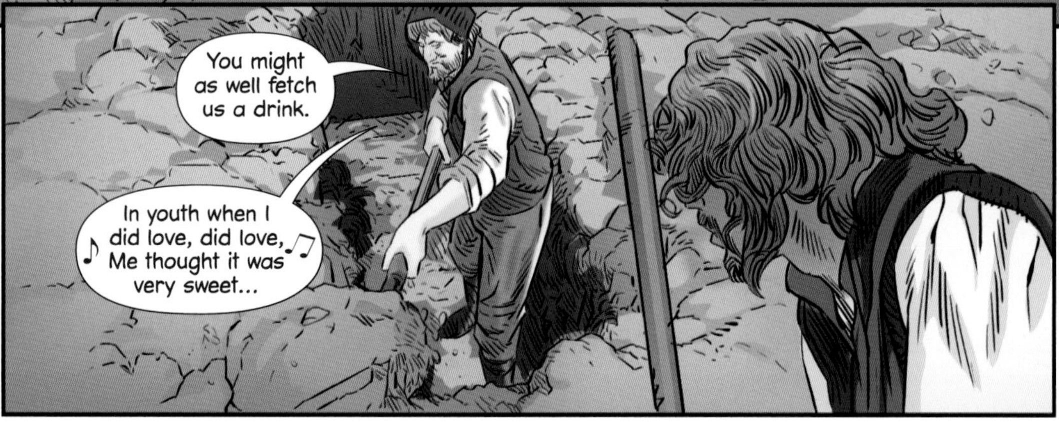
You might as well fetch us a drink.
In youth when I did love, did love, Me thought it was very sweet...

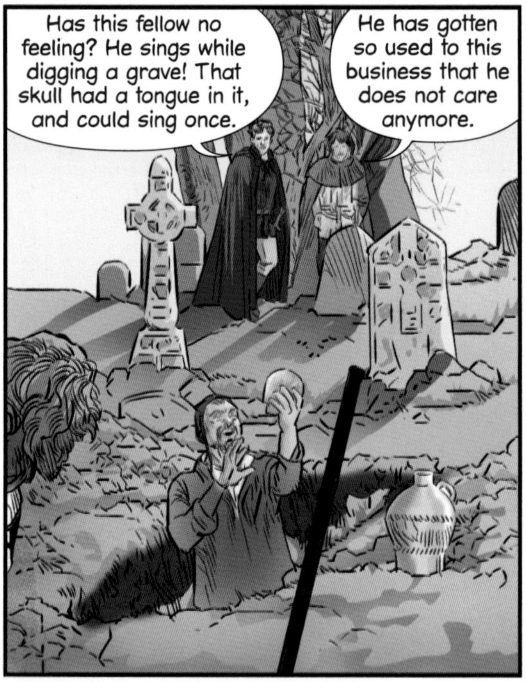
Has this fellow no feeling? He sings while digging a grave! That skull had a tongue in it, and could sing once.
He has gotten so used to this business that he does not care anymore.

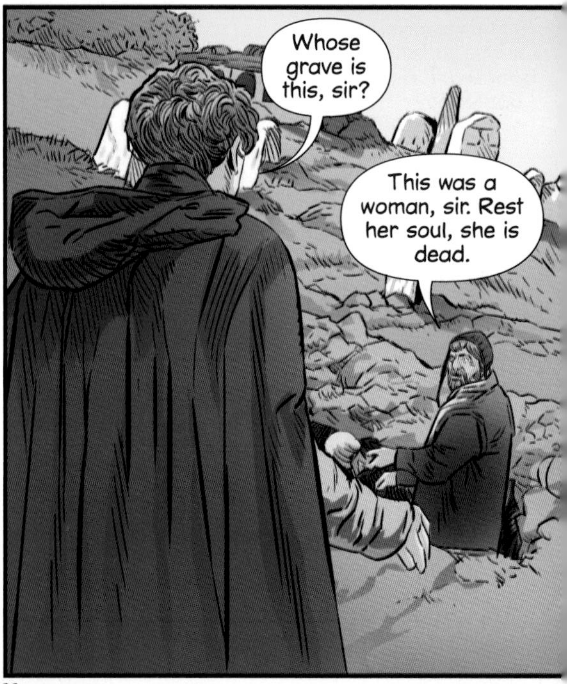
Whose grave is this, sir?
This was a woman, sir. Rest her soul, she is dead.

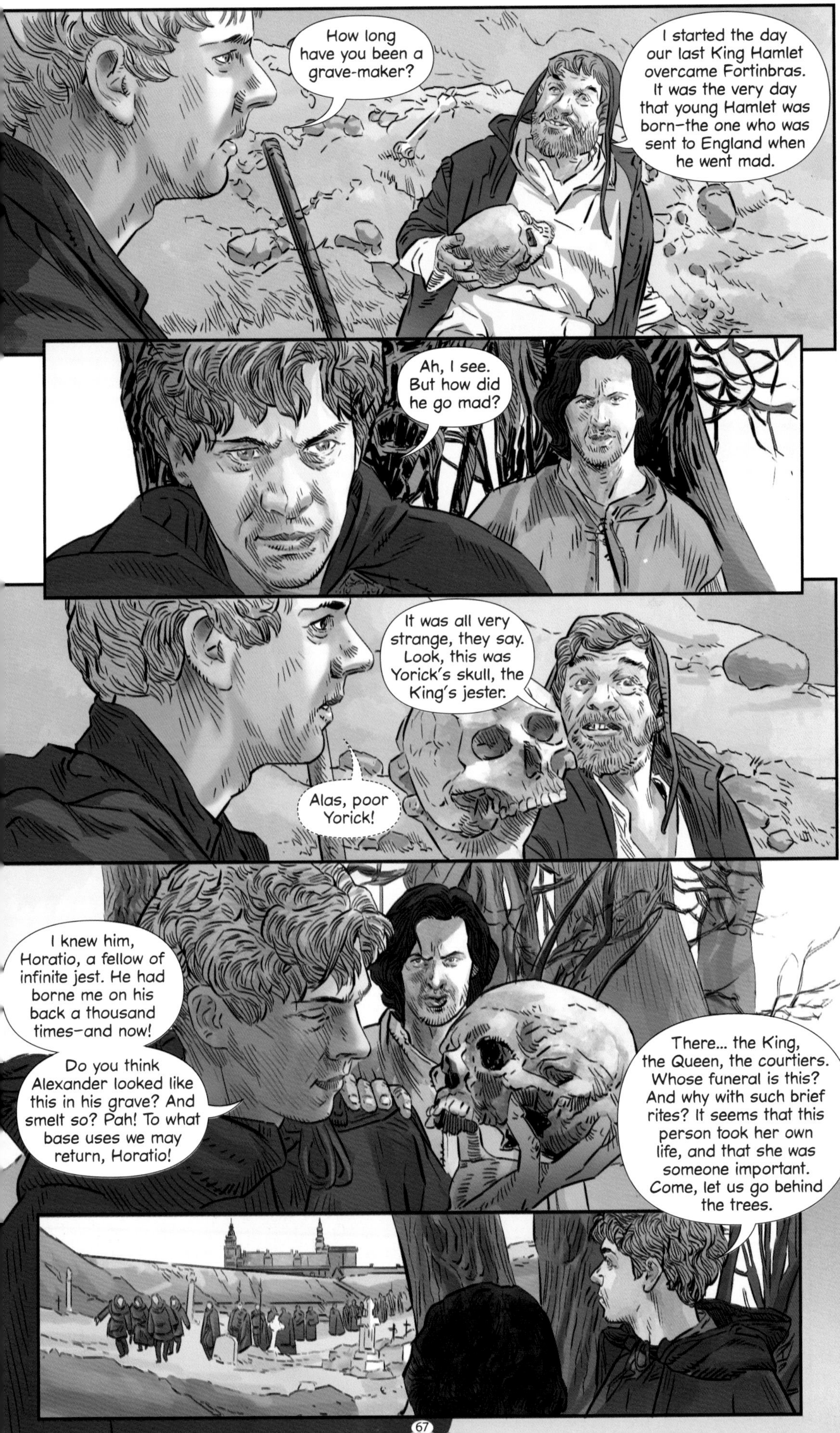
How long have you been a grave-maker?
I started the day our last King Hamlet overcame Fortinbras. It was the very day that young Hamlet was born—the one who was sent to England when he went mad.
Ah, I see. But how did he go mad?
It was all very strange, they say. Look, this was Yorick's skull, the King's jester.
Alas, poor Yorick!
I knew him, Horatio, a fellow of infinite jest. He had borne me on his back a thousand times—and now!
Do you think Alexander looked like this in his grave? And smelt so? Pah! To what base uses we may return, Horatio!
There... the King, the Queen, the courtiers. Whose funeral is this? And why with such brief rites? It seems that this person took her own life, and that she was someone important. Come, let us go behind the trees.

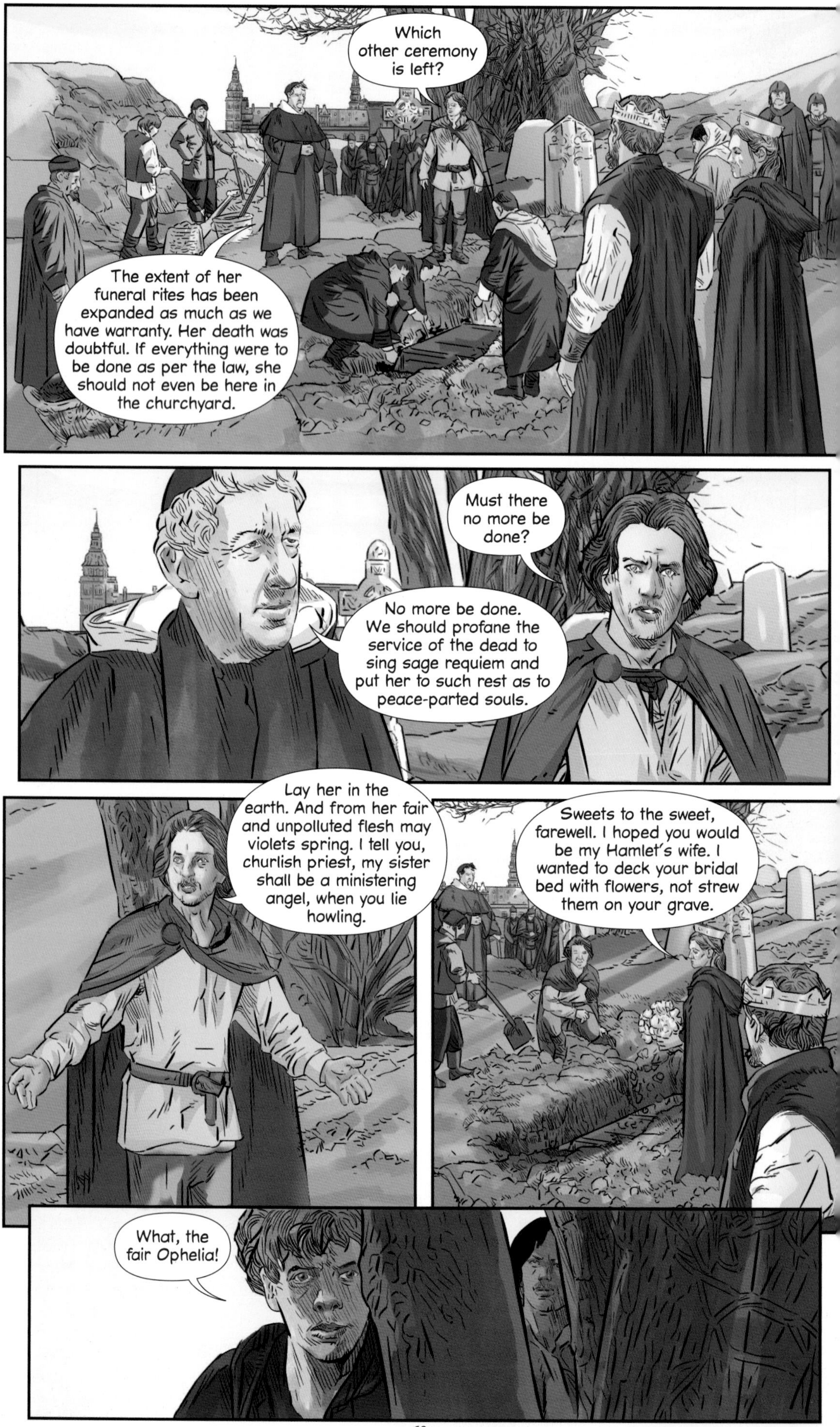
Which other ceremony is left?
The extent of her funeral rites has been expanded as much as we have warranty. Her death was doubtful. If everything were to be done as per the law, she should not even be here in the churchyard.
Must there no more be done?
No more be done. We should profane the service of the dead to sing sage requiem and put her to such rest as to peace-parted souls.
Lay her in the earth. And from her fair and unpolluted flesh may violets spring. I tell you, churlish priest, my sister shall be a ministering angel, when you lie howling.
Sweets to the sweet, farewell. I hoped you would be my Hamlet's wife. I wanted to deck your bridal bed with flowers, not strew them on your grave.
What, the fair Ophelia!

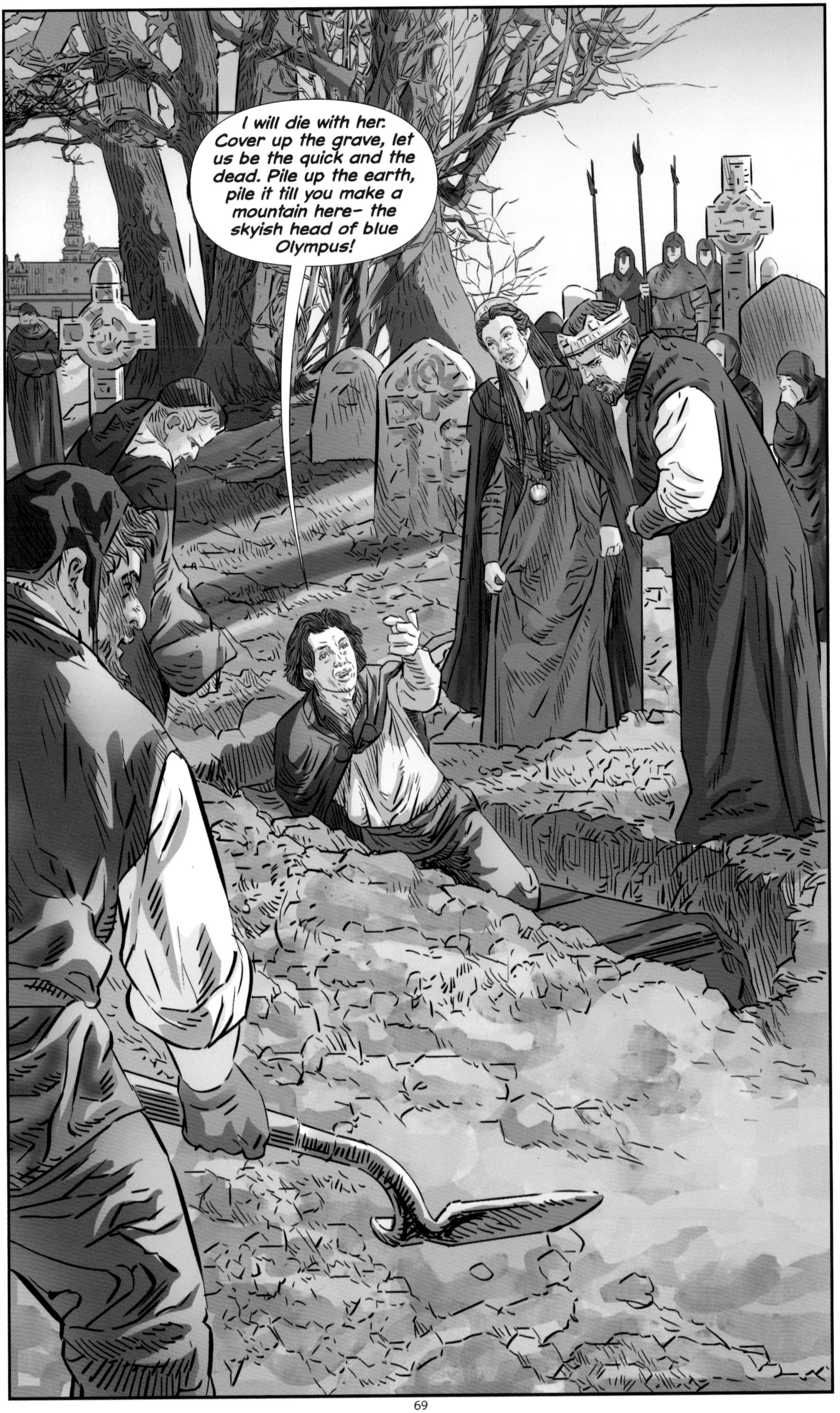
I will die with her. Cover up the grave, let us be the quick and the dead. Pile up the earth, pile it till you make a mountain here- the skyish head of blue Olympus!

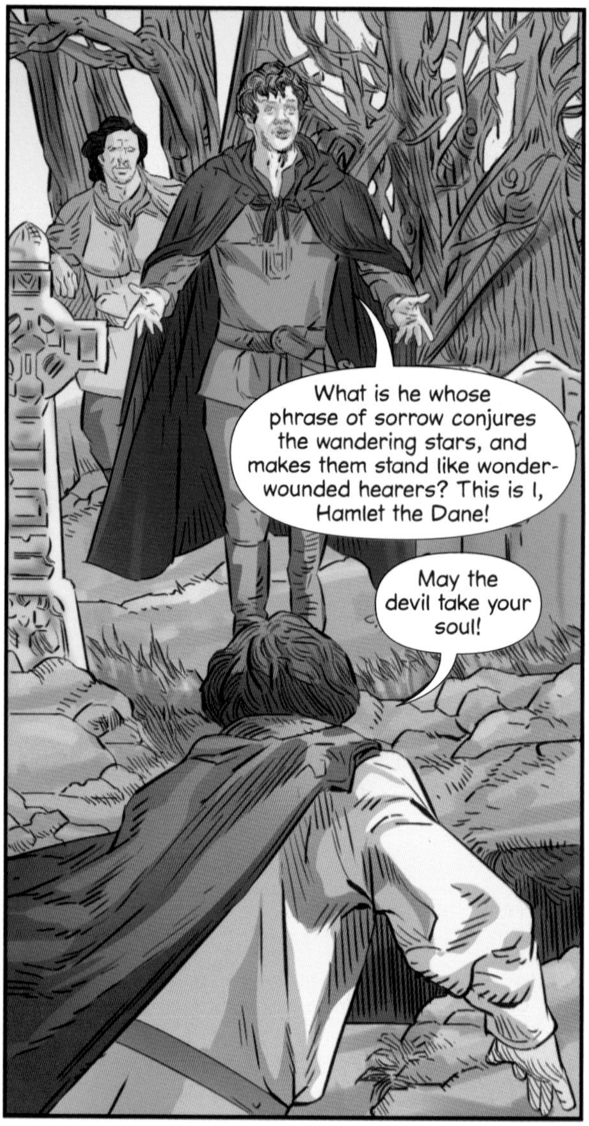
What is he whose phrase of sorrow conjures the wandering stars, and makes them stand like wonder-wounded hearers? This is I, Hamlet the Dane!
May the devil take your soul!

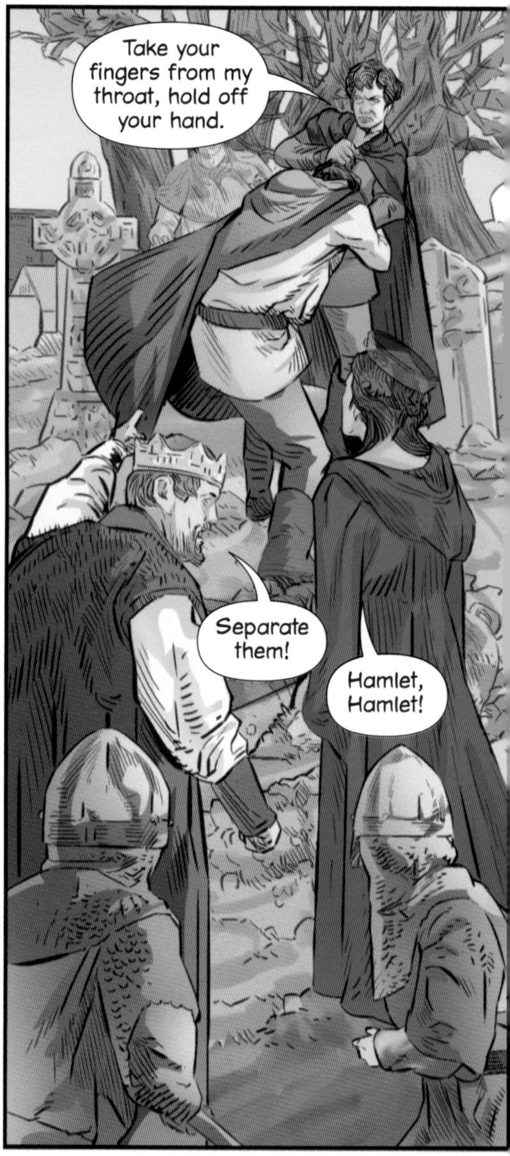
Take your fingers from my throat, hold off your hand.
Separate them!
Hamlet, Hamlet!

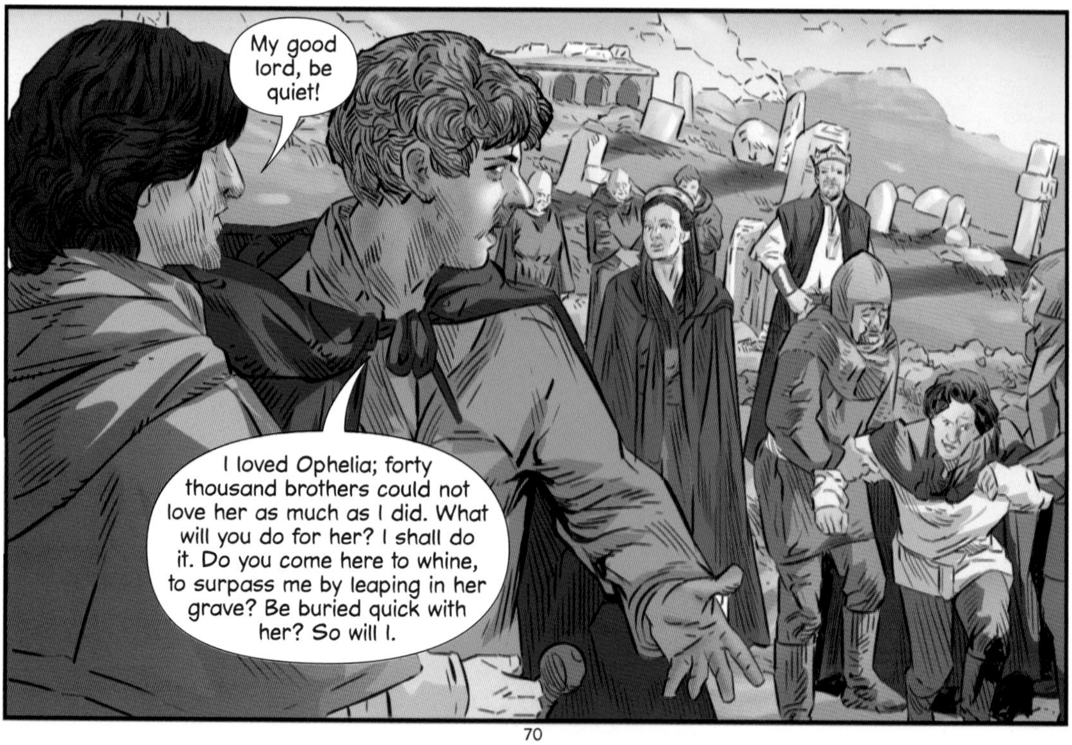
My good lord, be quiet!
I loved Ophelia; forty thousand brothers could not love her as much as I did. What will you do for her? I shall do it. Do you come here to whine, to surpass me by leaping in her grave? Be buried quick with her? So will I.

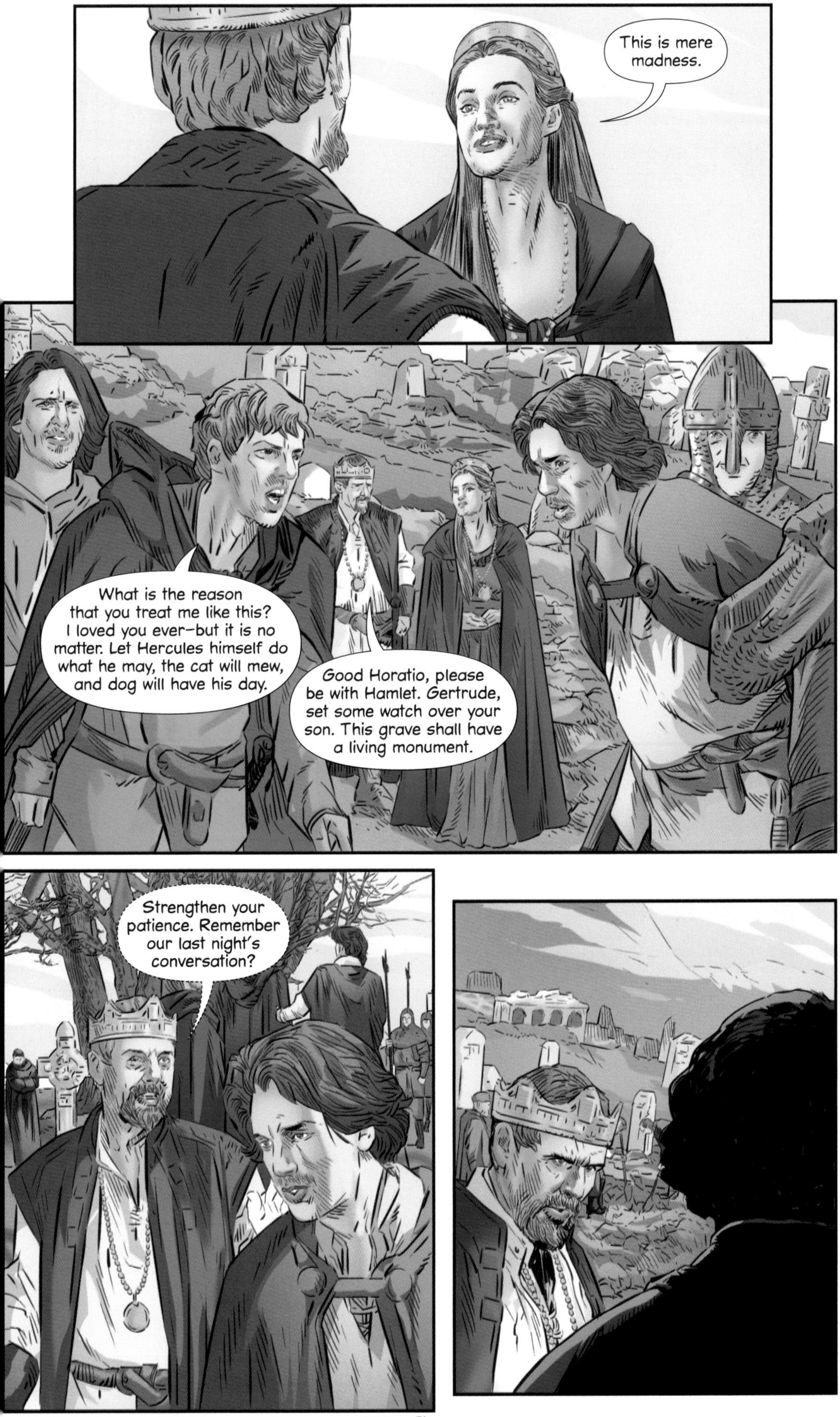
This is mere madness.
What is the reason that you treat me like this? I loved you ever—but it is no matter. Let Hercules himself do what he may, the cat will mew, and dog will have his day.
Good Horatio, please be with Hamlet. Gertrude, set some watch over your son. This grave shall have a living monument.
Strengthen your patience. Remember our last night's conversation?

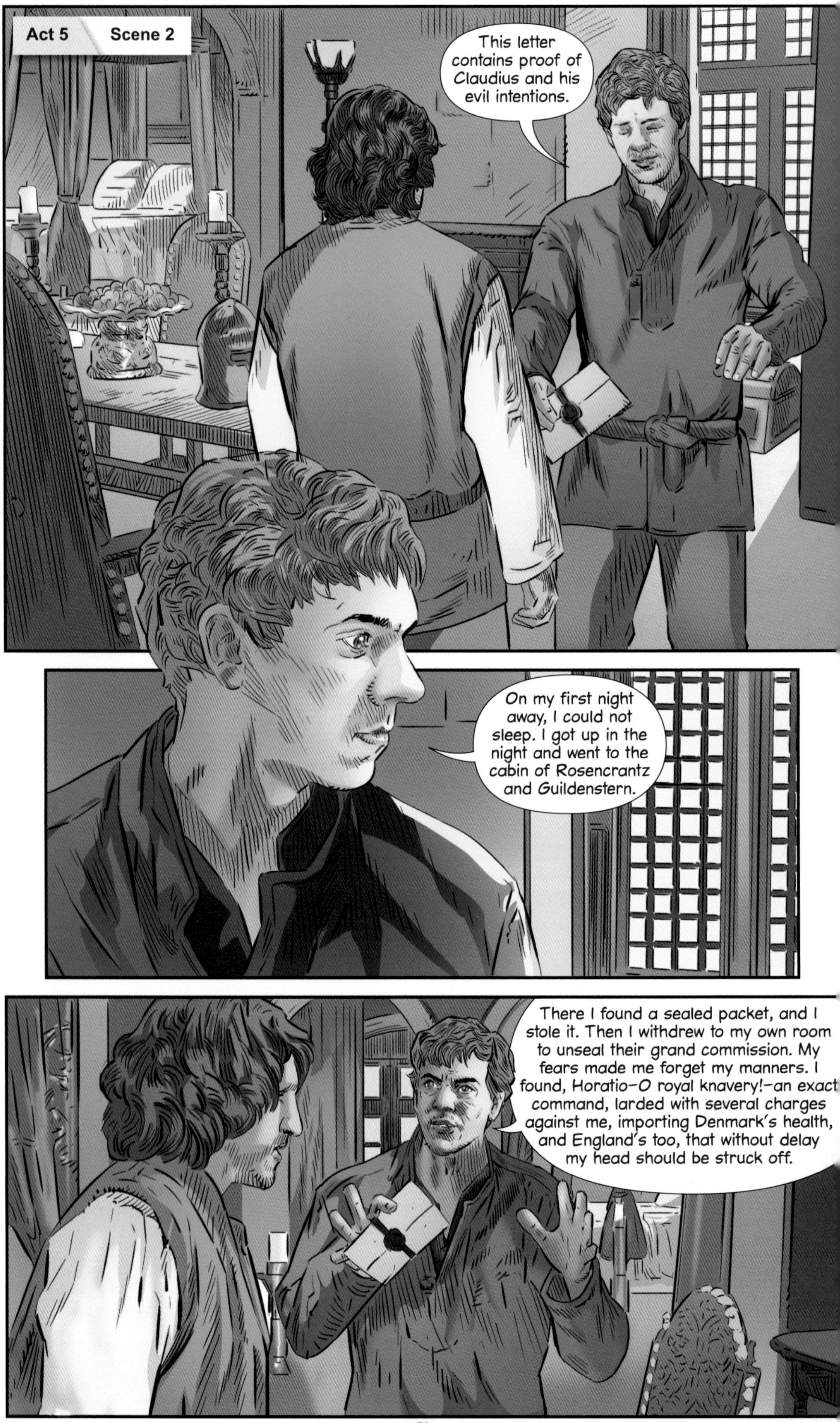
Act 5 Scene 2
This letter contains proof of Claudius and his evil intentions.
On my first night away, I could not sleep. I got up in the night and went to the cabin of Rosencrantz and Guildenstern.
There I found a sealed packet, and I stole it. Then I withdrew to my own room to unseal their grand commission. My fears made me forget my manners. I found, Horatio–O royal knavery!–an exact command, larded with several charges against me, importing Denmark's health, and England's too, that without delay my head should be struck off.

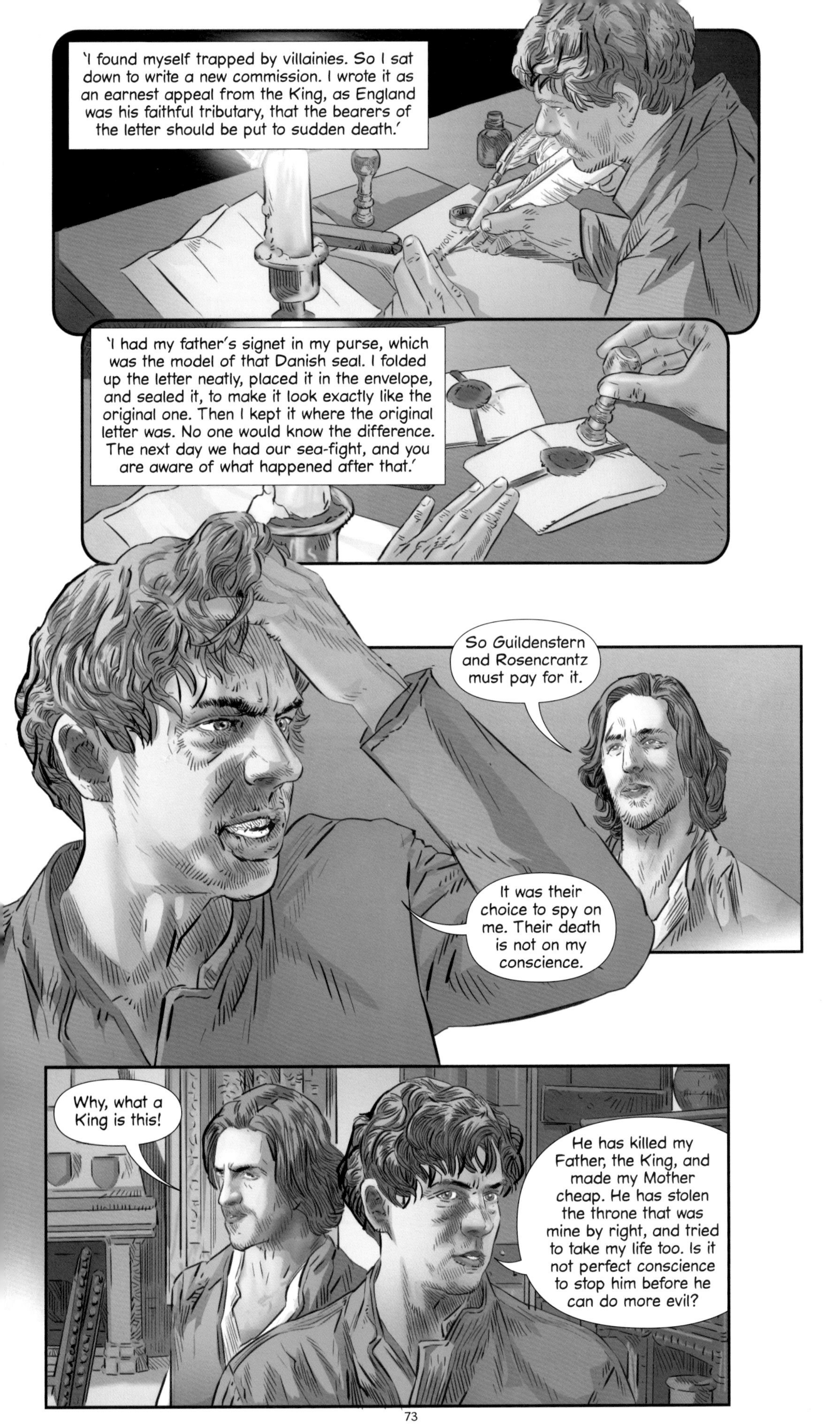
'I found myself trapped by villainies. So I sat down to write a new commission. I wrote it as an earnest appeal from the King, as England was his faithful tributary, that the bearers of the letter should be put to sudden death.'
'I had my father's signet in my purse, which was the model of that Danish seal. I folded up the letter neatly, placed it in the envelope, and sealed it, to make it look exactly like the original one. Then I kept it where the original letter was. No one would know the difference. The next day we had our sea-fight, and you are aware of what happened after that.'
So Guildenstern and Rosencrantz must pay for it.
It was their choice to spy on me. Their death is not on my conscience.
Why, what a King is this!
He has killed my Father, the King, and made my Mother cheap. He has stolen the throne that was mine by right, and tried to take my life too. Is it not perfect conscience to stop him before he can do more evil?

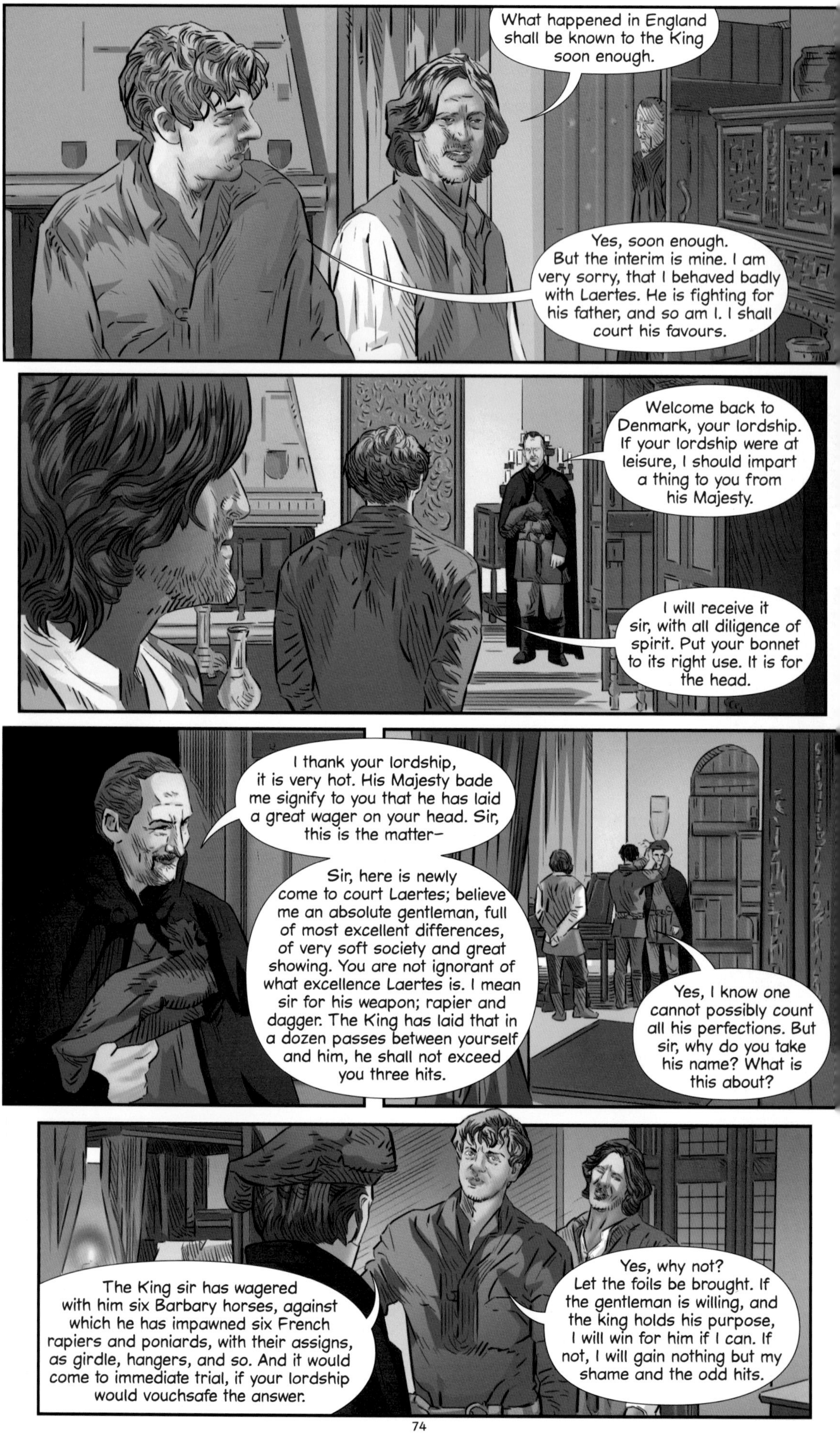
What happened in England shall be known to the King soon enough.
Yes, soon enough. But the interim is mine. I am very sorry, that I behaved badly with Laertes. He is fighting for his father, and so am I. I shall court his favours.
Welcome back to Denmark, your lordship. If your lordship were at leisure, I should impart a thing to you from his Majesty.
I will receive it sir, with all diligence of spirit. Put your bonnet to its right use. It is for the head.
I thank your lordship, it is very hot. His Majesty bade me signify to you that he has laid a great wager on your head. Sir, this is the matter–
Sir, here is newly come to court Laertes; believe me an absolute gentleman, full of most excellent differences, of very soft society and great showing. You are not ignorant of what excellence Laertes is. I mean sir for his weapon; rapier and dagger. The King has laid that in a dozen passes between yourself and him, he shall not exceed you three hits.
Yes, I know one cannot possibly count all his perfections. But sir, why do you take his name? What is this about?
The King sir has wagered with him six Barbary horses, against which he has impawned six French rapiers and poniards, with their assigns, as girdle, hangers, and so. And it would come to immediate trial, if your lordship would vouchsafe the answer.
Yes, why not? Let the foils be brought. If the gentleman is willing, and the king holds his purpose, I will win for him if I can. If not, I will gain nothing but my shame and the odd hits.

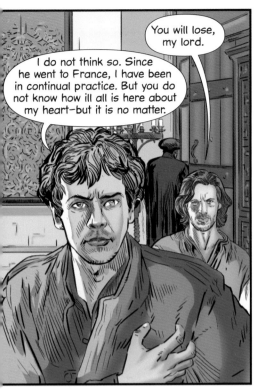

You will lose, my lord.

I do not think so. Since he went to France, I have been in continual practice. But you do not know how ill all is here about my heart—but it is no matter.

If your mind dislikes anything, obey it. I will forestall the match, saying you are not fit.

Not a whit, we defy augury. There is special providence in the fall of a sparrow. If it be now, it is not to come; if it be not to come, it will be now—the readiness is all.

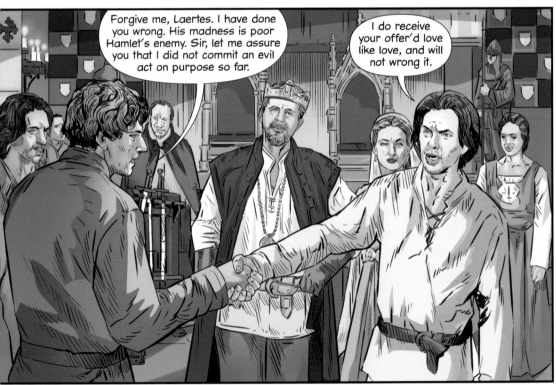

Forgive me, Laertes. I have done you wrong. His madness is poor Hamlet's enemy. Sir, let me assure you that I did not commit an evil act on purpose so far.

I do receive your offer'd love like love, and will not wrong it.

Give us the foils, come on. I will be your foil Laertes. Your skill shall shine against my ignorance like a star in the darkest night.

You mock me, sir.

Give them the foils, young Osric. Cousin Hamlet, you know the wager?

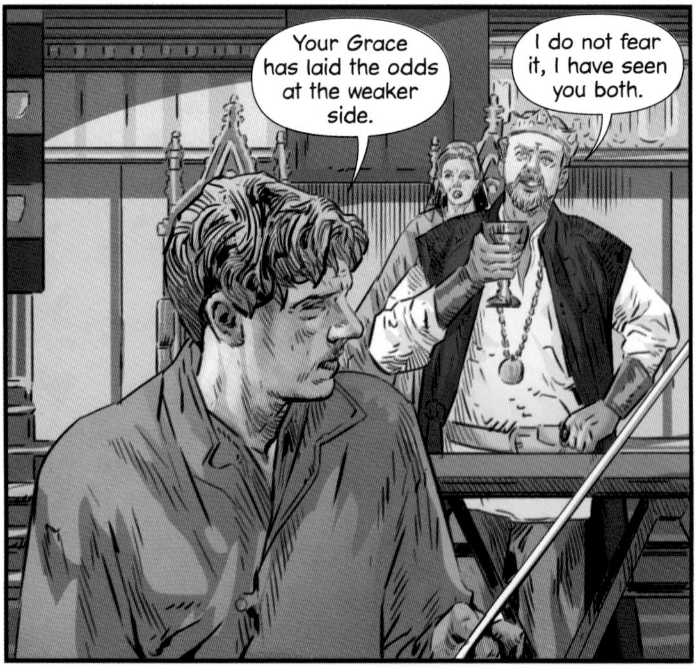
Your Grace has laid the odds at the weaker side.
I do not fear it, I have seen you both.

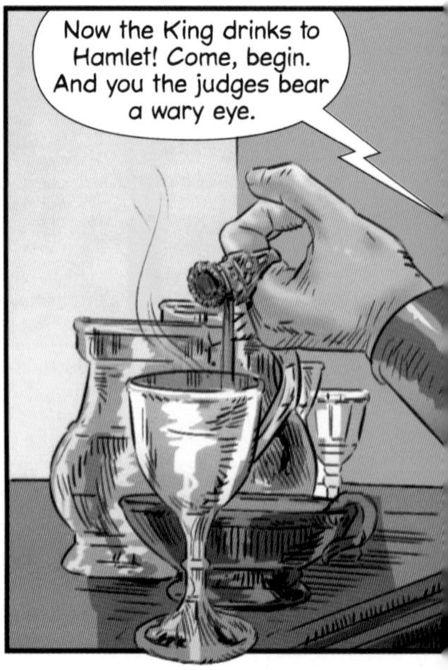
Now the King drinks to Hamlet! Come, begin. And you the judges bear a wary eye.

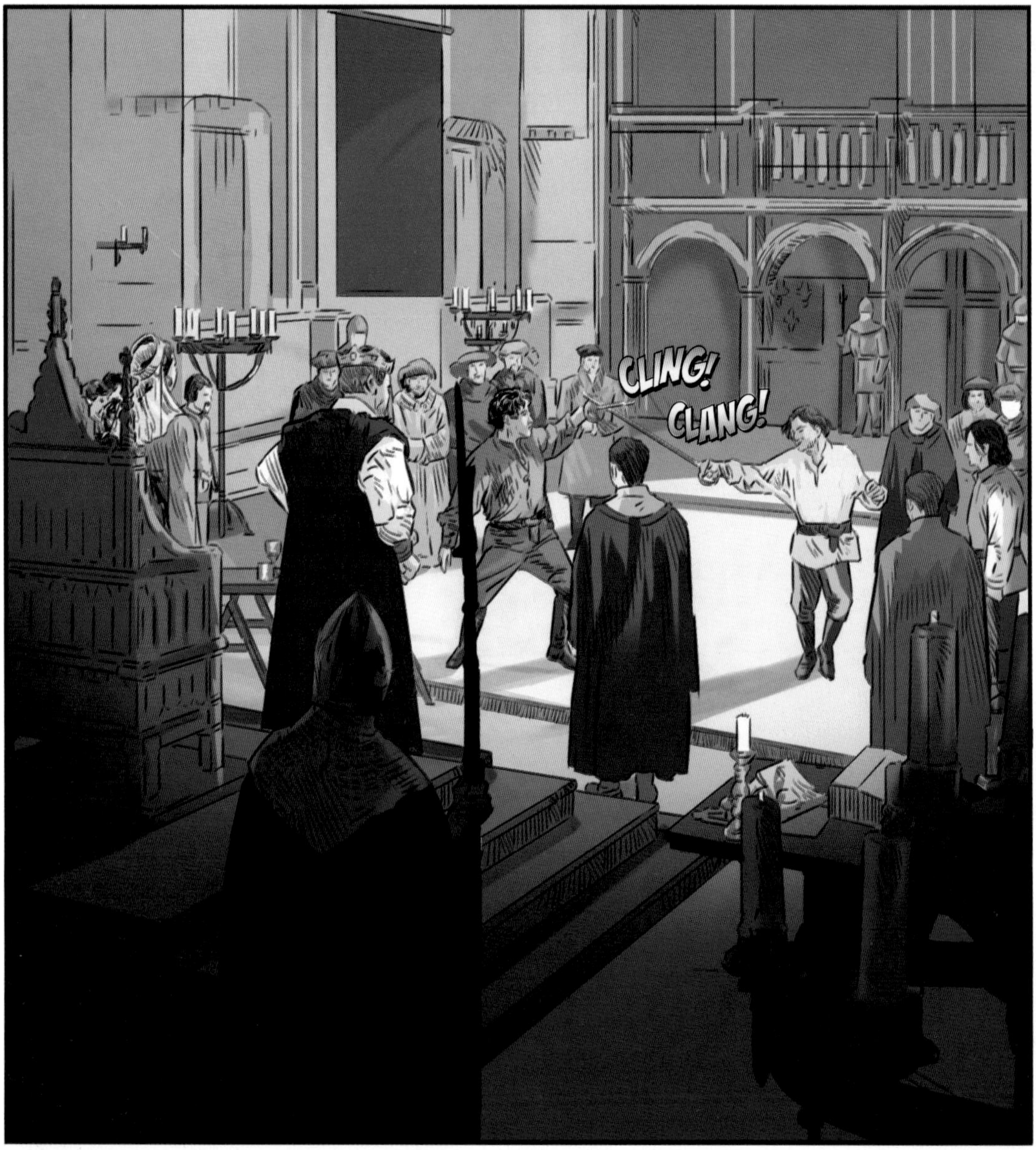
CLING!
CLANG!

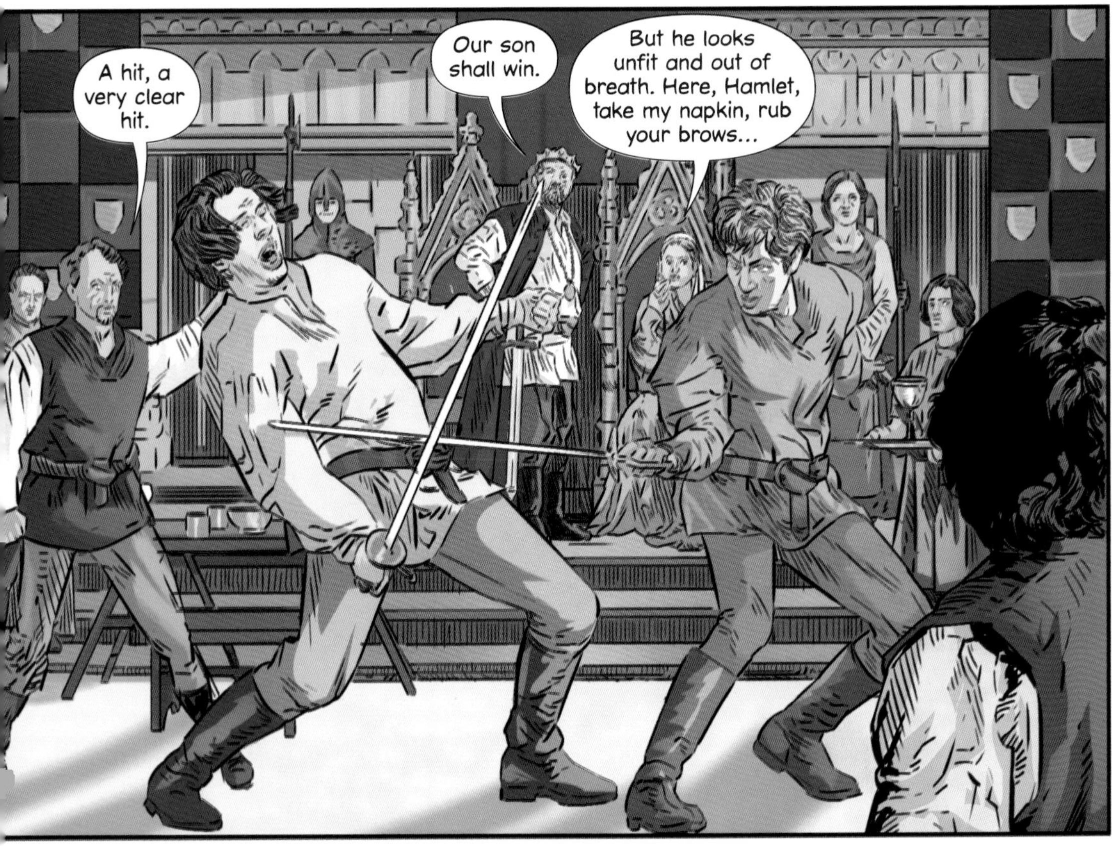
A hit, a very clear hit.
Our son shall win.
But he looks unfit and out of breath. Here, Hamlet, take my napkin, rub your brows...

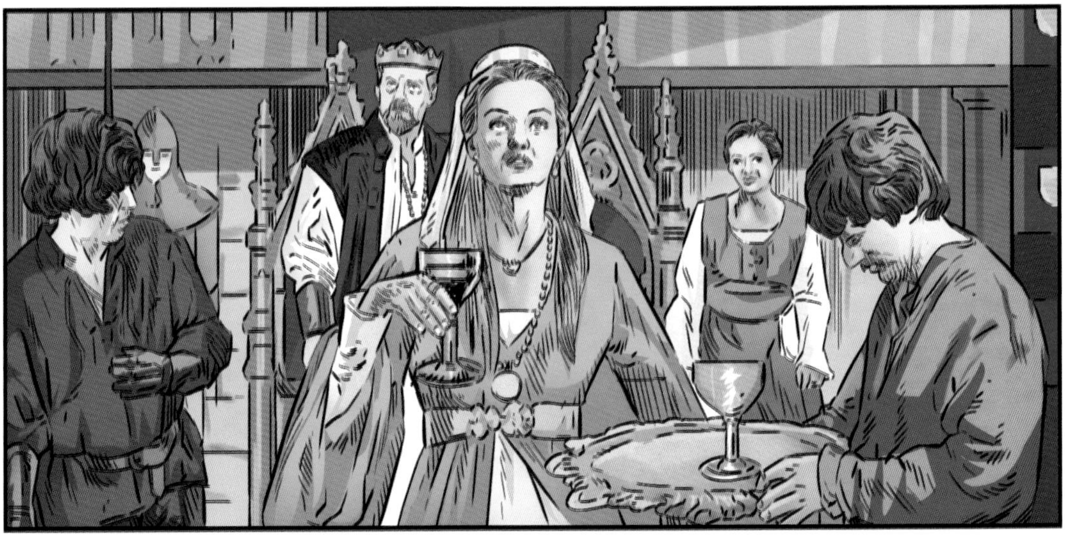

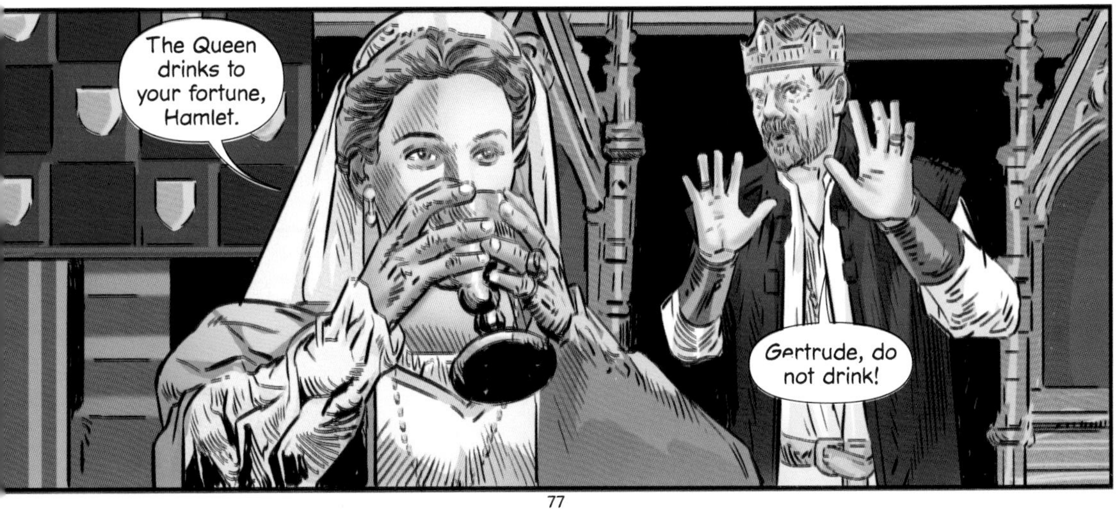
The Queen drinks to your fortune, Hamlet.
Gertrude, do not drink!

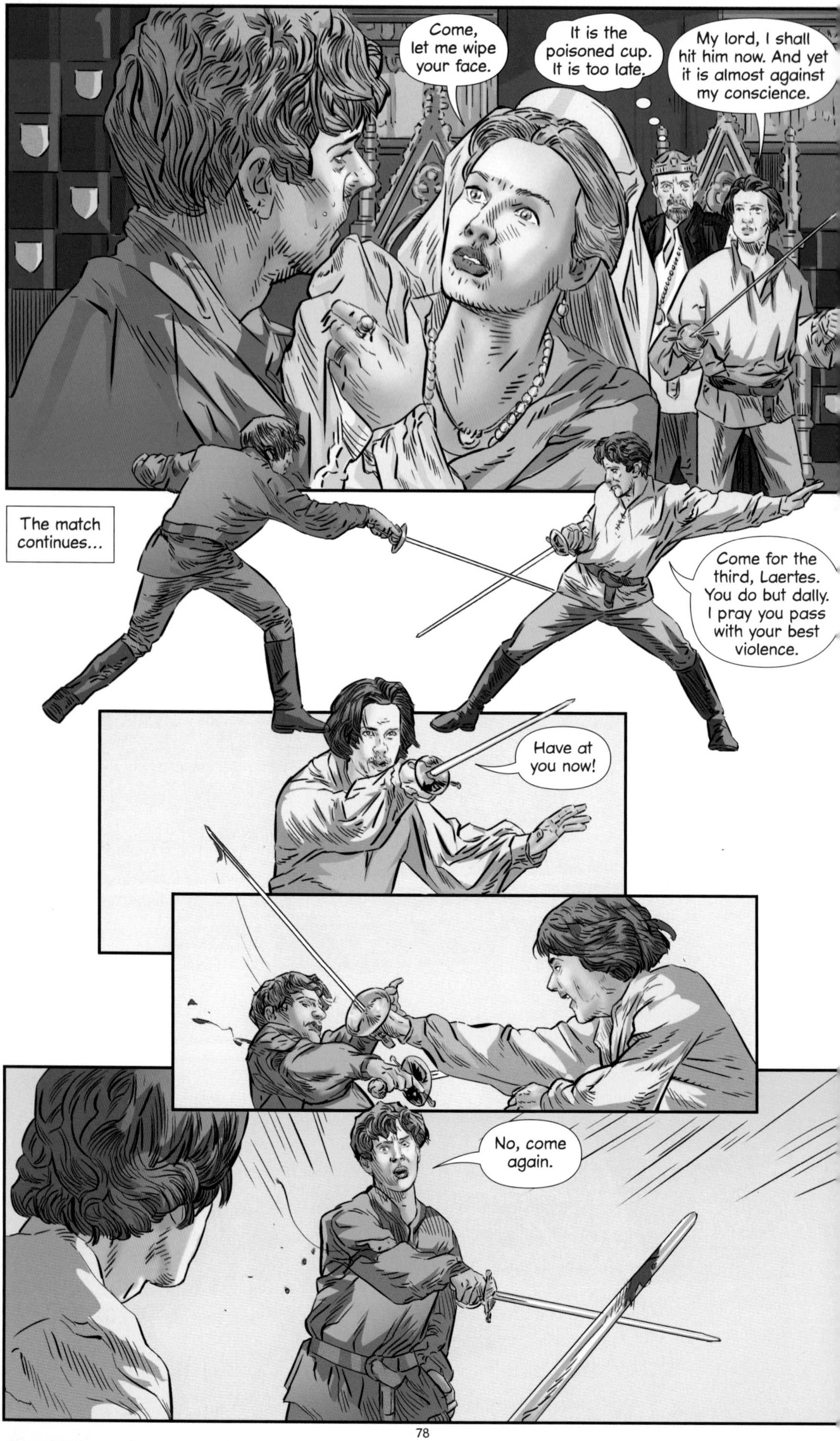
Come, let me wipe your face.
It is the poisoned cup. It is too late.
My lord, I shall hit him now. And yet it is almost against my conscience.
The match continues...
Come for the third, Laertes. You do but dally. I pray you pass with your best violence.
Have at you now!
No, come again.

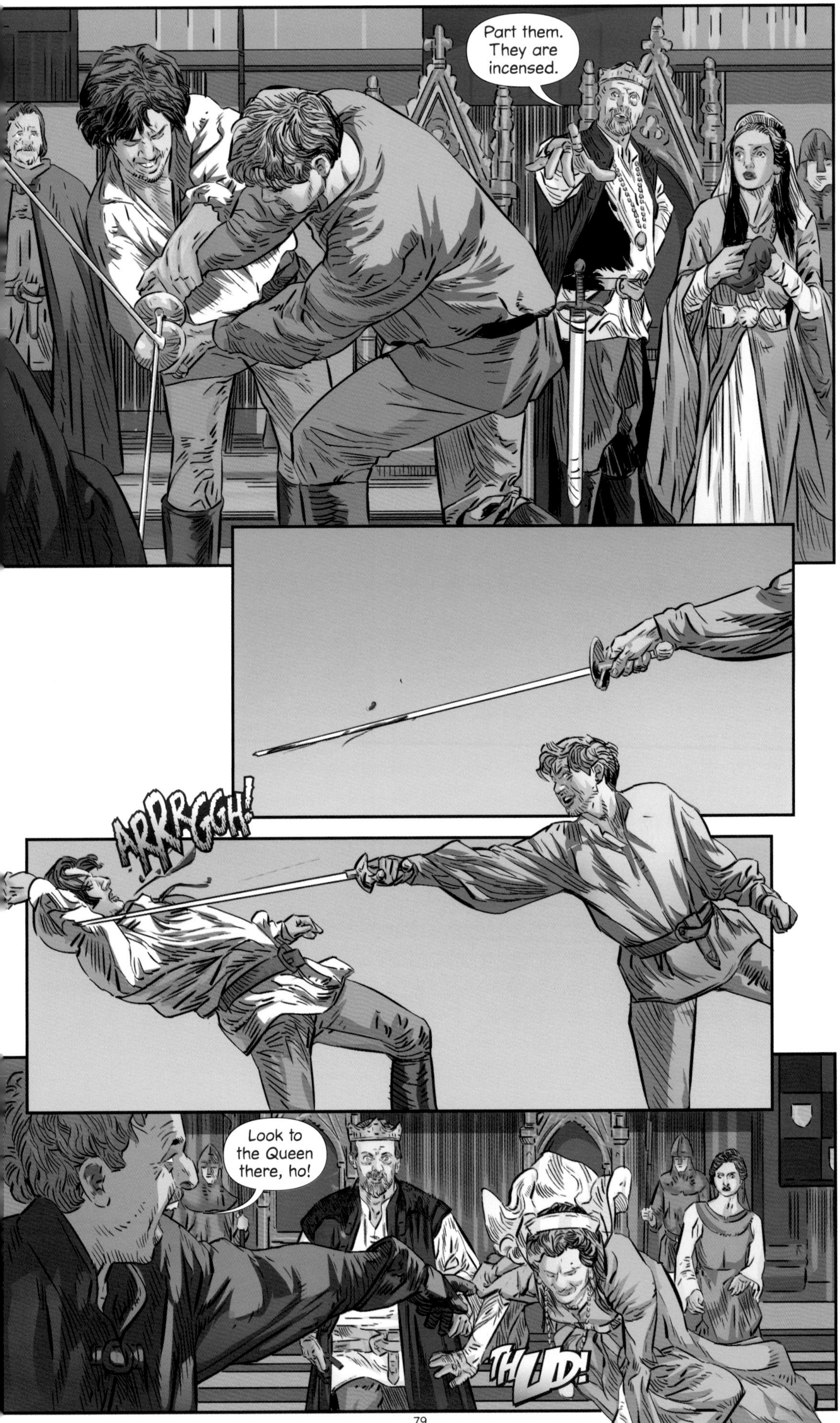
Part them. They are incensed.
ARRRGGH!
Look to the Queen there, ho!
THUD!

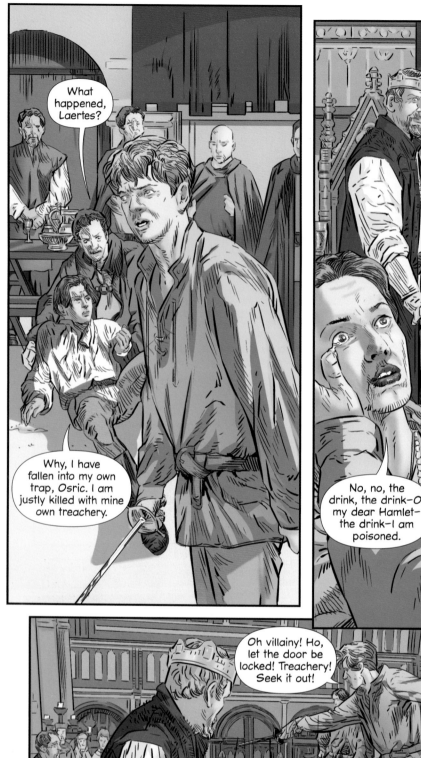

What happened, Laertes?

Why, I have fallen into my own trap, Osric. I am justly killed with mine own treachery.

What happened to the Queen?

She faints seeing you bleed.

No, no, the drink, the drink—O, my dear Hamlet— the drink—I am poisoned.

Oh villainy! Ho, let the door be locked! Treachery! Seek it out!

Glossary

Page	2	In arms: In full armor.
Page	10	Cousin Hamlet: Cousin here means 'nephew'.
Page	14	Green girl: Innocent and gullible.
Page	15	Rhenish: German wine.
Page	16	I do not set my life at a pin's fee: I place little value on my life.
Page	25	Satirical rogue: Clever and crafty.
Page	29	Hecuba: Wife of King Priam of Troy.
Page	32	Contumely: Abusive words.
Page	32	Bodkin: Thin dagger.
Page	32	Bourn: Borders.
Page	33	Arrant knave: Absolute rogue.
Page	44	For a Ducat: Bet upon a coin.
Page	45	Mildewed ear: Rotten ear of corn.
Page	45	Catpurse: Pickpocket.
Page	62	Rapier: A thin sword.
Page	64	Aslant: Lean over.
Page	64	Old lauds: Old songs.
Page	68	Requiem: Song for a funeral mass.
Page	74	Poniard: Thin dagger.
Page	75	Augury: Superstition.

For the curious ones...

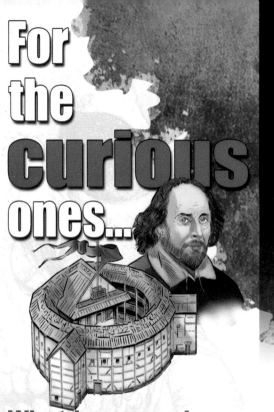

What is a tragedy?

William Shakespeare's *Hamlet* is known as a **'tragedy'**. The tragedy is a form of drama based on human suffering. It is known to invoke a sense of 'catharsis' or elation in the audience with the climax. The tradition of tragedy has a unique historical significance. It is strongly related to the cultural identity of the Western civilization. The form of tragedy originated in the theatre of ancient Greece 2,500 years ago. Since then, the tragedy has remained an important medium of cultural experimentation and change.

What is a monologue or a soliloquy?

A **'monologue'** is a long speech made by an actor in a play or a film. It is sometimes a solitary speech, used by a character to express his or her thoughts aloud. This is known as a **'soliloquy'**. However, sometimes a monologue is also directed at another character or the audience. The play *Hamlet* consists of many long monologues and soliloquies, some of which are quite famous. The "to be or not to be" soliloquy by Hamlet was even adopted as the plot device of a film called *To Be or Not To Be*.

The story behind Hamlet

Hamlet is one of the most well-known and poignant tragedies that William Shakespeare has written. Although there is dispute among scholars about the exact date of *Hamlet's* composition and performance, it is generally believed to have been composed around 1601. The play was performed at the wake of a religious upheaval – the Protestant Reformation movement.

There is also much debate on the text that influenced the play, but it is strongly believed that Shakespeare drew inspiration for Hamlet from the *Story of Amleth* written in the twelfth century, which first appeared in Saxo Grammaticus' *Historie Danicae* of 1514. The two stories have a lot in common. The Story of Amleth is about a prince who avenges his dead father by killing the murderer, his uncle, who is also the second husband of his mother. But the *Story of Amleth* does not end with the prince dying; instead, he becomes the next king. Shakespeare altered the ending to alleviate the play to the epic proportions of a tragedy.